# Mallory's Manly Methods

# Thomas Keech

**Real**
Nice Books
Baltimore, Maryland

ISBN 978-1-7355938-4-5 Hardback
ISBN 978-1-7355938-5-2 Paperback
ISBN 978-1-7355938-6-9 Ebook
ISBN 978-1-7355938-9-0 Audiobook

Library of Congress Control Number
2021949371

Published by

**Real**
Nice Books
11 Dutton Court, Suite 606
Baltimore, Maryland 21228
www.realnicebooks.com

*Publisher's note: This is a work of fiction. Names, characters, places, institutions, and incidents are entirely the product of the author's imagination or are used fictitiously, and any resemblance to actual persons, living or dead, or to events, incidents, institutions, or places is entirely coincidental.*

Cover photo by Shutterstock.
Set in Sabon.

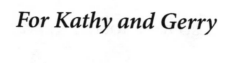

*For Kathy and Gerry*

Also by Thomas Keech:

*The Crawlspace Conspiracy*

*Prey for Love*

*Hot Box in the Pizza District*

*Doc Doc Zeus: A Novel of White Coat Crime*

*Stacey in the Hands of an Angry God*

*A New God in Town*

# List of Chapters

# Chapter 1: How May I Help You?

"Look. I already did all those things you are talking about. I made sure the power is on. I made sure the cable is connected. I rebooted the whole system. And I already indicated all that on the customer problems website. None of it worked. That's why I'm calling you at Customer Assistance."

"No need to get testy," Mallory replied.

"I've been waiting on the line for 35 minutes."

"Let me put you on hold while I check your billing status."

"No! Wait ...."

Mallory clicked him off. He smiled to himself. His customer would now have to listen to a recording repeatedly telling him to hold while the UniCast Cable Company checked his account information. Mallory had no intention of checking the customer's account information. But he was now free to visit the break room for as long as he liked. He congratulated himself for not being a slave to the phone or to his idiot customers, and for striking another blow against Algonquin J. Tycoon.

Mallory put both palms on his desk, rocked his large, solid stomach forward and at the same time straightened his legs to kick back his roller chair into the cubicle wall behind him. He had perfected this energy-saving method of standing up over the last few months. His supervisor didn't seem to care that he had battered a hole through the fabric on his side of the partition. But, of course, Nell cared.

Mallory knew the *thwack* of his chair on Nell's cubicle wall would bring her out. He didn't care. He didn't like Nell. She seemed to feel a special obligation to point out every way he failed to make the grade. Nell now stood in the opening to her own cubicle and tried to make eye contact as he made his way past her to the break room. He had always been a little afraid of the unsettling looks she sometimes shot at him from behind those large, black, rectangular glasses. But he didn't think she was pretty enough to demand attention in that way. Any chance she had of being attractive was sabotaged by those ropes of long, scraggly, black hair pulled back by that unattractive squadron of tortoise-shell barrettes.

"You know that gets on my nerves," she hissed as he passed by. But he knew she wouldn't yell. He doubted Nell had the self-confidence to confront him that way. He felt perfectly entitled not to return her look.

But she followed him to the arched entranceway to the break room, 27 cubicles and two turns away. She waited behind him until he had collected a cup of coffee and a cinnamon pastry from two of the machines lined against the wall. There were no windows in the break room. She sat down across the table from him. She wore a white collared shirt and grey cardigan sweater, as if she didn't want anyone to notice her figure. No one else was in the break room.

"Don't you understand how nerve wracking that is, to feel your chair slam into my wall when I'm talking to customers?"

Mallory slowly pulled apart the two sides of the cellophane wrapper around his cinnamon bun and peered inside. His mouth was watering, and he wished he could take a bite before dealing with her.

"You're not going to answer me?" She put her hands out flat, very close to the bun, and drummed her fingers on the laminated tabletop as if she were itching to snatch his snack away. Mallory pulled it back a few inches. Nell flinched. Then she smiled, as she had his attention. "I don't understand you." She was making an effort to talk calmly in the face of his silent glare.

Mallory broke eye contact, pulled the bun out of its wrapper, and took a huge bite, as if to say there wasn't anything a woman could offer him right now that was better than a cinnamon bun. But he knew that wasn't really true. In the fifteen years since high school, he'd been on a number of dates. He had even lived for a short time with a nice, tangy little piece who worshiped him night and day, until she didn't. He never missed her now, except late at night.

"That machine coffee is awful," Nell persisted. "Why don't you join the office coffee pool? We brew our own. For five dollars a week you can have all the fresh brewed coffee you want."

Since moving out of his ex's apartment and his mother's basement to an efficiency in Glenwood, Mallory had lived like he wanted to live and eaten what he wanted to eat. He exulted in choosing his clothes and in keeping his flaming red hair, including his facial hair, however he wanted, without having to listen to the opinions of any women. He carried the twenty pounds he had gained since living on his own proudly. Rather than hiding his protruding belly with oversized shirts or camouflaging overalls, he belted his pants tightly in front, carrying his extra weight in front of him like a protective shield.

"Coffee pool? Waste of money," he mumbled, avoiding her eyes. The truth was, he didn't know how to brew coffee.

"We've been sitting in cubicles next to each other for three months and we don't know anything about each other."

What did she mean by that? A faint tremor emanating from somewhere behind that protective shield teased his eyes up to meet hers. The penetrating look she gave him was disconcerting, even from behind those big, square glasses. His rush of excitement was now tempered with a little bit of fear. This strange, mop-headed woman was coming on to him, he was sure.

"I like this job," was all he managed to say. "You don't have to meet the customers. You don't even have to tell them your name."

She nodded. "But sometimes you can help them. Sometimes they're happy when it works. I like that."

"Hmm." Mallory had never had that experience. He believed his thinking was in line with the company's philosophy – to assume that the customer was always wrong. There was nothing more tedious than walking the customers through the list of questions UniCast had created to make sure the company didn't go to the expense of sending a technician to the home. But Mallory had found ways of using that list to his advantage. A good percentage of his callers hung up in frustration before supplying all the answers Mallory required – even though most of the information he asked for was already right on the screen in front of him. He also had a keen instinct for homing in on that one bit of information a customer hadn't gathered in advance, thus requiring customers to search frantically through their papers while he ate his donuts in peace. And if customers were completely prepared and organized, or persistent, he could just cut them off.

"We're all slaving away at just above the minimum wage," he informed Nell now. "Just so Algonquin J. Tycoon can make millions. And what's he doing with all his time? Searching the corporate world for a merger that will throw all of us out of work completely."

Nell's look was puzzled. "I don't know this Algonquin J. Tycoon."

He couldn't believe how stupid she was. Of course, Nell couldn't be above average, or even average, if she was working here – unless she was trapped here, just like he was, by the billionaire titans running the whole economy.

"Algonquin J. Tycoon. You know. The man. As in, *stick it to the man.*"

"Oh. You don't mean any real person." She sighed like she was reconsidering the wisdom of talking to him at all. Mallory hoped this little conversational glitch would cause her to stop probing any further. But he was wrong. "You might want to talk to the people you work with here." She caught his eye, and he could see she was a woman not easily deterred. "That way, you might enjoy being here more."

"I have nothing to say to them."

"There must be something. You must have opinions, at least."

His opinion was she'd look better if she let her hair down. She could be pretty. She had smooth, fair skin, dark lashes. But she looked like she was clenching her teeth whenever she was talking to him. And the way she stared at him through those glasses was disturbing. Mallory had not asked any woman out for months.

10

He saw women on Facebook all the time, chatting about their cats or their boyfriends or their stupid diet fads and exercise routines. Or posting semi-porno pictures of themselves on Instagram. Mallory preferred the real thing when he sat in front of his computer at night.

"I know it can be kind of lonely here," she persisted. "Talking on the phone to angry people all the time, with no one to talk to yourself."

She might be into him, he thought, but there was nothing sultry about the look in those piercing eyes. Manly Man said a woman will give off signs when she wants to be dominated, but Mallory couldn't read any signs like that yet.

"There are meetings, meetings where people talk," he contradicted her. At least, he'd heard announcements of meetings. He'd never been to one.

"Staff meetings, yes. I guess that's better than nothing. But I think people should try to make personal connections at work, too. I mean, for example, you and I spend all day, every day, at workstations that are no more than six feet apart. Don't you think it would be nice if we got to know a little bit about each other?"

She was into him, he was now sure, even though she was the last person he had ever suspected would be interested in him. He needed to let her know that was alright. He reached out and slid his fingertips lightly across her wrist. But she jerked her arm back, looking at him strangely. "Touch me again and I'll report you to Personnel!"

Mallory was humiliated beyond words, beyond even any rational thought. All he could do was flee. He quickly pushed his chair back, turned and escaped from the break room, propelling himself all the way back to his cubicle as fast as he could manage, swinging his protruding belly left, then right, almost as if he had two gimpy legs at the same time.

\* \* \* \* \* \*

Mallory had mastered the art of survival at UniCast Cable. He had been talking to customers for three months now without once giving out his real name. To those really obnoxious customers who demanded his name right off, he just made up something, usually "Bartifard Prescott" or "Bill Tell." It didn't matter what he said. UniCast Cable, which could keep track of, and bill for, every single television show watched by 750,000 customers at any given time, kept absolutely no track of customer's complaints. Customers who wanted to complain about Mallory might as well have tied their complaint forms to helium balloons and let them go in the breeze.

Mallory had been fired from eight jobs in the last fifteen years. He had attended community college and was usually way more qualified than the average person applying for the below average jobs that he sought. Fortunately, he had had so many jobs that he could pick and choose which former employers to ask for references. Most job references, of course, simply stated his last salary and the fact that he had worked there from $x$ date to $y$ date. But Mallory could always provide one actual letter of reference from one small previous employer. He had worked for a coffee shop until he aggravated a customer so much that she took a swing at him. The manager intervened and, in the scuffle, ended up punching him on the side of his head – unintentionally, he insisted. But Mallory sued. He didn't get any money from the lawsuit, but as part of the settlement he did get a lifetime supply of false, glowing reference letters.

Mallory was not bothered by his gradual economic decline over the past several years. He told himself he had no desire to become another Algonquin J. Tycoon. He liked being isolated in his cubicle with a phone that he could disconnect at will. He liked his efficiency apartment, though he was afraid of the Black family that had moved in across the hall. He kept his rooms exactly the way he wanted them. He picked up carryout from the Dough and Go almost every night. His mother called him once a week on Sunday night, and he usually answered. His father was dead. He remembered his father as angry, always complaining of getting the short end of the stick, whining about not getting enough respect from his wife, losing his job. Walking out when Mallory was ten. Mallory understood from his father's example that everything he had been taught to strive for would gradually be sucked away from him by the loafers and the parasites and the government and the Algonquin J. Tycoons of the world.

He made enough money to pay his rent, his tab at Dough and Go, and his car insurance. He didn't have health insurance, but he knew he wasn't the kind of person who got sick. He was sure some of his money was being taken away every payday to pay for other people's health insurance, but he wasn't sure exactly how that worked. What he was sure of was he was constantly being taken advantage of.

\*\*\* \*\*\*

The next morning, as he was sitting in his cubicle trying to finish his Dough and Go breakfast, a sudden quiet whisper in his ear roiled his digestion and made him jerk back in his chair. His legs straightened and pushed him back hard into the cubicle wall he shared with Nell.

"What the hell?" He jerked his eyes upward to see the smirking face of Nell. But it was a different, more frightening Nell.

"I know what you're doing. You're cutting customers off." She leaned in over his chair like she was telling him a secret – or making a threat. But it wasn't her accusation that frightened him. It was her appearance. Gone was yesterday's glob of thick ropey blackness swirled Medusa-like on top of her head. Instead, her abundant hair was cut just below the jawline and turned under smartly in a precise bob. And she wasn't wearing those clunky glasses. Mallory shrank back from the managerial gestalt she now projected. He took a deep breath and tried to remind himself that Nell was just another cubicon like him. Still, the sharp curve of her hair, her dark, defined eyes, the exposed jawline which now gave new definition to her face – it all suddenly penetrated his defenses and drew an instinctive tremor of fear out of Mallory's deep stockpile of denied emotions.

"I ... uh ... uh ...."

Her new face now broke out into a wide, non-managerial smile. Mallory had tried to put Nell out of his mind overnight. He had learned from Manly Man that non-flirtatious encounters with women were best forgotten, but he hadn't been able to leave aside her mortifying rejection of him the day before. Now she suddenly looked so pretty and sophisticated, and was acting so concerned – but she was still talking business. He didn't know how to deal with these mixed messages.

He swiveled his chair and stood up, reverting to his usual method of intimidation by filling with his sheer bulk the normal personal space between him and the person he was talking to. Nell did step back, and he felt a surge of courage.

"You don't know anything about how I deal with customers."

Nell seemed to lose her nerve. "I mean, you might be cutting customers' calls. I mean, everybody does that sometimes. But maybe you should be more careful. They do listen in on our customer interactions sometimes."

"You believe that bullshit?"

There was a flicker of surprise in Nell's eyes before she turned her eyes down, almost humbly. The juices in Mallory's internal ecosystem rebalanced themselves. He had put her in her place.

"Let's go to lunch," he insisted.

"It's only ten thir...."

"Come on." He reached out, intending to grab for her arm, but suddenly remembered and pulled it back. She cocked her head, coldly eyed him up and down. But then she turned to walk along with him to the break room.

"I have an idea," she told him as they stepped quietly past the 27 cubicles to the break room. "I think there's a way we can help each other."

There was a collection of electronic devices on the inside wall

of the break room just past the entrance, one of which was a surveillance camera. People joked about why the company wanted to
spy on them while they were eating lunch. There was a lot of spec-
ulation that it was just a dummy camera. Mallory had solved the
mystery his second week on the job. One afternoon, after he had
finished his lunch and left the deserted break room, he re-entered
it alone with a white plastic bag over his head with two jagged
holes torn out for the eyes. Wearing this disguise, he backed up
toward the camera, stood on a chair and put a piece of masking
tape over the lens. There were no repercussions. The other workers soon noticed. He heard a few snickering conversations about
the disabled camera. Mallory wished he had the nerve to take
credit.

He decided he liked the swing and curve of Nell's sleek new
hairstyle. He liked being able to look directly into her eyes. But
even more inviting was her idea of them helping each other out.
As he listened to her, he felt a strange warmth spreading slowly
in his chest. It wasn't exactly the same kind of thrill he got from
his porn sites every night. It seemed to be a little higher up. But,
despite this stirring new sensation, he couldn't remember anything
she'd said the day before. He ate his first tuna sandwich with his
usual gusto while he searched his memory.

"You've worked in the cubicle next to me for three months,
and I don't know you at all," Nell started. "Maybe it's none of
my business, but I don't understand why you want to risk getting
yourself in trouble with the company." As she talked, she tossed
her dark, glossy hair flirtatiously back from her face.

"You like me, don't you, Nell?"

"What?"

"I know you want to talk to me alone. I know you're lonely.
I know you need a man." Straight talk, right out of Manly Man's
playbook.

She rolled her eyes, shook her head. "I'm not comfortable
with this conversation."

"It's not always comfortable to grab for what you really want."

"Where did you learn this kind of talk?"

The first rule of Manly Man was not to talk about Manly Man. Mallory stayed silent, stared at Nell until she shrank back.

"Am I safe here? Can you tell me that?" she asked. Her eyes darted to the walls on each side of the empty room. "You're not going to try to touch me again, are you?"

He felt a surge of manliness. "I will not touch you, Nell, unless you want to be touched. That is the code of the true man. But think about what you really want."

"I want you to keep your hands on your side of the table. Please. That's what I want, Mr. Mallory." But she wasn't finished. She went on in such a low voice he had to lean closer. "Okay, I do want something from you, Mr. Mallory." A whisper of peppermint on her breath intensified his excitement. "Something that will help me, but that might help you even more."

His heart sped up. But he forced himself to remain calm, reminding himself that a man's true role is to assure the woman that her urges are completely natural, and nothing to be afraid of. "Don't be ashamed, Nell. We all have needs."

"I'd like to get to know you better," she confessed.

"Yes. Yes. Me, too. Yes." He hadn't felt this excited in years.

"A good way to do that, I'm thinking, is if I invited you ..."

"Yes? Yes?"

"... to join the Employee Cheer Committee."

\* \* \* \* \* \*

Mallory hadn't known there was an Employee Cheer Committee at UniCast Cable until Nell invited him to be a member. He told her right away what he thought of it. The Employee Cheer Committee was exactly the type of employee organization the Algonquin J. Tycoons of the world loved. Meeting only briefly during work breaks and performing most of its real work on their own time, and usually funding events with their own money, these committees performed their primary function very well. Their primary function was to convince employees they were not competent to perform any organized activities on their own – and so they had better let Tycoon make every important decision affecting their lives. Mallory had never had any intention of joining one of these docile employee volunteer groups.

"It's not like that," Nell defended her committee. "It's just simple things that make people feel better. Like coffee. And we send sympathy cards to each employee who has a death in the immediate family. And we're planning an employee holiday party."

"I don't know if I want to put my hard-earned money into all that."

"We only spend our money on things all members of the committee agree on. If you were on the committee, we would listen to your opinion too."

"No way."

* * *   * * *

Mallory was convinced that Nell's Cheer Committee invitation had been just an excuse, a cowardly way for Nell to learn more about him without acknowledging the instinctive rush of feelings that was drawing them together. After her invitation, he fantasized about her for weeks. He couldn't get over the fact that she'd cut her hair, ditched her glasses, changed her appearance, the minute he touched her hand. He had never had such a quick and dramatic effect on any woman before. He felt he had been given a strange, new power over her, and that it had ricocheted back inside his own soul and changed his world forever. He'd never known before what it was like to be in love. He suspected she didn't either. He had to find some way to reach her.

He decided to ask Manly Man. Manly Man was a website for men who were in touch with their inner virility, men who were sick of all the namby-pamby, politically correct woke-speak that weaker men were entangled in. Mallory visited the website every night, and he also was a dedicated follower of Man-Tweets, which gave him a constant, solid man-view of current events and trends. All of this valuable information and life advice was free.

Mallory had always thought only a sucker would pay for anything except porn on a website. But his lack of progress with Nell, even after he followed precisely the Man-dates posted every night on Twitter, convinced him he had to do more. He paid $13.95 for one-time personal advice from Manly Man himself. He could have gotten a month's worth of advice for $29.95, or a lifetime subscription for $59.95, but he felt like he wasn't that needy.

The process of asking a question wasn't as simple as they let on. He had to fill out a long questionnaire before he could even ask his question *Age*: 32; *Height*: 5'6"; *Weight*: 197; *Color Hair*: Red; *Color eyes*; Brown; *Type of Problem (pick one)*: Repressed Female; *Initial or Subsequent Approach*: Subsequent; *Accusations of Harassment*: No; *Age of Female*: Unknown; *Marital Status of Female*: Single; *Body Type of Female (pick one)*: Standard, lumpy.

The questionnaire aggravated Mallory so much he would have given up if he hadn't already authorized the $13.95 to be deducted from his credit card. But he plowed on. Why did Manly Man have to know so much about his past, his education, his dating history, his level of fitness, how many pounds he could bench press? When he indicated that the affair was taking place in the work environment, Manly Man asked so many questions about the workplace policies that Mallory was flummoxed. He had no idea what the workplace policies were, or even if there were any workplace policies. He answered these questions by checking the boxes randomly. This didn't seem to work too well. For every answer he gave about workplace policies, the questionnaire spewed out pages and pages of legalese and refused to allow Mallory to go on unless he checked that he had read it and understood it and that he released Manly Man from any and all responsibility for whatever might happen to him in the workplace from following his advice.

Just when he was about to give up, a box appeared on the screen. He was told to type his question in the box in 200 words or less. Mallory had never had a problem coming up with descriptions of his woes. He had deluged his previous employers with daily, multi-page memos detailing his grievances, memos so long his employers generally stopped reading them – giving Mallory yet another ground for grievance. But the requirement that he put his question in 200 words or less was the type of task he had never faced before.

He wrote and rewrote his question for hours, skipping all of his usual nighttime video game and other computer activities, skipping even the chocolate donuts he had bought from the Dough and Go for a midnight snack. In composing his question, he felt he was being forced to live all over again every detail of the last few frustrating weeks of trying to get close to Nell. Finally, by about 1:30 a.m., he was so groggy and sleepy he felt he just had to let it go, and he pressed *Send*. He pushed his chair back to get away from his computer, relieved that he had finally summarized his problem into a question that Manly Man would understand. But right then he heard a ding. He turned to look at the screen. Manly Man had already answered.

"Join the Cheer Committee."

# Chapter 2: Invitations

You had to be so careful these days. Mallory had forgotten his neighbors' names. He was groggy from staying up so late the night before and grouchy from the inadequate response he had gotten from Manly Man. When he ran into his neighbors' son on the landing the next morning, he almost called him "boy."

"Um, *sir?*" He felt this was the height of ridiculousness, calling a teenage Black boy "sir," but he just couldn't remember the kid's name. Mallory's mother had taught him not to be prejudiced against Blacks. "Who am I to be prejudiced?" she would ask. "Every time I see one of them on the street, I think, 'There but for the grace of God go I.'"

"Hi, Mr. Mallory." The kid looked about nineteen. Mallory was suspicious about why he was up so early. He was glad he hadn't left for work before the kid came out to lurk around near his door. To his credit, the kid was dressed in normal clothes and hadn't shaved his hair into some barbarous do. But he was carrying something.

"What's that there?"

"My backpack? Schoolbooks, running shoes, other shit."

Mallory stared at the backpack. He wished he had a scanner, or a drug-sniffing dog. "What are you doing with that?"

"I'm at Community Tech." The kid was thin, and almost six feet tall. Mallory didn't like having to look up to him. He was a graduate of Community Technical College himself, but he reminded himself never to mention this to the kid. He wished he could remember the kid's name, but it would be embarrassing to ask at this late point.

"Are you alright, Mr. Mallory?"

Mallory didn't realize he'd been staring. "Yeah. Sure." He turned to go.

"Oh, Mr. Mallory." The kid wouldn't let up. Mallory just had to turn back. "I see you forgot my name. It's Thomas. We're new here in the complex. I live with my parents."

"That's nice." At least it seemed like there wouldn't be any crack parties or shootouts across the hall.

"My parents and I get along okay. But it's just temporary. Parents there all the time. That kinda cuts down on the action, right?"

Mallory's stomach felt all squirmy at the thought of Black action right across the landing. He suspected Thomas was trying to intimidate him. He tried to think of something to say. He was annoyed that he had to try to think of something to say. He wished the kid would just leave him alone.

"Hmm," he managed finally.

"Well, I gotta go." The kid practically ran down the stairs, but then turned and called back. "My parents want to get to know you, Mr. Mallory."

Mallory's stomach churned at the thought. He made his way to the parking lot, only to see the kid far ahead of him, sliding quickly between the parked cars, jumping into a sporty looking new Corolla and powering his way off – all before Mallory maneuvered his way into the driver's seat of his ten-year-old Camry.

\*\*\* \*\*\*

Mallory was in more trouble at his job than he had let on to Nell. The customer he disconnected right before his first break room conversation with Nell had actually looked up UniCast Cable's chain of command and had written an actual letter of complaint. Of course, the customer couldn't identify him, but Mallory was called into his supervisor's office to discuss the complaint.

"Why would you think it was me?" Mallory acted offended.

"We don't know for sure," Mr. Teitelbaum, the Customer Service Supervisor, admitted. Teitelbaum was old. He looked like a person who had been laid off from a decent job in the last recession and was just hanging on at UniCast until he could retire. He was bald but for a silver rim of hair which he now scratched like he wasn't sure why he was spending what should have been the peak years of his career in this windowless three-story concrete building in a half-empty industrial park. And dealing with people like Mallory.

Mallory scorned Teitelbaum because he was nowhere near being any kind of tycoon, but still had to wear a suit. He waited for Teitelbaum to trot out the evidence against him. He suspected the company actually did record some customer calls, but he wasn't going to start defending himself until they showed him they had recorded this particular call. He thought Teitelbaum would have mentioned the recording by now if he had one. "You don't know for sure? So you're just guessing it's me. Do you think this is going to hold up in court?" Mallory loved to hint that he had a lawyer and that he was ready and eager to sue. This type of vague threat had gotten him out of a lot of jams with his previous employers.

"We don't have a tape," Teitelbaum admitted, adjusting his clear-framed glasses. But he didn't seem flustered. Mallory guessed he was too old and too far down the totem pole and had seen too many personnel actions gone bad to be upset if one more Customer Service representative got off the hook. Teitelbaum seemed calm because he really didn't care at all, Mallory was sure. "But we do have records of the length of each call from each line. The customer reported that it was an extraordinarily short call, after almost an hour of being on hold, and that it took place near the end of the shift, your shift. Our records show you were on a 52-second call at just about that time."

"What is that supposed to prove?" Mallory had never seen any benefit to making nice with any of his supervisors.

"It's not the smoking gun," Teitelbaum admitted. "But we received a similar complaint a few weeks ago." He picked up a file from his desk. "We looked up the telephone times on that one, too. And, interestingly, the customer service representative in both cases identified himself as Bill Tell. So, Mr. Mallory, are you Bill Tell?"

22

"Like you just said, I'm Mallory."

"Very well, Mr. Mallory. But I want to give you fair warning. We will be keeping close track of your customer assistance calls. We may well record them. We will check the timing of your calls more often."

\* \* \*   \* \* \*

Over the course of his career, Mallory had faced down and defeated more formidable supervisors than Teitelbaum. The coffee shop owner wasn't the only one to crack and take a slug at him. In one case, the State Secretary of Personnel had personally pounded him in the full view of news cameras. But Teitelbaum was not the type to use physical violence. And Mallory recognized that Teitelbaum was a burnt-out Boomer, just trying to eke out a few dollars to throw into his retirement account to ward off starvation in the coming years. He might increase the surveillance of Mallory a little, but he was not going to risk raising the kind of fuss it would take to get rid of him.

"Good morning, Mr. Mallory." Nell gave him her usual, brisk greeting as she passed his cubicle on the way to hers. But then she stopped, and he could tell she was still looking at him.

"Morning, Nell." He looked up and smirked. He had known she was still drawn to him, known she couldn't keep up her icy distance from him for long. He knew this purely by instinct. He hadn't taken Manly Man's advice to join the Cheer Committee. While he still believed in the free Manly Man precepts disseminated on the internet for all alpha males, Mallory decided that paying for advice was almost as bad as going to therapy.

"I see you're still drinking machine coffee." Nell's open smile belied her snarky sentence. She caught his eye and then glanced down toward the paper cup he had set down smack in the middle of his otherwise empty desk.

"Yeah. So what?" He curled his hand protectively around the quickly cooling cup.

"You might be interested in this. We had a meeting of the Cheer Committee yesterday afternoon."

"I'm not interested in the Cheer Committee." He was disappointed that she was still bringing this up. But he noticed that she still kept her hair styled smartly, tossing her head as she talked to him, the better to show off her smart new look. Her clothes, too, no longer seemed like things made by her mother.

"You have pretty eyes," he admitted. Mallory had never given a woman a compliment before. Manley Man said compliments should generally be avoided because they made you seem needy. If absolutely necessary, they may be used, but only on special occasions. And there were strict rules for compliments. No mention of body parts below the neck. No admission of any normal male physical reaction. No references to comic book heroines. Manley said if a woman is really attracting you, you must pretend the opposite, but you may admire something completely irrelevant such as a bracelet she's wearing or the color of her blouse – but even there, it was important not to try to name the color.

Her reaction was not what he expected. "Oh. That's a nice thing to say. My glasses were making my eyes look small," she explained. "I'm glad to be done with them." Then she smiled at him. Her eyes did look prettier, but the thing Mallory noticed most was this woman, by getting rid of her glasses, had taken the first step toward disrobing in front him. He couldn't believe how easily he was making progress.

But then she dropped her flirtatious tone. "We've been having long discussions at the committee. For weeks. We need members, and we want to encourage new people to join." When he just kept staring at her, she went on. "We finally came to a decision. Everybody agreed. We're going to pool our money and offer a financial incentive for new members to join."

Mallory's ears pricked up, but he wasn't going to show weakness by asking what the financial incentive was. Nell seemed to be trying to wait him out, but she couldn't hold back for long.

"We finally decided," she said, a big smile lighting up her face, "that the current committee members will pay new members' coffee pool dues for two weeks."

Mallory stared at her. "That's – what, ten dollars?"

"There's only seven people on the committee now. That means we're each going to have to give more than a dollar for each new member we get. Even so, we all agreed!"

Mallory didn't think ten dollars of free coffee made joining the committee worth it. And his fantasies of Nell surrendering to him any time soon were fading. She stepped back now and put a hand on her hip. And now she was talking about money. His compliment hadn't led anywhere after all. He reminded himself not to try that again.

He sloshed the remains of his coffee around in his paper cup. He didn't see any need to respond to her. And he was glad to see her begin backing up, moving on toward her own cubicle. He was still sure she was interested in him, but he could see she was obviously too socially awkward to make the first move. He finished the rest of his coffee. It was almost cold, and pretty bad.

Mallory tried to put Nell out of his mind. It seemed like she was pestering him, using the committee as an excuse to talk to him. He was especially sarcastic with his customers that day, but he didn't even enjoy doing it. And he came home to yet another hassle. When Mallory arrived back at his apartment building that evening, he saw Thomas sitting on the outside steps leading up to the landing between his apartment and Thomas's. Mallory did a double take before satisfying himself that he was in no danger. He really wasn't afraid of Thomas, he told himself. He nodded hello and tried to walk by.

"Mr. Mallory, I've been waiting for you." Thomas's easy smile helped smooth over the prickly edges of Mallory's anxiety, but he couldn't be absolutely sure Thomas wasn't challenging him.

"What? Something wrong with my apartment?"

Thomas stood up and walked with Mallory across the landing to his door. Mallory didn't understand why he did that. His suspicions were raised again.

"No. Everything's fine with the apartment, Mr. Mallory."

Mallory nodded. He didn't want to get his key out and open the door in front of Thomas. He struggled for the words to interact with this young Black man. "What's up?" he finally managed.

"My family's having a party. We're inviting our old friends and our new neighbors. My Dad is like, insisting I invite you to come."

"Oh. When is it?" Mallory reviewed his mental inventory of excuses why he couldn't come to events. "I'm kind of busy the next few weeks." He rarely went out of his apartment on the weekends, except to go to the Dough and Go, the Virtual Playground, and occasionally to the grocery store. How was he going to hide out from a party right across the landing?

"The party's not for three weeks, three weeks from this coming Saturday, on the 19th." Thomas met his eyes. "You're our closest new neighbor. Mom always wants to know our neighbors."

*Why would that be?* Mallory wondered. He'd passed Thomas's father on the steps once, a large, dark-skinned man in his late forties in a white, short-sleeved shirt and a tie, dark hair turning to silver, wire rimmed glasses, small moustache, a bulk to him that told he had a sedentary office job. Mallory hadn't greeted him at first because he was hoping he was just visiting. The man had sighed as he slowly climbed the stairs. He hadn't seemed overly friendly like his son.

"Good," Mallory finally replied. "I'd like to get to know you all too." He felt more secure now that he had a specific date, the 19th. He'd have time now to construct a conflict in his schedule.

Mallory generally didn't go to parties anymore. When he was in community college, and for the four or five years thereafter, he'd been to a few parties, but in his opinion the parties had degenerated over time. When he was slimmer and younger, he'd searched at parties for that elusive, beautiful girl who he'd take off to the side, make out with, fall in love with and eventually make a life with. In five or six years he had never gotten past the making out part, and only that far once or twice. Except for those few times, he'd never found a girl who was worth talking to. By his late twenties he realized there were no sweet, sexy girls to be had at parties, and the main fun was getting drunk or high. He had some really good times at those parties, though he did lose a job that way. But parties had degenerated even more since then. People at parties rarely even got high anymore. The main point of parties now seemed to be food. He could get better food anywhere. Women apparently came to parties now to gush over the awful salads they had made themselves, or else to gorge themselves on chocolate cream puffs or gooey homemade trifles that explained why they were mostly such lumpy bumpies now.

\* \*\* \*\* \*

Mallory was called into Teitelbaum's office once again. "I'm giving you an official reprimand." Teitelbaum's thin lips twisted in an old man's attempt at a smirk.

"You can't prove it was me who cut off that customer."

"Maybe we haven't proved that yet, Mr. Mallory." Teitelbaum spoke in a soft, self-satisfied, patronizing voice that reminded Mallory of being corrected by his mother or his aunts. Those soft words were always followed by concrete proof that he had done wrong, again. That tone had always made Mallory suspect that his father had been right to bug out.

"But we do have proof, Mr. Mallory, that your phone has been inactive for seven periods of an hour or more over the past week. As I'm sure you know, there is no excuse for that. We have customers waiting on the line for an average of 27 minutes to reach a representative like you. There is always a customer waiting to be served. You didn't pick up the phone for long periods of time on at least seven occasions."

"We're allowed break times."

Teitelbaum's smile was a thin line. "These seven instances are in addition to your authorized break times."

"If you reprimand me, I'm going over your head to the Operations Manager." Mallory recognized that Teitelbaum was only on his second or third career. The man probably had nowhere near the depth of experience in employer-employee relations that Mallory had. Mallory knew there was an Operations Manager, but he didn't know his name or anything else about him. He didn't even know if the Operations Manager could overrule Teitelbaum, but he guessed Teitelbaum didn't know either.

"I have the proof, Mr. Mallory."

"You don't know how the customer service operation really works on an hour to hour basis. There are lulls when calls don't come in. Sometimes the phone connection is bad. I'm sure you haven't checked anyone else's line like you checked mine. If you did, you'd see the same dead phone times, too." Mallory gauged the look on Teitelbaum's face to see if he was making a dent in his resolve. "Reprimanding me would be a mistake. All the employees will hate you. You'd blow up a smoothly running operation."

"Nevertheless, Mr. Mallory ...." Teitelbaum didn't finish his sentence.

# Chapter 3: Bunbury

Mallory nursed his coffee in the break room. He was actually on an authorized break. The candy and pastry dispensing machines were out of order. He wasn't that hungry anyway. He glanced up at the surveillance camera and noted with satisfaction that the tape he had put over the lens was still there. He was never surprised at UniCast's level of incompetence.

He saw Nell coming in through the open entranceway to the break room. He was sitting at a long, empty table and, just as he expected, she walked up and sat down across from him.

"I decided to wear contacts all the time," she explained. As if he had asked. And he didn't ask. He knew he was the cause of her new concern for her appearance. Manly Man said when females were fishing for compliments, a real man gives them only sparingly, and randomly. Intermittent reinforcement, Manly called it. When they can't quite predict what will bring on the praise they crave, females will try harder, be more inventive, go further to get your attention. It was something psychologists had learned while training pigeons. He hadn't made much progress in getting Nell to acknowledge the natural feminine urges he knew she was feeling for him. Mostly, she just kept hounding him about joining the committee. As he met her eyes, he curled his hand around his coffee cup as if she were going to steal it.

"Really, Kevin, how much did that coffee cost?"

"Buck and a quarter."

"Do you drink one on every break?"

"What? Are you going to do math on me now?"

Nell drew back, breathed out a sigh, looked out somewhere over his shoulder. He already knew the math. He was spending five bucks a day for coffee he could get from the Cheer Committee Coffee Fund for five bucks a week. But he'd have to stand in line at the committee's table while those finicky women measured their sugar and selected their spoons and stirred their creamer like they were in a biochemistry laboratory. He had finally gone on the internet to try to find out how to brew coffee, but there were so many types of coffee brewing machines he got confused. Today, he had been planning on sneaking a look at the brand name of the committee's percolator – or whatever their little machine was called – to narrow his internet search.

"The committee could use some new members," she persisted now. "It would be a chance to get to know people." Evidently, Nell thought that was a good thing.

"Would you please stop hounding me about the committee?" The force of his own speech shocked Mallory. But forceful was how he felt. He was sick of her pestering. Over the past few weeks, she had dolled herself up for him and pursued him relentlessly, but it was coming clear now she didn't even recognize her own instincts and was instead narrowing her focus to just the Cheer Committee. He could no longer take the tension of waiting for her to wake up.

Nell sat back with a look on her face like a patient big sister whose little brother was throwing a tantrum. Mallory could tell she was having a hard time getting a word out without mentioning the committee. And, he decided, she was such a Daisy Do-Gooder she could see in him nothing more than a potential committee member. Mallory decided he'd forget about researching the coffee machine.

"Okay, let's talk about something else," she surprised him. "What do you do for fun, Kevin?" He was thrilled that she was using his first name.

"You mean, outside of work?"

"Yes. Like, what do you do with your friends?"

"Gaming. Video gaming." He knew that sounded like a cliché. Now that she was interested, he needed to jazz up his story a little. "And the beach. I like to go to the beach." That sounded lame, so he added, "Especially when it's hot outside."

"Oh, that's nice. I like to go to the beach, too. I don't get too much of a chance anymore, what with my mother and all."

So, Mallory figured, neither of them went to the beach. Good. His fair, freckled skin would be burned in twenty minutes at the beach. But it might be worth it to see Nell in a bathing suit. He was confused about whether she was coming on to him or not. The thing to do was take control of the situation.

"We should go to the beach sometime."

Her eyes widened briefly, then quickly narrowed. "I go with my girlfriends once a year. We stay in a hotel right on the beach."

"Hit the clubs?" He thought this sounded like a cool thing to say.

"Oh, no. We rent one of those big beach umbrellas for the whole week. We make lunch and eat it out there and watch the ocean."

"What do you do at night?"

"We know three really good restaurants. They're hard to get into in the high season, so we make our reservations two weeks in advance." She glanced up toward him. "What do you do when you go there?"

"Uh, me and my best friend, we jet ski, do catamarans, deep sea fishing. At night we hit the clubs." Mallory hadn't been in a club in six or seven years. He'd never been deep sea fishing. He didn't have a best friend.

"Typical guy stuff," she rolled her eyes. He took it as a compliment. She had to be comparing her sterile world to the vibrant life he offered.

"Do you own your own house?" she asked suddenly.

"Yeah." He jumped instantly into that lie. Women loved houses. A man who owns a house has a 50% greater chance of picking up a woman, according to the Mandates.

"Oh, that's nice. Is it around here?"

"Uh, yeah. It's sort of behind Glenwood Village." He was careful not to be too specific.

"Oh, there are some nice homes in that area."

Bad luck. She knew the area. He now realized that lying about owning a house was a mistake. She would expect to see it someday.

Mallory was used to lying about his background when it suited him. But he was also practiced in backing away from a story that was no longer useful. If the ultimate goal was to bring Nell home to his apartment, and to his bed, he'd better start paring down her expectations right now. "My house is one of the smaller ones," he told her.

"Don't be modest, Kevin. Owning a home of any size is an achievement, and a responsibility."

*Achievement. Responsibility.* Why did she talk like that? Mallory finished his coffee and slid his chair back from the table. He gave her only a quick nod as he left the break room.

\*\*\* \*\*\*

It was a few days later that Mallory was startled to see a looming presence suddenly in his cubicle doorway. It was Teitelbaum in his dark suit, white shirt, sparse white hair, and clear-framed glasses, staring at Mallory's computer screen like he owned it. Mallory had installed pirate software he had bought on the internet called Loophole. With Loophole in place, Mallory could explore and play on the internet all he wanted. If any supervisor came near, he could, with one touch of the *Ctrl* key, instantly bring back the actual work screen he was supposed to be working from. Teitelbaum definitely glanced at Mallory's screen, and he did do a little double take when Mallory hit *Ctrl*, but Mallory was pretty sure the old guy had no idea what was going on.

"Mr. Mallory, I'd like to see you in my office." Teitelbaum's intense blue eyes provided the only color in his face.

"I'm on my break."

"You've worked in government agencies before you came here, I can tell. But this is a private business, Mr. Mallory. It's different. You have to do what management says here. Report to my office within ten minutes or I'll guarantee you'll be out the door."

Mallory took the opposite tack and followed Teitelbaum back so closely he was almost stepping on his heels. When Teitelbaum turned to enter his office door, Mallory almost bumped into him, and he thought he saw a trace of fear in the old man's eyes. Good. Teitelbaum scurried around his desk and sat down, and Mallory, after a moment's hesitation, sat down in the smaller chair facing him.

"Mr. Mallory, since we last talked, I've had our software people keep a record of your recent phone and computer usage. The records – and I have them right here on my screen – show that in the last ten working days, you have been off the phone, and not active on your computer, for numerous periods."

"We do have break times here."

"Many of these do not correspond to any of your break times."

"I'm not a robot. I do have to go to the bathroom sometimes."

"That's what break times are for."

"I'm not a robot." Mallory repeated. He doubted Teitelbaum wanted to go into any exploration of his bathroom habits. He thought he had fought Teitelbaum to a draw.

But the old man was not that easily deterred. "Actually, I anticipated that excuse. And so I checked the personnel records. Our application specifically asks if you have any disability that would prohibit you from remaining at your desk for a full eight-hour day, excluding breaks. You answered *no*." Teitelbaum clicked to a different screen. "Are you telling me now that you have developed a condition that requires you to leave your position in your cubicle for periods of up to 55 minutes, three or more times a day, every day for seven straight workdays?"

Mallory was surprised himself at how much time he had missed. Maybe he hadn't installed Loophole correctly. Maybe they were relying mostly on the phone records, which Loophole didn't cover. He didn't want to ask Teitelbaum to show him the data sheets. That would show weakness, as if he were afraid of their numbers.

"I have developed a condition. I'm consulting with my doctor about it."

"Do you mind my asking what the condition is?"

Mallory was caught off guard by this bold, intrusive question. His mind was an encyclopedia of workers' rights, and he realized he could possibly get away with refusing to answer. But now was the time, he decided, to confuse the enemy. "They haven't come to a definitive diagnosis yet, but my doctor thinks I might have Bunbury's disease. In rare cases, it can be fatal."

"Oh," Teitelbaum squinted at him with those cold blue eyes. He did not look sympathetic. "I've never heard of this disease. We'll need confirmation from your doctor, of course."

"I can't allow you to have that. The records of my medical condition are strictly confidential."

Teitelbaum picked up the phone. Mallory was alarmed to hear Teitelbaum speaking to Jim Starganoff, the Operations Manager for the whole company. Teitelbaum described Mallory's case in the worst possible terms. Mallory didn't like the way this was going. Usually, after preliminarily dealing with front-line managers like Teitelbaum, Mallory got the jump on his accusers by immediately filing his own complaints to the next higher manager in line. The first thing this manager would hear would be Mallory's side of the story. But Teitelbaum had already trashed Mallory first, and now Starganoff wanted to see both him and Teitelbaum, and right away.

Mallory felt strangely disoriented when he first saw Starganoff upon entering the Operations Manager's office. With his huge brow, thick nose, wide jaw, dark eyes and eyebrows, his black hair which fell naturally into a truncated mop top, and his crooked grin, Starganoff looked more like an ex-boxer than a corporate officer – but he also bore a disturbing resemblance to Bed Rock, Mallory's hero and the male protagonist in more than one porn site. Mallory had to put Bed Rock out of his mind. He could sense from Starganoff's attitude that this was not going to be one of those years-long personnel battles he was used to. Starganoff looked like he might actually fire him.

34

"You won't release your medical records of this disease, this Bunbury's disease that nobody's ever heard of, and that I can't find on the internet. You won't give us your doctor's name or allow him to release any information. Tell me, Mr. Mallory, why shouldn't I fire you right now?"

"Um ... I've been looking over the records where you allege that I was away from my phone," Mallory lied. "I admit those records may be accurate. But now that I have had a chance to look at the actual times, I realized it wasn't my Bunbury's disease that caused those gaps. Most of those times I was off my phone, and off my computer, were due to my duties as a member of the Employee Cheer Committee."

# Chapter 4: The Cost of Cheer

Mallory stood blocking the opening of Nell's cubicle. She was on the phone, staring at her screen, not noticing him. Mallory's smile faded as he realized it might be some time before she looked up. He became irritated. He thought she should be more considerate. Eventually, she noticed his shape in the entrance to her cubicle and looked up with a start. She held an index finger up as if to ask him to hold on for a minute. Mallory returned to his cubicle, furious. He decided to raise the price she would have to pay for his joining the committee.

The party that Thomas's family was planning right across the landing from his apartment was looming larger and larger in his imagination. He couldn't pretend to be out of town on the 19th because the party would be happening practically right in front of his door. He could go to his mother's house, but his mother had book club every Saturday night, and going there would require him to run the gauntlet of the old ladies' narrowed eyes and be forced to answer their pointed questions about his career and marriage plans. He'd rather be the only white person at an all-Black party. He wondered if they'd be smoking a lot of weed at Thomas's house. Mallory had spent 250 hard-earned dollars obtaining a prescription for cannabis, and he paid triple the street price to buy it legally at a dispensary, but he assumed most Black people smoked it illegally all the time.

Thomas had been sitting on the steps, waiting for him, when he got back from work the previous day. He had been practically forced to say hi.

"Mr. Mallory." Thomas closed his schoolbook. "My mother asked me to ask you what kind of food you like – for the party, I mean."

"Um, I'm not sure ...."

"Deviled eggs?"

"Oh yes. But ...."

"Barbequed pork loin. Oh, she makes that good."

"Oh, that sounds good!"

"She can make a chocolate lava cake. You like that?"

"Oh. Yes. Yes. Yes."

"Okay. Saturday, the19th, right? You'll be there, right."

"Right. I'll be there."

He had to go to the party now. But he was still a little afraid of Thomas and his father and their friends. He didn't want to be the only regular person at a Black party, and he was afraid to ask Thomas the race of every other person who would be there. He told himself it was normal for a white person to have this fear. But he had to go to the party. He knew he needed a plan.

\*\*\* \*\*\*

Nell finally appeared in his cubicle doorway a half hour after brushing him off. By that time, he had come up with a plan that would solve both of his problems at once.

"I've decided to join the Employee Cheer Committee," he announced.

"Oh. That's good. I'll bring your name up to the committee at the next meeting and recommend they vote you in."

"They have to vote someone in?"

"Yes. I find it best if all decisions of the committee are unanimous."

He had to *apply*? Mallory felt like he needed to turn the tide quickly, to show her that she was the one who needed this most. "Okay. On one condition. If you'll go to a party at my apartment complex with me, I'll apply."

Nell's face hardened. "You're saying I have to go on a date with you?"

"It's not a date. It's a social obligation. I have to go to this party. And I have to bring someone."

"You'll join the committee, right?" Nell shifted her weight to one leg and brought up one foot to scratch the back of her calf.

She gritted her teeth while she thought. And thought. "Can I just meet you there?" she said finally.

He smiled to himself. "Sure." He guessed they could meet on the landing. He felt he had her on the ropes now. But now was the time for revenge for her brushing him off earlier. "And one more thing. I want *four* weeks' free coffee."

"That's *twenty* dollars! The committee members would have to pay for that. That's almost two dollars each. I don't know if they will agree to that."

"You got *me* to join, Nell. I'm sure you can convince them I'm worth it."

*** ***

"*Are-you-sure-there-is-not-to-be found-a-splicing-in-the-LAN, sir?*" Mallory was doing his best imitation of an Indian accent. He sensed that he was in trouble with the Operations Manager, and he was trying to lie low. He was afraid Starganoff would check out his Cheer Committee excuse right away. He had assumed Nell would be thrilled to put him onto the Cheer Committee instantly, but then he had blown the timing by insisting on extra free coffee. Now, Nell was adamant that she couldn't act on something that would cost that much money without a vote of the whole committee. Mallory could have solved that problem by dropping his free coffee request, but he knew that manly men never backed down. Besides, he thought he might have some time before anyone could check out his story. Teitelbaum and Starganoff had looked up in surprise when he came up with this excuse for being away from his desk. Apparently, neither one of them had ever even heard of the Employee Cheer Committee.

"I don't think I understand what you just said, young man."

"The-LAN-sir. Would-you-please-to-find-out-for-me if-there-a-splicing-in the-cable-to-the-LAN, sir?

"I am a woman."

"A-thousand-pardons-Ma'am."

"I'm an old woman. I just know my cable TV went dark. I don't know what a LAN is, or where the cable to it is, or what a splicing would look like."

"Hold-please-for-technical-advisory."

Click.

He hadn't even had to make up a name. And the old woman probably thought he was twelve thousand miles away. He liked his new gambit. No customer would ever suspect it was he who cut them off. He could shorten these tedious conversations with these stupid strangers. He could spend more time fantasizing about Nell. He was now imagining rescuing her from Thomas's ghetto party, putting his arm around her waist as she shook in fear, ushering her to his place right across the landing. A couple drinks there to calm her down. The worshipful look of gratitude. The suppressed passion smoldering in her eyes, then suddenly leaping into flame as his lips touched hers. The fire spreading everywhere.

But the screen indicated he'd gotten another call.

"It-is-my-pleasure-to-help-you-sir-whom-may-I-ask-is-calling?"

"Reginald Coates, customer number 7EX43 ...."

"Please-not-to-say-the number-yet-sir."

"Okay."

"What-is-your-customer-ID-number-sir?"

"My customer number is 7EX4329772554-7788."

"7EX4329772954-7788?"

"No. 7EX4329772554-7788."

"I see. You-are-correct, sir. Undoubtedly-is-causing-your-problem the-error-in-your-customer-number-sir."

"There wasn't any error in my customer number. You just heard me wrong when I said it right now."

"It-is-not-needful-to-insult-your-customer-service-representative-sir."

"I didn't insult anybody. And pray tell, what is your name?"

"Apu."

"Apu what?"

"Apu ... Krishna. Please-to-tell-me-your-correct-customer-number-now-sir."

"Okay, Mr. Krishna. 7EX4329772554-7788.

"One-moment-please-sir." Mallory took a long, slow gulp of his coffee. "I-am-not-seeing-that-number-listed-to-Mr.-Reginald-Coates-sir."

"Well, that's my name, and my number."

"Please-to-obtain-your-actual-bill-from-company-sir-and-read-it-off-to-me."

"That'll take me a minute."

Mallory could hear Reginald rustling papers and mumbling under his breath. As soon as those sounds stopped, and he could hear Reginald clearing his throat to speak, Mallory hung up.

Time for a break. He had noticed that morning that the vending machine was back in order. He checked the surveillance camera in the break room as he entered. The tape was still there. He shook his head at the stupidity of UniCast, trying to prove the exact times he was taking breaks by going through call records when all they had to do was remove the tape from their own camera.

He had tried to pressure Nell into hurrying up his application to the Cheer Committee that morning. But her face seemed to go suddenly blank, her eyes dull and cow-like. He supposed she got that way from dealing with customers. He knew he could save her from this passionless life of droning on with customers. The job of Customer Service was to keep the customers from slowing down the UniCast profit machine – without making them quite angry enough to unsubscribe. He often saw Nell frustrated, her jaw set stolidly as she dragged information out of one idiot customer after another. But now she looked at him like he was a customer himself. She told him there wasn't another committee meeting for two weeks.

"You can't call a special meeting to let me join?"

"The meetings are scheduled three months in advance. We have to make sure everybody can be there."

"I thought you *wanted* me on the damn committee," he growled – but low enough so that the worker in the next cubicle wouldn't hear.

"We feel we can do a better job with wider employee representation."

"That's it? There's nothing special about me that you want?"

"Every person has their own perspective, their own unique and valuable way of seeing things. We gain a lot by hearing each person's point of view."

"I thought it was just about the coffee."

He really needed to get on that committee before Teitelbaum or Starganoff started investigating. But he could sense that the more pressure he put on Nell, the harder she would resist. He decided to talk up the party he was going to at Thomas's parents' apartment. He knew Nell was fond of animals. He told her the party was intended as an occasion to set up a committee to advocate for the county to set up a no-kill shelter for homeless animals.

"Is this part of the ASPCA?"

"No, not the ASPCA."

"Is it part of Our Friends the Felines?"

Mallory had never heard of Our Friends the Felines. "That's cats, I guess. No, it's not cats. It's some kind of new organization they're thinking of starting."

"Is it like, a specific animal they're trying to protect?"

"Yes," he responded. Then he immediately realized his mistake. He should have kept the whole thing vague. He decided to just hope she'd drop the conversation.

She didn't. "What kind of animal? What's the group's name?"

"I'm not sure. It's not your usual group you've ever heard of or anything. It's like, a new group. A group that isn't even started yet."

Nell's expression showed that her level of interest had dropped down a bit. "Well, it's nice that your neighbors are thinking about the welfare of the animals. But there are already a lot of organizations they can join without starting a new one."

"Um ... I think this one is specific. I mean, specific to an animal problem in our Glenwood neighborhood."

"But you don't know what problem?"

He put his hands out, palms up. "No." Then he realized this made him sound stupid. "Nell, I don't know for sure, but I think it might be ... ferrets. Yeah, I think they said we're having a ferret problem."

"I never heard of that."

"Me neither. I'm not sure they want word of it to get out yet. You know, property values and all. When we go there, we're not supposed to start talking about ferrets right away." Mallory fervently hoped by the time she had a few drinks she would have forgotten about ferrets. Maybe some of Thomas's marijuana would help, too. He wondered if he should have warned her that Thomas's family was Black. But there might be a good side to her being surprised. Once Nell was traumatized by the situation, she would more easily flee across the landing to his apartment and melt into his arms.

\* \* \* \* \* \*

Mallory had not always used Manly Man's theories in his relations with women. Three years before, he had met his old girlfriend Rose at a setup his mother had arranged at a lunch hangout near the office where both women worked. At the time, he had run out of roommates, and money, and food. Besides, if he went to this lunch, it would count as fulfillment of his monthly duty to have dinner at his mother's. It was not that he didn't feel any attachment to his mother. But he had discovered that the more he stayed away from her, the more he liked her.

"Hello." Rose was already seated on a leather bench next to his mother. They both pointed to the chair he was to sit in opposite them. Rose seemed fit enough. As she turned to greet him, a thin gold chain slid across her black ribbed sweater. She had short black hair and an olive complexion, muted lipstick. She gave off the no-nonsense vibe of a businesswoman; but she looked right into his eyes, and her graceful, precise gestures seemed to be inviting him closer. It was the kind of alluring enticement that women almost never offered him. He hated that it was happening now, with his mother right there.

"Rose works with me. Well, on a different floor. It's a big place," his mother explained. "We got here early so you could sit right across from us. There's more room for a big man on that side of the table."

Mallory ignored the reference to his weight. He was sure he and Rose wouldn't like each other, but he didn't mind looking into those dark, inquisitive eyes. "The chicken cacciatore is their best meal here," she explained at once.

"You work with my mother?"

"We both work for Accounting Associates, but in different divisions. Where do you work?"

He didn't realize there would be a quiz. But he wasn't going to leave before the food came. "I'm starting a new job next week. Assistant manager at Starbucks," he lied.

"Oh. Does their 401(k) have an option to invest in company stock?"

He had never heard of a 401(k). "I'm not sure."

"You should find out right away. A lot of people have lost all their 401(k) savings when they had it invested in company stock."

"I see what you mean," he said.

"At least, it shouldn't be a default investment. Make sure you check the detailed terms of the plan, if they have a plan."

"You should get a job," Mallory's mother interjected from her seat next to Rose, "with some kind of vested pension plan, not just a 401(k)."

"Of course, Mom." Mallory glanced at the menu as the waiter hovered over them. "The French dip looks good."

"No. You want the chicken cacciatore," Rose commanded.

He let her order the chicken cacciatore for him. Rose was cute, smart, and a little flirtatious, but she worked in the Audit

Department and seemed to have strong opinions about how everything should be done. He felt he had already endured a lifetime's worth of a woman's strong opinions. But he liked sitting across from Rose. She talked with her hands and, as she moved, the slim gold chain bounced between her breasts. And her opinions were at least focused on him, to the point where he almost forgot his mother was there.

The chicken cacciatore actually was very good. He had a small scoop of ice cream for dessert while Rose kept nibbling on her salad. She explained exactly how many calories were in each serving of each of their meals and what should be the appropriate balance of protein and carbohydrates for each of their body types. His pulse quickened at her every flirtatious smile, but his brain told him he should not go out with her. He had a premonition that living with her would be like being audited twenty-four seven. He waited until his mother got up to visit the ladies' room, then pushed back his chair and began to stand up to leave.

But Rose reached out to him. "I'd like to get to know you better. We should go out for a drink sometime. Tomorrow night would be the best time for that." She touched the tips of her long fingers, their nails painted a subtle shade of frost, to his wrist.

It had been years since he'd been touched like that. His knees wobbled. He obeyed.

# Chapter 5: Party Protocols

As he edged his way between the final row of cars in his apartment parking lot, Mallory saw Thomas run ahead of him and leap up the steps to the landing three at a time. Then the young man started jogging in place on the landing while he looked back, apparently waiting for Mallory to catch up. Mallory was in a good mood as he trudged up the stairs himself. He knew Thomas would be thrilled when he promised to show up at his family party.

"Why are you running around so much?" he started.

"They tore up the track at school now that semester's over. Redoing it."

"You run ... *track*?" Mallory had always thought running track was the stupidest thing he'd ever heard of. That's why they invented cars, so people wouldn't have to run.

"Eight hundred meters." Thomas had stopped doing jumping jacks but was still breathing hard. "This is my first year. I came in fourth in the CCCC division championship meet. Coach says if I can cut off four tenths next year I can probably get a track scholarship to State."

Mallory could understand that Black people might have more reason to run than whites. He wondered for a second about Latinos. He'd never heard of any Latino track stars.

"So you run in the street after school?"

"The streets. The park. Sometimes, if I have gas money, I drive over to the State track, but it's 25 miles away."

The whole thing seemed like a waste of energy to Mallory. But he wondered if he could make use of Thomas to run to the store occasionally – though he wasn't sure if Thomas would be very good at buying white things. Thomas paced the landing, smiling, making eye contact, and Mallory remembered the good news he had for him.

"I'll definitely be there on the 19^th," he announced. "And I'm bringing a woman."

"Your *wife*?" My Mom will be jazzed to meet her. There's a lot of food. It's gonna be a big buffet."

Buffet? Wife? This whole party thing was getting out of hand. Mallory had counted on blues music, marijuana smoke, leering Black men who would send Nell scurrying to the safety of his own apartment across the landing. He started to tell Thomas that Nell was just a co-worker, but something about Thomas's energy and optimism made him not want to disappoint the young man. Thomas seemed to believe he was a standard, sturdy citizen, and Mallory decided to pretend to be one.

"Girlfriend. Her name is Nell. She works at UniCast Cable, just like me."

"Nice. Hey, do you think you can get us a deal on HBO? Just kidding, man."

"Yeah. Ha ha. Well, I'll be seeing you around."

Thomas took the hint and moved aside so Mallory could get to his door. Once inside, Mallory breathed a deep sigh of relief. Thomas certainly wasn't threatening, but something about him made Mallory uncomfortable. He didn't like having to pretend he cared about things like families, neighbors, or track. Besides, if he somehow became Black Thomas's friend, Nell might be afraid to be his girlfriend.

\* \* \* \* \* \*

The next day, Nell still wouldn't budge about letting him join the committee immediately. Then he saw Teitelbaum in the break room for the first time ever, and he suspected he was being watched. He couldn't finish his snack. But he was happy to find that the tape was still on the surveillance camera. He wondered if explaining his tenuous job situation to Nell would nudge her to get him admitted to the committee more quickly, but he decided against this show of weakness.

Nell glanced up at him as he blocked the entrance to her cubicle. He expected her to cut off the customer she was talking to, but instead she turned right back to her screen again. He decided to stand there silently until she was finished. But Nell's conversation with the customer went on and on. He shifted his weight from one leg to another and grabbed the top of her cubicle wall for balance.

"Have you tried unplugging all of the cables and plugging them in again, then rebooting everything?" she asked the customer now. "Yes? Well, okay. Are you getting a light that indicates that the cable box is on? It's supposed to be a red light. Oh, you say a yellow light. Oh, that's possibly an indication that there may be a hardware malfunction. I'm going to connect you to the service department. Make sure you have your account number, router number and the serial number of your cable box handy. It looks like you'll be 27$^{th}$ in the queue for the service department. Thank you for letting me serve you. Have a nice day." She clicked off. Then she swiveled her chair in Mallory's direction and slowly took her headset off like she was removing a delicate diamond tiara.

Mallory knew how much she needed him on the committee. He doubted anyone on that committee could match the ideas he could come up with. She probably told herself that her excitement was due to having a man of his experience and boldness to guide the committee. But he knew what she really longed for was something much deeper and more instinctive.

"I'm looking forward to this party Saturday night," he started.

"I guess so. Is it a special occasion? Am I supposed to bring a present?"

"No. No. Nothing like that."

"Is the dress formal? Casual?" She seemed aggravated about the whole deal. "Is this more like a barbeque or a fancy sit-down dinner? Am I supposed to bring a dish?"

Mallory had no idea. "No, no. Don't bring any food." Then he did have an idea. "But it's not casual. I think most of the women will be wearing fancy, slinky dresses."

"Slinky?"

"You know, like the lady judges on those reality talent shows."

"They're going to dress like Shakira?"

"Something like that, I guess. Of course, if you can't dress up like that ...."

Her look was suddenly stern, her voice flat. "I can dress in any number of styles."

"Good. Good. And you only have to stay as long as you want." Provided, he thought, she partook of some pot, or some wine, or any other substance that would ease her way across the landing into his flat.

# Chapter 6: An Unexpected Ally

Mallory's knowledge about what was going on in Glenwood, and in pretty much all the rest of the world, came entirely from Spike, the son of the owner of the Dough and Go. Spike's father was a Greek immigrant who moved between the kitchen and the counter so fast he kind of blurred himself into the background. He talked to the customers a lot, but he spoke very fast, and Mallory was afraid of people who talked with an accent. His son, Spike, whose real name was Spiro, was much more American and laid back. He was a college student who played in two soccer leagues. On those occasions when Mallory sat at one of the small Formica tables that lined the interior wall of the Dough and Go, Spike would sometimes come over and talk to him.

"How's it going?" Mallory called out to him one morning as he passed by carrying dishes back from another table. Spike immediately dropped the dishes on an empty table and turned to answer.

"Fine, Fine, Mr. Mallory." It wasn't hard to distract Spike from his duties at his father's eatery. "Can't talk long. Have to get these dishes to the back so they can get washed. You know ... so they can get dirty again ... so they can be washed again ... and the money can continue to dribble, dribble in ... and so on." He rolled his eyes as he gestured with his head over his shoulder in the direction of his father. Spike would never openly talk disrespectfully of the restaurant in his father's presence, but he had confided long ago to Mallory that he was sick of the family business and was taking courses to prepare himself for a career in finance.

"Anything going on?" Mallory seemed not to notice that Spike had just told him that nothing – except his father's most boring, repetitive business – was going on. But Mallory sensed that any piece of information, no matter how small, might help him cope with the mysterious, alien world all around him.

"Hm. Not much. Well, people say there was a suspicious character lurking in the alley behind the restaurant. I didn't see him."

"Call the police?"

"Nah. They wouldn't do anything anyway. Not unless somebody's shot, I don't think. You want something to eat?"

One of the benefits of Mallory's mindset was the ability to focus on a problem. He felt that, without the burden of any tedious knowledge of current affairs, or history, or politics, or economics, or science, to clutter his mind, he could immediately grasp the hidden meaning behind almost any situation. Spike's warning about the suspicious character lurking in the neighborhood colored all of his thoughts for the next few days. Although Spike hadn't described the lurker, in Mallory's mind he was wearing a hoodie. His own experience was that people wearing hoodies were scary. He fantasized that he and Nell would encounter the lurker in the parking lot when she came for the party. Nell would be afraid to come out of the car until Mallory scared him off. Then, she would be so juiced up and excited he would take her directly to his place, where her pent-up urges would be stoked, then stroked, then satisfied.

Mallory was suspicious of anyone who moved fast. At the many offices he had worked in, he found those quick-breathing, keyboard-clacking, teeth-clenching co-workers to be nothing but a bunch of show-offs and brown nosers. And after his first few days on each job, when they were formally polite and pretended to be interested in him, these show-offs soon found something more interesting to look at each time he passed by, even if it was just solitaire or a newsfeed on their screen. But it wasn't just the fast movers in offices that bothered him. He hated waiters in restaurants who walked up to your table thirty seconds after you sat down and asked you what you wanted to eat. He hated people who walked fast, and he was especially scared of people who ran. Mallory himself hadn't moved as fast as a jog in fifteen years – not since the time he got out of his car in the drive-through lane of a fast food restaurant and forgot to put the transmission in park.

Now, the sight of people running in the street made him uneasy. His recent anxiety about the lurker merged with his dislike of runners, and in his mind the lurker in the alley behind the Dough and Go was not only wearing a hoodie but was also running fast.

At least it was something to talk to Nell about. Nell had been avoiding him lately, as if the excitement of their coming date was too much for her. She declined to go on break with him one day. The following day, she did go with him; but when he started to describe how he had struck a tiny blow against Algonquin J. Tycoon by taping over the surveillance camera, she put her hands over her ears. She later brought a girlfriend to one of their breaks. But Mallory could see no point in having a conversation with two women at the same time.

But the other woman, Kathie, a tall, skinny blonde with a thin face, a strong chin and blue eyes, seemed uninterested in either Nell or Mallory. She picked at her sandwich and looked around like she was hoping Brad Pitt would suddenly walk in and carry her away. She was actually talking about Brad Pitt with Nell, but in a resigned way that signaled to Mallory that she knew she was in a lower caste than Brad and could only dream of being ravished by that movie star. Manly Man had taught Mallory that many women were caught in this logical and emotional trap, believing that famous movie stars were magical men who could fulfill their needs better than the real man who might live right next door. This type of woman could be freed from her fantasy world only by the attentions of a real man. Although there was no manly rule against satisfying two women at the same time, Mallory decided that Nell's attraction for him was too intense for her to deal with a rival for his affections. He decided not to go after Kathie romantically, and so he lost all interest in her and didn't even pay any attention to what she was saying.

"What do you think?" Nell looked over at him as if he had been part of the conversation.

"What do I think about what?"

"Do you think we ought to have a movie star motif for the

holiday party? People dressed up as their favorite movie star?"

This question did interest Mallory. He figured all the girls would want to pretend to be J. Lo, or Shakira. Since they were all so much uglier than those gorgeous creatures, they'd have to whore up their costumes to give the men the idea of what they were trying for. He was actually kind of excited about the idea. But there was that thing he wanted that Nell wouldn't give him.

"You won't let me be on the committee yet, but you still want me to give you my opinions?"

"Oh, come on. What do you think?" He was startled that Kathie spoke to him now. Hadn't he already decided that she didn't even exist for him?

"Nell wants my ideas for the Christmas party," he complained to Kathie. "Pretty soon she'll be asking me to help set up decorations. But she won't let me on the committee yet. It's not fair." He didn't know why he was explaining this to Kathie, when he had already decided he was not interested in having sex with her. He had noticed she was much more aggressive than Nell. He didn't like that in a woman, but he found himself complaining to her anyway.

"Why can't he be on the committee?" Kathie looked like she was trying to read Nell's face.

Nell sighed. "I explained this to him. He would be welcome on the Cheer Committee. But I need to make sure everybody's in agreement with it first. And we can't do that until the next meeting, which isn't for two more weeks."

"Why don't we just email everybody on the committee? I'm sure they won't mind another member."

Mallory decided he liked her commonsense approach – but then a sudden thought made him panic. "No. Wait," he interrupted. He had a vision of scores of emails flying around with the subject line: *Kevin Mallory As New Member of Employee Cheer Committee?* That wouldn't do. Teitelbaum was bound to notice – and bound to notice that Mallory had not been on the Cheer Committee three weeks before, when he used it as his excuse for being away from his desk so often. Teitelbaum would pounce on this documentary proof that he had lied to the company managers. Now Mallory wished this Kathie woman had just minded her own business.

"Using email, that's so impersonal," he suggested. "I think you should just call the other members of the committee and ask them. How many members are there, anyway?"

"Seven." Nell clasped and unclasped her hands uncomfortably on the lunch table. She made a little noise in her throat almost like a growl. It seemed like she wasn't used to being in a conversation she could not control.

"That's not enough people even to set up a big party, anyway," Kathie offered, shifting forward in her seat. "We're going to need more members." Mallory could see that her bright, can-do attitude annoyed Nell as much as it did him. But he saw the advantage in taking her side now.

"Just call the other five people." Mallory's look was incredulous. "It can't take you more than a few minutes. Then I can be on the committee and give you the benefit of my ideas."

Nell's lips compressed into a thin line. She obviously didn't like people arguing with her, even when they were right. "I'm president of the Employee Cheer Committee." She said it like she was President of the United States. She closed her eyes for a moment. "But if you call the other five members, Kathie," she breathed out hard, puffing out her lips in a gesture of patronizing exasperation, "and if they agree, we can maybe let Kevin join right away."

\*\*\* \*\*\*

No one objected to Mallory joining the committee. He still feared there would be a flurry of emails congratulating him on his appointment as a new member, but nothing happened. And Nell never asked him again for his ideas about the holiday party. He was glad the next meeting wasn't scheduled for two weeks. He didn't plan to attend.

# Chapter 7: Hoodie Insurance

"Yeah, the government pays for those hoodies," Spike assured Mallory when he asked. He spoke with the certainty of someone without the slightest bit of knowledge about the subject. "You can buy 'em with food stamps now."

"No food stamps here." Spike's father overheard the conversation between Spike and Mallory and injected his comment from twenty feet down the counter.

"Yeah. Right, Dad." Spike, looking at Mallory, rolled his eyes. He went on in a lower voice. "You can buy clothes now with food stamps. Hoodies included."

"They're paying people to hide their faces and skulk around our neighborhood?" But Mallory got over his instant of amazement. There was nothing the government wouldn't stoop to just to keep on the good side of those who didn't really want to work for a living.

"The neighborhood?" Spike looked puzzled. He had forgotten about the person seen lurking in the alley the previous week. And he had never said the guy was wearing a hoodie. He figured Mallory was talking about something else. "You have people in hoodies hanging around on the streets in your neighborhood?"

Mallory took Spike's question as a statement of fact. After all, Spike was the sole source of all Mallory's knowledge about what was really happening in the world. Mallory was surprised at the news; but if people were hanging around his neighborhood streets in hoodies, he was glad he had found out. He hadn't seen any of these yet, but a little tremor of foreboding ran down his spine. What would he do if they blocked his parking space at the apartment complex? What if they confronted him as he got out of his car?

"My apartment complex doesn't have a security force."

"They're afraid," Spike announced authoritatively. "Real estate companies are afraid to hire a security guard. What if he arrests the wrong person, or if he questions a suspicious looking character who turns out to be innocent? Then they'll get sued and, the courts being what they are these days, they'll be out millions of dollars. It's not worth it to them. Your safety is not worth it to them."

"They really don't care about ordinary people like us." It was presented as half a question, half a statement. Mallory had found it convenient to phrase his convictions in such a way, so he could seem to be agreeing with the speaker without committing himself, just in case that wasn't what the speaker meant.

"Big real estate investment companies, the bottom line is all that matters. The top execs are paid on current value, and current value depends on cash flow – and of course on manipulation of all the special tax breaks built into the U.S. Code."

"Yeah," Mallory guessed at the meaning of what Spike was saying. "It's all set up for the big guys. Regular people like us, nobody cares about."

"Yup." Spike stood tall with his hands on his hips. Mallory thought he puffed out his chest a little. "But I'm not going to be a little guy forever. I'm going to make it to the top of that financial food chain."

"Hey! Mr. Food Chain! Tables 6, 7, 10. Now." Spike's father's command from behind the counter ended their conversation.

*** ***

The apparent invasion of the streets by men in hoodies jangled Mallory's nerves in the days before the neighborhood party. He now questioned whether he would be a hero to Nell or whether he would end up cowering in the car while the hoodlums pounded and thumped on the hood and the roof.

He stopped in at Guns-R-Us on his way back from work one afternoon. Mallory had never owned a gun, and he sat outside waiting in the parking lot, hesitating, for half an hour. His father had owned guns, two rifles and a shotgun. He remembered it was a constant source of tension between his mother and father. His father said he was a hunter, but Mallory had never seen him go out hunting. He remembered his mother made his father buy a locking gun rack so Mallory couldn't get into the guns. He remembered them fighting over that. When his father left when Mallory was ten years old, his mother insisted he take the guns; but on the day he left, his father couldn't find the key and ended up ripping the whole rack off the wall. It was months before his mother got the gaping holes in the drywall repaired.

When Mallory asked his father why he was leaving, his father had looked at him like it couldn't possibly be any of his business. "Living with your mother," he grudgingly explained, "it's like everything's too tight. Everything's got to be done the right way every time, and the only right way is her way." He noticed Mallory looking at the stack of guns hooked together and covered in drywall dust on the floor.

"Do you ever go hunting?" Mallory felt brave even for asking.

"Of course." He knitted his brow and stared at his son and shook his head. "What the hell else would I have these 30-30s for?"

"I just ... never saw you hunting."

"You don't hunt inside the house, nitwit."

Mallory wanted to explain to him that he knew that, but he couldn't get the words out. He felt so stupid he just stared down at the floor. He didn't blame his father for wanting to leave such a stupid kid.

His father put his hand on his shoulder and told him to look up. Their eyes met. His father's mouth opened, but no words came out. It looked like he had opened his mouth before deciding what to say. Mallory dreaded the words that his father was forming in his mind. The son already felt like he was nothing but a little accidental speck of humanity. One more honest word from his father and he'd be blown away into nothingness. If he could have done it himself, he would have disappeared from the face of the earth at that moment.

56

"Tell you what, Kevin."

It took all of his ten-year-old strength to ask: "What?"

"Tell you what. I'm not coming back here much. Your mother's picking, picking, picking at me all the time. It's like to drive me crazy. I'm not going to be one of those make-an-appointment-to-see-your-son dads."

Mallory wondered what his life would be like with his father completely gone. His father had always been there – or, at least, the *idea* of his father had always been there – and even if he didn't compare well with the other dads in most ways, he had at least always taught his son not to be bothered by anyone's opinion. His father had always been there, at least in the back of his mind, as a safety or backstop against the disapproval of others. Without his father, it seemed like all those put-downs would be true.

"It's just not in me. I can't be one of those *visitation* fathers," his father spat the word out. "Taking a kid out to a restaurant on Saturdays when he'd rather be with his friends. I'll let you off all that crap."

This was all new to Mallory. He didn't have time to think about whether this was crap or not. He wanted to ask about this Saturday restaurant thing – but what was the point when it wasn't going to happen anyway? He just didn't qualify for the Saturday restaurant thing; his father had just told him. No point in even thinking about it. He just nodded blankly at his father.

His father sighed. "But maybe we can do a more manly thing."

Mallory looked up, his eyes locking on his father's.

"Yeah, forget this *visitation/restaurant* crap. Why don't I take you hunting? Teach you to shoot, then take you hunting once in a while? Yeah, we'll do that. Manly stuff. This 30-30 here's practically got your name on it already."

After that, for a year, he waited excitedly for the day. Then, for another year, he resolved to remind his father, but he saw his father only for brief moments, during most of which he was arguing with his mother, and he didn't have the nerve to interrupt. For another year he blamed himself for not reminding his father earlier. Then it was too late. His father never took him hunting.

Mallory sat there in the parking lot of Guns-R-Us and wondered if he was even qualified to own a gun. He didn't mean legally – almost anybody was legally qualified to own a gun. But for some reason he simply hadn't passed muster to learn to shoot his father's 30-30. But now he had a sudden wild idea that with one bold stroke he could reverse the course of his own history and buy that exact 30-30 deer rifle he had once been promised.

"That rifle ... eh ... might not be exactly what you want for protection," Gus, the middle-aged, buff, bearded owner suggested. "It's difficult to carry, even in your car. If you're worried about young toughs hanging around the streets in hoodies, you might do better with a pistol." He gestured toward a whole wall of pistols.

"I want this rifle."

"Okay. Okay."

"But I still need something I can carry in my car."

"Right. Well, you could buy both."

"What's the cheapest handgun you have?"

The cheapest handgun was $375. He didn't have that kind of money, especially after putting $399 on his credit card for the rifle and a lot more for the carrying case. He drove home with the rifle in his trunk, feeling strangely elated, but uneasy. He finally had something he had always wanted, but he still didn't have what he needed for protection from the hoodlums. He consulted Manly Man but didn't find any advice on anything close to his problem. He sought relief from his anxiety in his porn site, imagining it was Nell on screen, begging for domination. But even this vision didn't drive away the fear about his safety that was now haunting him. He visited Manly Man again and was told that he shouldn't worry, that if he ate right, thought right and worked out at least three times a week, his anxiety would gradually dissolve, his male pheromones would multiply and he would be ready to face down any and all challenges to his manhood.

# Chapter 8: Dumping the Evidence

He could tell Nell was miffed about the way he and Kathie forced his way onto the committee early. The day after their conversation in the break room, she shoved onto his desk a thick manila file loosely packed with all the committee notes for the past several years. She bluntly ordered him to go through the papers and see what type of activity he was most interested in. Over the next few days, however, she became more upbeat. "Joining was really a constructive thing for you to do – even if Kathie stretched the rules to get you in. I'm sure you'll benefit by the experience of working together with us."

Mallory didn't open the meeting minutes file. He did go to the coffee bar and carefully observe how their coffee machine worked. He was overjoyed to see that his name had not yet been put on the coffee payment schedule that was thumbtacked to the wall. His coffee was free for now, and it was much better than the vending machine coffee.

All was going well, but then he saw Teitelbaum skulking around again. The supervisor arrived at Nell's cubicle and stopped. Mallory slid his chair back toward the partition between his cubicle and Nell's – gently this time – to listen in.

"Ms. Pickens." Mallory imagined Nell putting up one finger as she finished her conversation with a customer.

"Ms. Pickens!" Mallory heard a sudden rustling as Nell rushed to click the customer off. "Thank you, Ms. Pickens."

"I was with a customer, sir."

"I understand, Ms. Pickens. But we have an important personnel matter to clear up. I have learned that you are the Chair of the Employee Cheer Committee."

"Yes. I have been the chair for three years. We have had many successful events. We strive to keep morale up in good times and bad, especially with remembrance cards. The company pitches in only $750 a year, and the committee members and the staff themselves pay all the rest of the expenses."

"That's all .... Well, that's all very good. But I need to see some of your records."

"We keep a strict accounting of all funds. Emily Schiff in accounting goes over our books twice a year."

Listening from the other side of the partition, Mallory imagined Nell's prim little smile.

"I'm not interested in the funds right now. What I want to know is the date that a certain person joined the committee."

"Oh. Who?"

"Well, I can't tell you the name." The balance of power in the conversation seemed to have suddenly shifted. "It's a personnel investigation ... I mean a personnel matter. Confidential. Just give me all the records."

"The notes from our meetings, there's a lot of personal stuff, about deaths in the family, personal milestones, family issues. They're pretty confidential, sir." Nell picked up on Teitelbaum's word. "I'm not sure I can release them without the agreement of all members of the committee." Mallory imagined Nell's smug little smile.

"You're telling me that this is a secret committee?"

"It is a very open committee, sir. Everyone is invited to join."

Teitelbaum hesitated. "Open committee, huh?"

"Yes. People come and people go. People sometimes leave and come back later."

"So your records won't show ...?"

"... exactly who joined, and when? No."

Mallory wanted to jump over the partition and give Nell a hug.

"Um ... well...." Mallory could tell Teitelbaum didn't want to go through a bunch of records about whose grandmother died, whose niece graduated from high school, whose puppies were paper trained. "Alright for now. But if there's a formal investigation later, we may have to call you in to the Personnel Department and look at those records."

Mallory now glanced at the loose stack of papers in the Cheer Committee file. On sheets of sometimes crumpled pieces of paper of different sizes and colors, he saw random notes in different handwritings about coffee purchases, holiday party plans, plans for morale-boosting events, not to mention a host of personal events in the lives of committee members. No, Teitelbaum would never take the time to go through all of this. Nevertheless, just to be safe, Mallory dumped the whole file in the recycling bin on his way out of the office that evening.

He kept the rifle in the trunk of his car. He didn't want Thomas to see him carrying a gun into his apartment and get the idea that he might be a racist. Before he left work, though, he opened his trunk just to look at it. Even hidden in its $199.95 carrying case, it gave him a feeling of a renewed connection with his father. It was as if, even though his father had never come through for him, he had learned to come through for himself. He was sure that was the manly thing to do.

But he realized the rifle hadn't solved the security problem in his neighborhood. He wouldn't be able to get the rifle out of his trunk quickly enough if those Black hoodlums in hoodies started thumping on his car. And he wasn't sure how much good it would do if he got it out. The owner of Guns-R-Us had asked Mallory a lot of questions about his experience with firearms. Mallory told him he had practically grown up with guns. Although that statement was technically true, Mallory had never actually shot a firearm, and he had never even seen a gun go off, except in video games. The owner asked him whether he wanted a lever or a bolt action, and Mallory had answered "30-30." He asked him what kind of sight he wanted, and Mallory, after a few moments' hesitation, said "plain." They talked for a great while about the merits of that leather carrying case. But Mallory was pretty sure the whole deal wouldn't really do him any good against the street toughs that were apparently trying to take over his neighborhood.

Mallory dined at the Dough and Go, where he quizzed Spike about the hoodlums running through the residential streets at night in the neighborhood. Spike seemed to brush him off, saying he didn't know much about it. Another customer blurted out that he'd seen a Black man running on his residential street late the evening before.

"Wearing a hoodie, right?" Mallory's voice was tremulous.

"No, I don't think so. But the ones you saw had hoodies, right?"

"Um ... yeah." Mallory's voice was tentative at first because he couldn't remember what he actually saw. "Yeah, hoodies."

Mallory looked down at the menu, which he had long since memorized. But he couldn't get this fresh news out of his mind. There must be different groups, hoodies and non-hoodies. How dangerous was this neighborhood getting? Mallory thought about this and stared at the menu until Spike got tired of waiting and said he'd check back with him later. When he finally did get his fried shrimp sub, Mallory was too anxious to take much pleasure in it.

\* \* \*   \* \* \*

He grew more anxious when he saw Thomas outside his apartment building, even though he couldn't find any specific thing to dislike about the kid. Thomas's father, Edison, still wearing the white, short-sleeved shirt and tie from work, was with him. Edison was not unfriendly, but he was gruff, as if he were still at work, dealing with people he had to deal with. The two had piled up three or four coolers at the bottom of the stairs and were carrying them up one at a time, one guy on each side.

"Looks heavy," Mallory contributed.

"Oh, hi, Mr. Mallory!" Thomas had started to act like they were friends. "It is heavy! It's ice. For the party." He grunted his way up the steps with his father. "The other ones aren't so bad. One person can carry them." Mallory watched the pair drag the cooler of ice inside, then come back and take two more. Thomas came out alone to get the last cooler. Mallory watched him carry

62

it in, then waited, hoping the kid would come back out.

"My mother is a *good* cook," Thomas assured him when he returned. Mallory, who still held his prejudice against parties whose main focus was fancy food, grunted in assent. Thomas's mother's food was not going to get Nell into his bed. But he needed to talk to the kid.

"I need to talk to you for a minute about something that's come up. Come on inside."

Thomas eagerly followed Mallory into his apartment; but, ten feet in, he stopped still. "Jesus fucking Christ! What's that smell?"

"Smell? I guess that's my cat. I haven't cleaned his cage." Mallory walked over to the cage in the opposite corner from his video setup.

"You keep your cat in a cage?"

"Sure."

Mallory hardly ever noticed the smell. He thought Thomas would get used to it pretty quickly. He was disturbed, though, when Thomas followed right behind him and looked into the cage.

"That's not a cat." Thomas squatted down at a safe distance.

"Yeah, it's a ... big cat."

"Somebody tricked you, Mr. Mallory. This here's a ferret."

"Oh. Oh. Well, it's not really mine. I'm keeping it for a while for my friend, Bunbury. It's a ferret, you say?"

"Yeah. And them suckers are mean."

"My friend left me this harness I'm supposed to use when I walk him, and these gloves to wear when I'm dealing with him. He told me he was a big cat."

Thomas stood up and faced him. "If I were you, I wouldn't tell anyone else about this, Mr. Mallory. The only animals allowed in this apartment complex are cats and dogs."

"Thank you. I'll tell my friend what you said. But there's something I wanted to talk to you about. Have a seat, Thomas." Mallory looked around. There was only one chair in his place, a wicker computer bench his mother had been ready to throw out.

It faced his oversized computer screen and was half entangled in its wires. Mallory was struggling to turn it around when Thomas told him he could just sit on it as it was.

"Thomas, there's a crime problem in this neighborhood."

"I haven't heard of any. That's why we moved here, because it's supposed to be safe."

"Apparently, the problem's just starting, but it's growing. I'm thinking we have to start some preventive action." Mallory paused for a second while he pondered whether he'd used too big a word for Thomas. "People have seen groups of hoodlums harassing people on the streets. We want to stop it before they start coming into this complex." Mallory thought Thomas's family would be the perfect partners in this venture. They lived in the complex, they seemed half-respectable, and they were Black and therefore might have some idea of how to deal with these people. If they joined with him, he couldn't be accused of being some type of vigilante.

"Oh. Okay." Thomas's eyes seemed to lose focus. "I been all around this neighborhood, and I haven't seen anything. But I'll talk to my Mom, Mr. Mallory, see if she's seen anything."

Mallory didn't want to come off as a scaredy-cat in front of Thomas, so he didn't press the issue. He would talk to Thomas's mother the next day, at the party, about the criminal elements in the neighborhood.

But he had to do something about the ferret that night. He'd bought it in the mall a few months before. He'd been pretending to look in a pet shop window so he could get a look at the reflection of the cute girl standing next to him.

"They take a lot of dedication, and skill," the cute girl had said as their reflections made eye contact. He couldn't believe she was actually talking to him. But he didn't know what she was talking about.

"Umm."

"Some people are scared of them – because of their beady eyes, I think. But I think certain men, men who know how to channel an animal's urges, can get a lot out of a relationship with a pet like that."

"Yeah. I can see that." He could finally see past her reflection into the store. He recognized the beady eyes right away. The scrawny little grey creature seemed to be staring back at him. He saw by the tag on its cage that it was called a ferret. He turned to face the girl. "I've done ferrets before. I know what you mean." He gave her a knowing smile. Anything to keep the conversation going.

"Oh, this one might be just right for you. Why don't you step inside the store with me now? We've been having a sale, and this is the last ferret available."

Within ten minutes, she convinced him he could have a strong relationship with this fierce little predator. He bought it and its cage and some food and took it home that night. The cute girl offered him the link for a website that had detailed instructions for its care and feeding, but he had to pretend he already knew all that. He named it Coco. The girl didn't say if Coco was a he or a she, and he was too embarrassed to ask. When he tried to find out at home, Coco bit him.

Every morning, he pushed some ferret food through the bars, but otherwise he kept the animal in his cage except for taking it for a walk two or three times a week. He hadn't noticed the smell until Thomas mentioned it. But Nell wouldn't like the smell either, and she would probably also find some picayune objection to the way he was caring for the disgusting animal. He knew she would be skittish and maybe even try to keep her distance when he first brought her back to his lair. Women were skittish by nature. He didn't want Coco freaking her out.

After Thomas left, Mallory dragged the ferret in its cage out to his car. He'd gotten the name of the nearest animal shelter from Nell. She had warned him that it was not a no-kill shelter, and they put animals to sleep if they had to. Mallory looked up their hours on the internet to make sure he didn't get there until well after closing time. His plan was to drop the ferret, cage and all, at the front door and just leave it there. He brought a white plastic bag to put over his head in case there was a security camera.

The shelter was in a one-story brick building that used to be an elementary school. Slowly, Mallory circled the block several times to make sure there wasn't anybody inside. He thought he saw a security camera, which made sense because the building used to be a school. He parked under some trees around the corner and about a half a block away. He opened the trunk and wrestled out the ferret cage. The animal was growling or hissing or something, and it snapped at Mallory's heavy leather gloves each time they came near the bars of the cage. Mallory set the cage down in the darkness behind his car. A hundred yards away, the front of the shelter was well lit, and he knew he'd have to put the bag over his head before he got there. He walked up to the passenger side door of his car and got out the plastic bag. He had to make the eye holes bigger because of the darkness. The bag frightened the ferret even more, and he frantically snapped at Mallory's fingers every time they came near the cage. Mallory could carry the cage only a few feet at a time before the animal figured out where to bite, forcing Mallory to put it down and find a new handhold. He hadn't made it halfway to the shelter when the street was lit up with swirling red light and a police car pulled up behind him and he heard an amplified voice tell him to stop.

"I repeat. Stop. Drop the object that you are carrying. Put your hands in the air and face me."

Mallory set down the cage and did as he was told. The plastic bag got twisted in the process, and he couldn't see anything, but he was afraid to adjust it with his hands.

"Walk toward me, slowly."

Mallory walked toward the sound of the voice.

"Take that thing off your head."

Mallory pulled the plastic bag off and threw it down. The policeman told him in a regular voice to step forward.

"Is that your car over there with the trunk open?"

"Yes, it is." Mallory could see nothing but the business end of the flashlight the cop was shining in his face.

"We got a report of suspicious activity in the neighborhood. Possible Ku Klux Klan activity."

"No. No."

"You want to explain why you were wearing that white thing on your head?"

Mallory figured the truth wouldn't help him here. There was probably some kind of law against dropping a ferret at the door of the shelter in the middle of the night. Admitting that he had been disguising himself by wearing the bag on his head might look suspicious, he thought.

"I got a problem with mosquitoes."

"So, you wear a white bag on your head to keep the mosquitoes off?"

"Yes, sir. They're particularly bad when I'm taking my cat out for a walk."

"You take your cat for a walk by carrying it in its cage?"

"Yes, my cat has a bad foot problem. Infection. Feet can't be allowed to touch the ground outside."

The cop had Mallory walk slowly back to the cage, where the ferret cringed in a corner against the bright beam of light.

"You sure you own this …. Wait, this isn't a cat! What the hell kind of animal is this?"

"I call it a cat. Some people call it a ferret."

"It *ain't* a cat. You got any kind of papers on this animal?"

"I bought it at the mall."

"Put it back in the car." The policeman followed with the flashlight as Mallory placed his cage in the trunk. "Whoa! That gun in there? Is it yours?"

"It is mine. I just bought it today."

"Step away from the car! Leave the cage inside the trunk." Mallory heard the policeman utter some numbers into his phone, and the word "backup." He then told Mallory to turn around and put his hands behind his back. He felt himself being handcuffed. "I'm putting you in the back of my car."

"Am I under arrest, officer?"

"Yeah. For suspicious activity, imminent danger. You name it."

From his seat in the back of the squad car, Mallory saw the policeman in the headlights. The first thing he did was chase down the white plastic bag, which had started to blow away. Then he approached the trunk, but he didn't pull out the rifle. He walked back and got in the squad car and waited.

"I don't think suspicious activity is a crime," Mallory offered.

The policeman tuned his head. For the first time, Mallory could see his features in the glow from the dome light. Short, very dark hair, dark eyebrows, a look on his lips like he'd had it up to here with smart talk. "You're going to wait right here until we get a straight story about what you're doing with that gun and that Ku Klux costume and that animal."

"It's a ferret."

"You said it was a cat. Giving false information in the course of an investigation is a felony."

"It's kind of a cat."

The cop turned toward him again. His dark eyes were piercing. He had a half-day's growth of beard over a ruddy complexion that was gradually becoming redder as they conversed. He looked like he had been exercising, or was aggravated. Mallory had never before been in a position where his behavior might have immediate detrimental physical consequences.

"I'll keep my mouth shut." His voice came out weak. The cop smirked and turned away. Another cruiser arrived and, after a long conversation with the first cop outside the car, the new cop approached the trunk of Mallory's car. He photographed everything inside, then put on a pair of rubber gloves and carefully pulled the rifle out and put it in the back of his own car. He left the ferret in Mallory's trunk, and they took him to the station.

He sat with his hands manacled behind his back in a straightbacked chair near an empty desk. He heard one of the cops say he was going out to get something to eat. He realized he was hungry himself, but he decided not to ask for anything. He told the first cop, whose name he found out was Selby, that he had just bought the gun the day before.

"Yeah. Doesn't look like it's ever been fired."

"No."

"What's that ferret got to do with that gun? We're you planning on shooting it?"

"No."

"A lot of people hate those animals."

"Actually, it's not my ...." Mallory had planned on saying it was Bunbury's, but he suddenly realized what a bad idea that would be. This was the police, not some namby-pamby employer. They would immediately ask for Bunbury's phone number and identifying information. He could of course say Bunbury was out of town. That was where Bunbury always was, but he sensed that story wouldn't work here. They would figure out in the end there was no such person. He would be caught in yet another lie. They'd never let him out until he said something that made sense.

"Actually, I confess." He told Officer Selby exactly what he had been doing on the side street near the animal shelter, white plastic bag and all.

Selby blinked hard with both eyes. "What about the gun?"

"I bought that gun for protection against those gangs that are running around our streets."

"Gangs, huh?"

"Yeah. Everybody says so. I just bought the gun yesterday."

"Why don't we sit right here while I call the owner of Guns-R-Us?" Selby punched in the number. "I'll put him on speaker." The employee who answered the phone put the owner on immediately. "Gus, Selby here. We got a call about a suspicious character, and we got the guy, and he says he bought a 30-30 from you yesterday."

"Yeah. I remember that guy. 30-30, case, the works. Hunting rifle. But he's never been hunting."

"Did he say what he was going to use it for?"

"He talked on and on. Can't remember all of it. Something about his father."

"Was he having an argument with his father?"

"No. Nothing like that. Some weird kind of family memory thing, I think."

Selby turned to Mallory, his face flushed with scorn. He turned his head back to speak to the owner. "Psycho talker, huh? I'm trying to decide if this guy's posing a danger to the community with that gun. You think he is?"

"Oh, absolutely not. Absolutely, positively not."

"How can you be so sure?"

"I wouldn't sell him any bullets."

# Chapter 9: Post-Release Syndrome

Mallory reached the interstate and sped past three exits before he stopped at a rest stop. He'd heard that ferrets had strong homing instincts, and he wanted to make sure he never saw that animal again. He parked at a distant parking spot just out of range of the halo of light in front of the small rest stop building. He took the cage out and carried it across the grass and into the brush. He put the cage down and started to unlock the cage door – but then he had a vision of that damn animal following him back to his car. He turned and walked away, vowing to leave the damn animal to its fate. But he got only as far as the door of his car before remorse set in.

Another car pulled in and parked next to him. He jumped into his Camry and locked the door. He was suspicious of this car being parked next to him at the end of the lot where the light was so dim. He'd heard that robbers sometimes stalked the rest stops on the interstate. He breathed a sigh of relief as the potential robbers got themselves together and walked slowly away toward the lighted building. He decided to wait until he got over his jitters. As he waited, and his heartbeat gradually slowed down, his mind wandered. He hadn't eaten since dinner. He wondered what kind of food was in the vending machines inside. He wondered if Nell would ever appreciate the courage he'd shown tonight. One day he'd tell her about the incredible efforts he'd made to have his apartment clear of the ferret cage, and smelling as good as his aftershave, all for her.

He wondered if he should introduce Nell to his mother. His mother had been heartbroken when he had split up with Rose, and this strengthened the fear he had felt all along that his mother preferred Rose over him. Once in a while, his mother still dropped a hint that maybe she would call Rose to see how she was doing. Mallory had not expected this; but he went with his first instinct, boldly lying to his mother, insisting that Rose wasn't fond of her at all. He was going to be more careful about what he told his mother this time, once he hooked up with Nell. He was determined she would never meet his mother until he and Nell were fused together in the all-consuming passion they were destined for.

Mallory slowly opened his driver's side door. He thought of getting his rifle out of the trunk for security, but then he changed his mind. He wondered why Gus, the owner of Guns-R-Us, had sold him just about every piece of equipment you could buy with a gun, except bullets. Keeping in the shadow of the nearby car, he crept toward the grass lawn, then quickly scrambled across it into the darkened bushes. He had barely breathed a sigh of relief when he tripped and fell forward into something that he soon realized was a sticker bush. The harder he thrashed about, the more he was stuck in his arms and legs. He lay there moaning and trying to look around, but this brought on more little stabs, now to his face and neck and arms. Lying still didn't help either, as his weight pushed him relentlessly onto the stickers.

He forgot the pain when he heard a terrifying, high-pitched scream right next to his ear. An adrenaline surge pushed him upright, and he started to run. Then something caused him to stop suddenly. He recognized that scream. He'd heard it before when he had once caught Coco's leg in the apartment door. Coco was screeching in the darkness somewhere right at his feet. He still couldn't see the cage in the darkness, but the ferret continued to scream. Then he stumbled onto the cage, and Coco screamed even louder. Mallory was afraid the ferret would attack him, but even more terrified that someone would hear and call the police. He steeled himself to feel around for the contours of the cage without getting his fingers too close. Coco's eyes glowed yellow and stared at him like a demon who had come for his soul.

He felt around for the latch and opened the cage door. Nothing happened at first, so Mallory leaned down to look in. He suddenly felt a blow to his head, and everything went black. The ferret had jumped on his face. Then it clawed away at him until it got enough traction to escape. The skin of his face felt like it was on fire. The animal quickly disappeared into the dark undergrowth. Mallory didn't have any way to examine his wounds, nor did he have the time. He stood up and turned toward the parking lot, where the robbers and the police posed an even greater danger. But the robbers' car was gone, and the police were nowhere in sight.

\* \* \*  \* \* \*

Mallory was certain now that he deserved all of Nell's love, affection, and submission. He raced home and made his little Camry's engine roar as he screeched to a stop in the parking lot of his complex. It was after eleven. He still had to clean up his place if it smelled as bad as Thomas had said. The only kind of cleaner he had was Windex, which he used for all purposes. He opened all the casement windows wide to get any remaining smell out of the place. He hid the Manly Man and porno sites in case Nell wanted to look at the computer. He didn't have a vacuum, but he thought he could borrow one from Thomas the next morning.

By midnight he was really hungry, and the Dough and Go was closed. He drove out to the 7-11, revving his engine and screeching his wheels just as manfully as he had before.

"Man, what happened to you?" the cocky young guy behind the 7-11 counter remarked when Mallory approached with a box of donuts.

"Oh, just a sticker bush. Nothing." Mallory pretended not to be interested in the young man's astonishment.

"Looks like you got into a fight with a tiger. Or one hell of a mean woman."

Mallory just threw the box of donuts down, threw eight dollars on top of it. "Keep the change." He felt free, breezy, in charge. He found a way to make his tires squeal pulling out of the 7-11 lot.

His manly hormones were still flowing when he screeched to a stop on entering his apartment parking lot again. Inside, the smell of Windex had replaced the ferret smell entirely. He had already filled his refrigerator with a six pack of Heineken and a six pack of an IPA, as he wasn't sure what kind of beer Nell drank. He decided things were going too fast and he was worrying too much. He gulped down one of the Heinekens, then decided he needed to drink an IPA, too. As his heart rate slowed, he decided he needed to remind himself of the point of all his courageousness. He brought up the link to his porn site from where he had hidden it in the "Sunday Services" folder. He watched the lurid scenes with new interest. He wondered if the women's moans and shrieks of pleasure were real, and if Nell would make sounds like that once she dropped her prudish pretenses. But there was more to women than that. Even Manly Man said so. He pulled the Manly Man link out from where he had hidden it as "Father's Day." Women were physically weak, and their deepest instinct was to seek protection from a confident man, Manly Man said tonight. All their talk, talk, talk was just a way of hiding from themselves this basic need. Listen for clues in their babble, babble, babble – and be ready to pounce.

\* \* \*   \* \* \*

"What time is this party going to be over?" He recognized Nell's voice on the phone, though she didn't introduce herself.

Mallory had drunk four more beers and had been in a deep sleep until the phone woke him up at ten o'clock the next morning. His Saturday mornings had been completely free ever since he had gotten rid of Rose. He was annoyed that Nell apparently felt she had the right to call him any time she wanted.

"It starts at five o'clock."

"You already told me that. I need to know, is it an afternoon or an evening party?"

"Uh, it starts at five o'clock."

"I still need to know what to wear. If it's an afternoon get-together, I can wear a skirt and flats. If it's primarily an evening party, I'll need to wear heels, and something more formal."

"You mean like a strapless dress with those ... *star things* ... sequins?"

"I'm not dressing like some kind of sex doll, if that's what you mean. But yes, I have some outfits that are a little fancier, if it's that kind of party."

"Wear those."

He wanted her to just meet him inside Thomas's apartment, but she refused.

"Do you want me to pick you up, then?"

"No. That would be too much like a date."

He said he'd wait for her on the landing outside the hosts' apartment. He gave her the address to put in her phone. She said she could only stay for about two hours. He figured she'd be terrified of Thomas and his friends and he'd be comforting her back in his own apartment within an hour. He'd read once that nothing was a better aphrodisiac than a racing heart from danger overcome.

# Chapter 10: Cognac Syndrome

Soon after he clicked off from his conversation with Nell, Mallory jumped to hear a knock at his door. The only people who ever knocked on his door were the apartment maintenance men and Jehovah's Witnesses. He had not let the maintenance men in for weeks because of the ferret. He did have a problem with his air conditioning. He was shocked when he opened the door to see Thomas standing there. But Mallory could tell he was getting to like Thomas because he didn't flinch even on a subliminal level when he saw that Black face at his door.

"My mother would like to know what kind of thing you like to drink."

"Oh. Beer."

Thomas's face fell just a fraction. "Oh. Okay. We'll get you any kind of beer you want." Mallory noticed Thomas grit his teeth like he was trying to hold something back; but obviously he couldn't. "But my Mom makes an awesome mint julep."

"Oh, that sounds great. I'll drink mint juleps then."

"And my Dad drinks nothing but Hennessy."

"Oh, Hennessy. I'll take that."

Thomas's face went blank, as if he had given up on understanding his new neighbor. Mallory felt a sudden small tinge of desperation as he saw that uninterested look, that look so similar to that he saw on scores of faces every day at work. Thomas's enthusiasm for their new friendship looked like it was dying out. Mallory desperately searched his mind for the name of some exotic drink he could ask for. But Thomas was turning to go, and he couldn't think of the name of a drink, or of anything.

"Why don't you come in for a minute?" Mallory blurted out.

"Okay." Thomas seemed to be regaining some of his usual enthusiasm; but then he went quiet again. Mallory started to tell the story of his adventures with the ferret, but it suddenly hit him that Thomas might be an animal lover. He wanted to tell him the whole story about his father and the gun, but he worried that the whole story, especially the part about buying a gun without any bullets, was not manly enough.

"Smells different in here. Like Windex or something."

Mallory could see Thomas's question in his raised eyebrows. Mallory panicked. Determined not to tell the ferret story, he searched his soul for something to say, quickly. Then he had a brilliant idea. It was so simple! He would start asking Thomas questions.

"Aren't you kind of old to be living with your parents?"

Thomas turned toward him, his face lit up with a broad, toothy smile. "Actually, they're kind of living with me."

"What?"

"It was supposed to be my apartment. Had a roommate lined up and all. My parents were going to pay half the rent as long as I stayed in college."

Mallory was intrigued. "So why are they living there now?"

"They sold their house. They're building a new one. But the new one wasn't ready and they had to get out of their old one. I already had the lease on this place, so they moved in with me in the meantime. And they pay *all* the rent as long as they're living here!"

Mallory was jealous. He had lived in his mother's house all through community college. He had slept in his old room at first, then moved to the basement. But that woman hadn't let him alone. She came down all the time on the pretense of cleaning, and she always wanted to have what she called "heart-to-heart" talks with him at dinner. The theme of all these talks, he gradually realized, was that he should *not* grow up to be like his father. She was going to make sure of this, it seemed, by controlling his every move. The best thing about his current life was that he was totally independent of her. But, to this day, whenever they saw each other, she was always on the verge of going on a rant about his shortcomings.

"That seems like a good deal," he told Thomas now. Mallory

was not in the habit of encouraging fellow human beings along their own paths. But he was starting to believe he was kind of a hero to the young man.

"I'll be out on my own soon. It was supposed to be only 30 days before their new house was finished, but it's going on 60 now."

"Those real estate people are all a bunch of robbers."

"I think it's really the construction company." Thomas turned his head slightly, his eyes went out of focus. He clearly wasn't comfortable contradicting his new mentor, but he stuck to his point. "It's not the real estate people."

Mallory nodded. Even a hero, he realized, sometimes got a fact or two wrong.

\*\*\* \*\*\*

The party wasn't anything like he expected. While he waited on the landing for Nell to arrive, he saw only three people arriving, and two of them were from the apartment immediately below Thomas's. It was a warm, bright, late September afternoon. There was no smell of marijuana or hint of other drugs in the air, no loud music, no sketchy characters coming or going.

Nell arrived on the dot of five, clicking up the stairs in heels. Her dress had no glitter on it, but it was made of a powder blue, shiny fabric that ended just under the knee and showed just a bit of her shoulders at the top. She wore a rhinestone belt and silver, open-toed heels. "Hello," she called out to him as she reached the top of the stairs. He was sitting on Thomas's empty cooler on the landing.

"What happened to your face?" She backed off as if the scratches were contagious.

"Oh. Um … just a run-in with some gangbangers in the parking lot trying to steal my dinner."

"Gangbangers? Did you call the police?"

"Um, no. I scared them pretty good. I don't think they'll be

78

back around here for a while."

"You should always call the authorities so they'll know what's going on."

He didn't like the way this conversation was going. It was too much like so many conversations with his mother. Even when he was the hero of the story, his mother had always seemed to find something lacking in the way he had acted. Now, Nell was ignoring his bravery and his fighting skill and focusing on his failure to file a useless police report. If Nell wanted to be his girlfriend, she'd have to realize he knew what he was doing.

"I don't need to call the police for every little scuffle." When he stood up, he noticed she was now as tall as him. His heart skipped a beat. She stood there twisting her fingers together at her waist. Impatience? Or fear? He could use either to his advantage.

"It's in here," he said, pointing to Thomas's door. "Listen, if you feel uncomfortable at any time, for any reason, let me know and we can leave."

"Why would I feel uncomfortable?"

He opened Thomas's door. People turned to look. Apparently, you were supposed to knock. Thomas looked up from where he had been talking with another guy and jumped up to greet them. The apartment was much larger than Mallory's. It had two bedrooms, an open kitchen and a large living room with a balcony. There was a buffet table along one of the walls, piled high with food. Thomas shook his hand and looked expectantly between Mallory and Nell. There was an awkward silence. Mallory wondered why Thomas was eyeing her. Nell looked at Mallory for a few seconds for an introduction, then sighed.

"I'm Nell," she introduced herself. "Nice to meet you. It looks like a nice party."

"Nice seeing you, Nell. Hey, Mr. Mallory, this woman been scratching on you?"

His attempted joke fell flat. Thomas seemed to shrink down, and he drifted away to the other side of the room. Mallory was relieved that his scratches were not going to become the focus of the conversation. At the same time, he thought it wouldn't hurt his reputation with Thomas if the young man thought he was involved with a dangerous, clawing cat woman.

"This does look like a nice party," Nell admitted.

Mallory's first impression was that it looked like a party his mother and her old biddy friends would waste an evening on. Thomas had brought only one friend his age, a guy who seemed to want to stand in the corner and argue with Thomas about politics. Thomas's father wore the same short-sleeved white shirt and tie that he wore to work every day. It didn't look like the party was his idea. He came up to Mallory and handed him a stiff drink of Hennessy. "I hear you like the good stuff." Mallory just smiled.

Thomas's mother introduced him to the couple who were their neighbors on the ground floor. "We've passed each other on the parking lot for weeks without a word," the husband said. "Nice to meet finally meet you."

"Nice to meet you," Nell filled the silence when Mallory didn't answer. "I don't live here. I'm a co-worker with Mr. Mallory here."

"Hey, your boyfriend here looks like he was in a fight or something," the husband smiled at Mallory. "What happened?"

"Just a little altercation in the parking lot last night. Ruffians."

"Last night! Yes, I told Audrey, my wife here, I heard a commotion in the parking lot last night. Doors thumping, tires squealing, like. Just real quick, though."

"Yeah. I took care of it. We all should watch out for these gangs running around the neighborhood committing crimes."

"You don't say? I hadn't heard about any gangbangers until now. I guess you experienced it first-hand. Glad you weren't hurt. Thanks for the heads up."

"Gangbangers? You say something about gangbangers?" Ava, Thomas's mother, looked up from her position next to the food table. "You know, I don't want to start rumors or anything, but my friend Edie called me last night. She said the police arrested a guy wearing a Kluxer outfit right on her street. She said she called the station and they said it was just some foolery. But I don't know."

"You're right to be concerned. We all should keep our eyes open." Audrey's husband nodded agreement with his own opinion.

There were only ten or twelve other people, including those leaning on the railing on the balcony looking into the woods. A few of them introduced themselves as neighbors, and almost all of them commented that they should have gotten together like this months ago. But the main event of the party seemed to be the food. Thomas's mother, a tall, solid woman with a wide face and wavy black hair, stood by the table and basically answered questions about the food. She had made it all, and word was quickly getting around that it was great. Nell asked her a few stilted questions while Mallory scanned the table. He skipped the ribs and pork roast and potato latkes and went straight for the desserts. He sank his teeth into one of the cream puffs and instantly changed his opinion about the party.

Nell pulled him aside. "I'm the only one here in heels and a party dress. You made me come here looking like your floozie."

Mallory was dumbfounded. He thought she looked great, but he couldn't get the words out because his mouth was full. He did notice then that all the other women were wearing shorts except for Thomas's mother, who wore a long, dark skirt. He looked at Nell in her bare-shouldered dress and high heels. She had definitely dressed to be flirty. What the hell was wrong with that?

"It's a party," he offered.

"You know what I mean. I don't like coming across as your sex doll. Get your hand off my arm."

The plan to get Nell into his bed was going to hell, but Mallory found himself easily distracted by the food. After he finished his dessert, he headed for the pork loin. There was a glaze on it like nothing he had ever tasted before. He was so moved he broke through this natural reticence and started up a conversation with

Thomas's mother. It was almost entirely about the food. "I didn't know Black food was so much better than regular food."

"Mm hmm."

He could see Nell across the room. He noticed by the set of her mouth that she was trying hard not to exude any sex appeal. Each time a couple approached her, she would acknowledge the man quickly, then immediately turn toward the wife – as if to emphasize that she was not trying to flirt, even though she was wearing that alluring dress. She seemed to be trying to start a serious, non-flirtatious discussion with yet another couple, but within a minute they also turned away. Mallory saw his chance. He poured a huge slug of Hennessy into a water glass and approached her as she stood alone, leaning against the wall. Her mouth was screwed up in either boredom or desperation. Mallory decided it was desperation, loneliness. He approached her with the extra drink in his hand.

"No, thank you. I don't drink before sundown." But she took the glass and held it, almost as a prop, he thought, so she'd look like she had something to do. She suddenly turned to him. "I thought you said people here wanted to talk about a no-kill ferret shelter. Nobody I've talked to here knows anything about that."

Mallory had forgotten he had said that. "I don't know. Maybe the ferret people didn't come." He tried to act like he knew nothing about it, like she was the one who had predicted the ferret people would be there. He also kept his voice low so Thomas, who was standing against the wall just a few feet away talking with his buddy, wouldn't hear anything about ferrets. But Thomas had very good hearing.

Thomas approached timidly. His attempt at a joke about the scratches on Mallory's face had not gone over well at all, and he hadn't talked to either of them since. He had misjudged how close Mallory and Nell were. "Nell, I'm Thomas. I heard you talking about something. Are you a ferret lover, too?"

Nell turned toward him and said in a low, flat, almost preachy voice, "I have respect for all members of the animal kingdom. I don't know anyone who has a ferret, but I understand they make wonderful pets."

Thomas's eyes shifted from Nell's to Mallory's and back. He glanced back at Mallory again. This time, Mallory mouthed the words *shut up*. Mallory hated to see the rejected look on Thomas's face when he did that, but he was afraid Nell would totally freak out if they got into the whole ferret story. Mallory stared at Thomas until their young host retreated back to the corner he shared with his friend from school.

"I don't think your friend likes me," Nell sounded resigned. "I don't think anybody here likes me. Except for Ava, and I can't get too near her or she'll keep stuffing food down my throat."

"It's great food, though."

"It is," she admitted.

"I got an idea. Why don't we go back to my place? It's right across the landing."

Her eyes suddenly widened, in shock, or fear, or something else Mallory couldn't figure out. This female psychology stuff was over his head. His next words were those of an utterly confused, defeated soul. "If you don't like anybody here, you can go home and we can forget this party ever happened."

She seemed to take his words as a challenge. She raised her chin. "I haven't even had my Hennessy yet." She swallowed it down in three huge gulps and came up practically gasping for air.

"I thought you didn't drink before sundown."

"This is a special occasion. Oh God, I feel better! I wonder if there's any more of that food."

"Ava said I could take some with me when I left." He thought he'd try one more time. "How about we take some back to my place, where we can eat and talk without all these strangers?"

"Why not, my man?" She was already feeling the effects of the alcohol.

Mallory rushed over to the food table, grabbed a plate, and piled it high with pork ribs, chicken, mashed potatoes. Then he remembered that Nell was a woman, and he piled on some women's food, salads and other green things. He took the last two chocolate cream puffs. Thomas saw what he was doing and came over to help. "Your girlfriend don't seem to like me."

"No, no, man." An idea crossed his mind, something to make Thomas feel better: *it's not you, man, she's just prejudiced*. But he didn't say it. It wasn't fair to Nell. He didn't really think she was prejudiced. And he had this fantasy that all three of them would one day be friends. Even as he watched Thomas pile the food high on yet another plate for him, he realized he'd have to take the trouble to say something that wouldn't make his young neighbor feel worse "No, man. She likes you. It's just the ferret talk. She's just freaked out by ferrets."

Thomas caught his eye, then tipped his head toward Nell, asking if he should bring one of the plates to her. Mallory nodded yes. Nell had started a second drink and seemed barely capable of carrying the plate across the hall, so Mallory asked Thomas to do it. Nell went along, breezily waving goodbye to the other partyers. She apparently had forgotten how miserable she'd been just moments before.

He sat down on his sofa bed. Nell sat down on the other end. She had taken her second drink with her, but she was no longer swilling it down.

"Smells like Windex in here."

"I just had the windows cleaned," he lied. "Should we eat? There's two kinds of salad."

"I'm gonna start with one of those cream puffs." When Nell said she was going to eat her food out of order, Mallory knew he was on the right track. There was a wicker bench he usually sat on in front of the computer, and he pulled it over so they could use it as a table. He smiled when he noticed this forced them closer together. He wasn't going to try anything until she finished that drink. Manly Man said certain kinds of liquor could set the female sex drive on fire. He could wait. Besides, he wanted that other cream puff.

Nell raised her eyebrows when he opened a beer. "You're

going to drink beer with a creampuff? And after all that cognac?"

"That's all I got to drink here. I'll be fine." He raised the bottle to his lips to emphasize how unconcerned he was. But the beer taste didn't mix well with the taste of the sweet cream filling, and he gulped the whole mixture down to get it over with. Then, a sudden pressure inside pushed its way back from his stomach and ended in a huge, loud burp. He glanced sideways at Nell to see how she would react, but she just stared straight ahead, the line of her lips compressed like she knew what she had to ignore.

"Do you want some" – he was going to say *pork loin*, but he remembered who he was talking to – "salad?" He was happy to see she was still sipping on her drink.

"Do you have any plates and silverware?"

She glanced toward the doorway to his kitchen. He had plates, and silverware, of course, but he didn't have a kitchen table. Or any table. On those few occasions when he ate in the kitchen – usually when he had to microwave something and the bowl was too hot to carry – he just ate standing at the kitchen counter. But it might ruin the mood to do that with Nell right now. And the wicker bench was too small for plates and silverware both.

"We can use the computer stand." He stood up quickly and pulled his monitor off the stand. He moved to put it on his sofa bed, but then he hesitated. It was probably a bad idea to clutter up the bed. He felt a little dizzy, so he roughly set the monitor down on the floor, in the process pulling the computer itself to the edge of the stand. Nell let out a little worried yelp. He turned around and reached out and grabbed at the computer, but he lost his balance and slid to the floor, enmeshing himself in a tangle of wires.

"Are you okay?"

"Yeah, I'm fine. I think I need another beer." He was surprised that Nell was noncommittal about his drinking another beer. Neither his mother nor Rose would have allowed it. Neither of them drank much themselves, and they seemed to have no idea why anybody would want to. Nell was finishing up her drink and obviously enjoying it. But he noticed something worrisome about her behavior under the influence. Instead of getting woozy and lovey after the two stiff drinks, she seemed to be getting more contrary and self-assertive.

He pushed himself up off the floor and made his way to the kitchen, where he found some plates, forks and knives. He decided he didn't need another beer. He looked through his cabinets for something to settle his stomach and came across an old bottle of crème de menthe. He quickly wiped the dust off the outside of the bottle and swallowed a few gulps. Feeling a little better, he carried the bottle and plates and silverware out to Nell.

Nell was still on the edge of the sofa bed, where she was leaning tight against one armrest as if to make sure there'd be no chance of touching him.

"You lied to me."

"What?"

"You told me you owned your own house in Glenwood."

"This is Glenwood."

"Don't give me that nonsense, Mallory. I remember that conversation very distinctly now. We talked about how mature and responsible it was that you own your own house."

Mallory looked her straight in the eyes. "Oh, I see. You thought this was *my* place. Now I understand your confusion. No, this is my friend Bunbury's apartment."

"This isn't your apartment? Then why are you here?"

"I'm just watching it for Bunbury. While he's in the hospital."

"In the hospital? Oh, is your friend very ill?"

"Actually, they can't figure out what he has. It's been a couple of weeks." Mallory watched her face closely. "He had me taking care of his pet ferret. Until his sister came and got it last night."

"Oh, that's so nice of you. I'm so sorry I accused you .... Sometimes, when I drink, I get a little aggressive ... and I was nervous around all those new people."

"I noticed they weren't very nice to you at the party. That's why I brought you here."

86

"Oh, Kevin. Can I call you Kevin? Yeah, they weren't very nice to me. They acted like I was crazy every time I mentioned the word ...." She sat up so quickly she spilled the last dregs of her drink on her dress, but she didn't seem to notice. "Ferrets! They didn't want to talk about ferrets. I think you got it wrong, Kevin! I think it was your friend Bunbury who wanted to start a no-kill ferret shelter. That's where you got the idea. It wasn't the neighbors! It was Bunbury you were thinking of!"

Mallory could not believe his luck. Nell had come up with an explanation even he couldn't have dreamed up. An explanation for everything. And an explanation only a woman in love could believe.

Mallory did his best imitation of a man who had just been overwhelmed by the genius of the woman in front of him. And he could tell from the soft look in her eyes, and her deep, steady breathing, that she believed she was worthy of this admiration. She had progressed from dark suspicion of him and anger at his neighbors to an epiphany of understanding and love for all. He had engineered all this in the best tradition of manliness. And she was looking at him now like he, Mallory, held the key to understanding the world around her and unlocking all of her own frustrated emotions. She needed him, and she knew it.

He wished they were finished their food so he could put his arm around her. He put the plates on the computer stand, and she practically jumped off the sofa bed to sit down next to him on the wicker computer bench. He ate a little bit of salad to demonstrate what a well-rounded man he was. Then he dove into the pork ribs, eating with his hands. Nell laughed and ran to the kitchen to get paper towels for him. The ribs were still good, but they had gone cold since they left the party. The greasiness was more noticeable, and it started to bother his stomach. He asked her to get him another beer. While she was out of the room, he tried some of her potato salad. It was warmer than he would have liked. She bounced back into the room, jumping over the computer cables, and handed him his beer. He couldn't concentrate on the conversation, if there was any. The room started to swirl. He woke up the next morning with a pounding headache.

# Chapter 11: The Morning After

Mallory opened his eyes against the harsh early morning light. The first thing that startled him was the lack of bedclothes. Even more startling was Thomas's face not two feet away. Thomas sat on his haunches and stared at him, his eyes wide with concern. Mallory jerked himself up so quickly that Thomas recoiled and fell back against the wall.

"What ...? What are you doing here? What time is it? Who did this to my head?"

"You don't remember? Mr. Mallory, you were very sick. Your girlfriend came over and asked me to help her get you to bed."

"I don't remember any of that. Did she say ... uh ... what we did?"

Thomas looked puzzled. "She said you were eating and drinking a lot and then you got sick and then you passed out."

"My head is killing me, Thomas. Can you find me some aspirin?"

Thomas went to the medicine cabinet, didn't find anything, then went next door to get some of his mother's aspirin. Mallory remembered very little of what happened in his apartment after he and Nell left the party, but he was sure of one thing – he had made her fall in love with him. That was more important than his throbbing head or the acid burn in his throat. But what had they actually done? He sensed that Thomas didn't know. And even if Thomas did know, he might be too chill to ever mention it. Mallory had been looking forward to this morning after, planning on bragging in a subtle but masculine way to show his young Black neighbor that a white man could get a woman too.

"Where are my sheets and bedspread?" he asked when Thomas returned. He had apparently slept with his face pushed against the rough texture of the sofa arm.

"We took them off. Your girlfriend and I took them off. My mother washed and dried them. They're folded up on your computer bench."

Mallory decided right then that his new neighbors were an exception to everything he had always known about Black people.

"Thank you, Thomas." Thomas just nodded. Mallory wondered what Thomas wanted in return for all his help. The young man didn't seem to need anything. Except maybe the approval of this older, wiser man. Or maybe to be let in on some of the secret wisdom such a real man possessed. Mallory sat up, bracing himself with a hand on either side to try to stop the dizziness. Thomas stood up and retrieved the computer bench and brought it near and sat down. "Thomas, I don't know what happened last night."

"After the party, you and your girlfriend came here. She said you – I mean both of you – were drinking a lot. Then you passed out."

"Did she pass out too?"

"I don't think so. She said she thought you had beer and crème de menthe and potato salad and ribs and a hell of a lot of Hennessy."

"But what I need to know, Thomas. And it's important to me. Did Nell and I ... did we ... make love?" Mallory restrained himself from using the *f* word. He used the softer, girlie term instead. He wanted Thomas to understand that he was a respectable white man. A respectable man who was groping in the dark about what happened. He was going the extra mile to let Thomas in on his worries. His understandable, manly worries.

Thomas began to speak, then shook his head and fell silent. "I don't know what to say, Mr. Mallory."

"You can call me Kevin. I've been after that woman for a long time. I'll have to see her every day at work. It would help me to know what happened last night."

Thomas gave the slightest shake to his head. "I can't tell you, Mr. Mallory. I didn't see anything. Nobody said anything. Honestly, man, I don't know."

90

\* \* \*   \* \* \*

Mallory was depressed that he now had to sit through Cheer Committee meetings. Nell introduced him and allowed him to give his opinions about the holiday party; but, even though the party was two months off, it seemed that most of the decisions had already been made. The rest of the group all just sat there like cows and stared at him like he was a man from Mars. Then Nell tediously explained the history of the discussion, including what kind of party each member of the committee had advocated for, the discussions that ensued, and what the final decision was. By the time it was over, Mallory was wondering if being on the committee was too high a price to pay for keeping his job.

Mallory was glad to see Kathie at the committee meeting. He had guessed from their conversation in the lunchroom that this long-faced blonde wasn't a complete cow. He had hoped she would interrupt Nell's tedious recitation of everybody's past opinions about the holiday party, but she spent the entire meeting flipping through pictures on her phone. Occasionally, as she stared at the screen, her eyes would grow larger and her breathing deeper. He guessed it was Brad Pitt again.

Mallory had been avoiding Nell in the days following the party. He had imagined her coming up to him glowing with the cognac-inspired admiration he'd seen in her eyes the evening of the party, her face flushed with memory of her sweet surrender to him. But Nell was unusually quiet in the following days. He wanted to ask Manly Man what to do, but he couldn't afford yet another $13.95 charge. He didn't want to come right out and ask her what happened. A real man should remember what he'd done with his woman. Maybe Nell had been shocked at the depths of buried passion he had released and would need some time to reorient her life. He decided to let her readjust in peace. He lowered his eyes and murmured a quick "hi" when they passed in the hallways. He even stopped rolling his chair back into her cubicle wall.

"I've got a complaint." One of the cows at the committee

meeting suddenly slapped her hand gently on the table, gaining everyone's attention. This was Jennifer, a heavyset woman with blue-framed glasses, a white, wrinkled blouse and a broad white face. Mallory guessed that her range of interests didn't usually extend beyond the dinner table. He was sure she was going to bring up the issue of party food again, but he was wrong. "We decided last time to send a card to my niece on her fifteenth birthday. It didn't come. Wait, listen to me. I didn't buy her one myself because I expected to be able to sign our employee card. I don't know what my niece thinks of me now. Is this the way we treat members of the committee itself?"

"I don't remember deciding that." Nell's voice was like a sigh.

"Well, you wrote it down at the time. I saw you."

"I can't find the committee notes right now."

"Let bygones be bygones." This was Bob, a shriveled man in his late fifties with furrowed, tanned skin, grey hair and bizarre, white-rimmed glasses. "I don't complain myself. I didn't complain when the committee voted down my Fourth of July desk flag idea."

Jennifer closed her eyes and took a deep breath. She removed her hand from the table.

"This is not the way the committee operates." Nell's voice was firm. "We need to get along, and there's no need for criticizing or attacking anyone." She suddenly seemed out of breath, threatened by the sudden commotion in her committee. She paused, then went on in a defeated voice as if she had just lost a battle. "I'll check the records about your niece. But I don't know what we can do about it now. Her birthday's long since passed. Can you just explain it to her, tell her the committee meant to wish her a happy birthday?"

Jennifer's mouth was set in a grim line. "I don't know what good that'll do."

\* \* \* \* \* \*

He was in the break room alone, trying to manipulate the committee's machine to get his free cup of coffee. He looked up and saw Nell entering, coming straight toward him. He checked the surveillance camera to make sure the tape was still over the lens. He told himself you never could tell what a woman in her situation would want.

"Can I talk to you for a minute, Kevin?"

She motioned with her head toward one of the tables. He followed and they sat down. She seemed to be waiting for him to start talking, but he had no idea what to say.

"I've been thinking about this for a couple of days," she began. "I wanted to apologize to you about what happened after the party." His heart jumped. "I drank too much, too fast," she went on. "What happened got me a little too full of myself, and I somehow felt entitled to take such ... *liberties*. Then, to make things worse, I left without ...."

It was everything he had hoped for! The only bad part was he didn't remember any of it. But he would never tell her that. "There's nothing to be ashamed of." He tried to make his face a model of manly confidence and serenity. "Breaking down the barriers to love is sometimes frightening. It'll take some time for us to get used to it."

Nell's eyes went wide. "*Love!*" She looked around to make sure no one had entered the break room and heard her exclamation. "Love? What the hell are you talking about?"

Mallory realized Nell was not willing to admit her sexual submission to him had anything to do with love. It wasn't actually the word he intended to use anyway. "It doesn't have to be love," he assured her now. "We had a good time, didn't we?"

Nell looked at him evenly. "We had a good conversation. When you explained about Mr. Bunbury's ferret, it helped me understand why people were looking at me so strangely at the party. I felt so relieved. We were both laughing about that, I think. Then you passed out on your sofa bed, and ... um ... threw up all over your sheets."

Mallory strained all the muscles in his face so as not to look totally defeated.

"I went back to the party and asked your friend Thomas for help," Nell went on. "His mother took the sheets to the apartment laundry in the basement. He did most of the cleaning up of the sofa, and of ... of you."

"Oh, my God, I'm sorry." He really was.

"Before the sheets had come back from the dryer, Thomas had you cleaned up and lying on the bare sofa bed. But I just ran out then. I shouldn't have. It was only seven o'clock. I could have waited until the sheets were dry. Thomas said to go, and I just ... fled."

# Chapter 12: A Semi-Beautiful Mind

"I turned my computer off and rebooted it like you said, Mr. Tell, but the screen is still black."

"I'm assuming you have Thunderwire 2.0 or above, and your IOXX system is compatible with that."

"Um ...."

"Did you direct the modulator to the USB port?"

"What? I have no idea what you're talking about."

"Okay, if you have an old system, there might still be something you can do to fix this yourself, Miss. Can you hit Control-Alt-Delete on your keyboard?"

"Sure. Okay. Got it. What next?"

"Now, press the power button on your router. It's usually on the side, near the bottom."

"Um, okay, but the computer's on my desk and the router is down on the floor."

"You have to press Control-Alt-Delete and the power button at the same time."

"Um. Hmmm. I can just barely reach .... Uh. Okay, I think I got it."

"You did get it! I can see the error code on my screen. I think one of our trained service technicians can handle it from here. I'll get one on the phone for you right now."

"I'm really stretched out here. How long do I have to hold this position?"

"Just until he gets there."

Mallory clicked off and pushed back his chair, visions of cinnamon buns already dancing in his head.

Nell appeared almost immediately in his cubicle entrance, her hazel eyes wide with alarm. "Kevin!" she whispered fiercely. "What are you doing? You can get fired for messing with a customer like that."

He avoided her eyes, stared straight at his screen, fingered his goatee. "Yeah, I guess I could get fired for that." His tone indicated he might not care.

"And, you know, they're still looking for the customer rep who used that fake Indian accent."

He turned toward her. "You're such a tattletale, Nell. Why don't you turn me in?"

Nell started to say something but gulped back her words. Her face turned red. She wasn't embarrassed because he called her a tattletale. Everybody called her a tattletale. She was embarrassed because she had *not* turned him in. He wondered why she hadn't.

"It's almost like you're trying to get yourself fired."

"Maybe I am," he surprised himself by saying. Of course, he was an expert at making it more trouble to fire him than it was worth. Teitelbaum was dying to fire him but hadn't yet gotten a thing on him. And Mallory was looking forward to a long personnel battle with him. But insulting customers would make it easier for his supervisor to fire him, and insulting customers was exactly what he had done.

"Really, why are you risking your job?" Nell couldn't have looked more perplexed if someone on the Cheer Committee had said a bad word.

"I was thinking you wanted me gone."

Nell's eyes widened in alarm. "I don't want you gone, Kevin. Did somebody tell you that?"

"No. I just thought ...."

"I hope you stay here at UniCast, Kevin." Mallory's sudden surge of hope was extinguished by her next sentence. "You are a valued member of the Employee Cheer Committee."

\* \* \* \* \* \*

He stopped rolling his chair back into Nell's cubicle wall. He decided to try a little harder to keep his job. He ditched the character of Apu Krishna except for callers he didn't like. He decided that Algonquin J. Tycoon was never going to spend the money to

96

pay someone to actually listen in on his conversations with customers. But it cost almost nothing for the company to do a com-
puterized search for the length of time he spent on the phone with
them. So he took a new approach to the customers.

Could I have your full name and customer number, sir? Which
type of plan are you on? I don't think that's a plan we support
anymore, sir. Do you have more recent paperwork showing a current plan? What is the number on the upper right of your most
recent bill? I will also need the serial number of your modem. It
should be stamped on a small plate on the bottom of your modem.
Yes, I will wait. It's not there? Do you have a UniCast modem or
an aftermarket modem? If it's an aftermarket modem that's where
the problem is, and you'll have to call the manufacturer. You do
have a UniCast modem? Are you sure? And the number is not on
the bottom? Then look at the back of the modem, where the cables attach. Sometimes the serial number is stamped on the plate
next to the connections. Sometimes it's on a small metal tag, and
sometimes the tag falls off it the modem has moved. Have you
moved the modem since it was installed, sir?

Mallory had no idea where the serial number would be found
on a UniCast modem. He had never even seen a UniCast modem.
But he was sure he had tripled the length of his average call by
using this method. He spent his time on his favorite websites or
looking at YouTube on his phone while sending customers scram-
bling for information that he already had, or that didn't exist at
all. But the best part of this strategy was he rarely had to cut off
customers anymore. The customers usually hung up themselves
after a half hour or so. He figured the company couldn't blame
him if the customers would not provide the information on their
account that he needed.

Nell was unfailingly polite to him, even when he confessed he
had left the Cheer Committee notes on the floor of his cubicle and
the janitorial crew had tossed them out.

"Oh," she said, looking right past him. "There was a lot of
personal information in those records."

"I don't think the dumpster people will be searching out whose dog had puppies last year."

Nell puffed herself up. "Puppies are important to people."

"I guess so." He tried not to smirk. It was hard to listen to this drivel coming out of her mouth. But he found himself doing so, pretending to be interested. It wasn't that he was interested in this trivia. He was interested in her. She didn't think like he did. That probably meant her mind was defective, but he was still interested in finding out how it worked. He'd never taken an interest in another employee at any of his previous jobs. But now he was intrigued by how her mind worked, at least enough to distract him from the drudgery of Customer Service.

\*\*\* \*\*\*

Mallory wore an old-fashioned goatee that covered just the bottom of his chin and was just thick enough that he could plait it into a thin strand that twisted its way down toward the neck of his shirt. It was red, like the rest of his hair. His mother said it was repulsive. "You got a round face. If you want to grow a beard, you should grow a full beard like your father."

"Why do you want me to be anything like him? He left us, didn't he?" Mentioning his father's desertion was usually enough to shut her up. Actually, Mallory had tried several times to grow a full beard, but he couldn't.

"It makes you look like the devil, is all I can say."

At his original job interview at UniCast, Ms. Marcie, a young female personnel assistant, after first glancing very quickly back at Teitelbaum, had stated very delicately that his appearance would have to meet standards "that will present an attractive and professional image of the UniCast team to the public." Mallory had strung a few colored beads onto the end of his plait just for that interview. He fingered them as he nodded gravely at the personnel assistant.

"You object to the way I dress?" It was always best to challenge an employer's minions head on. It was even better if you could T-bone them by deliberately misunderstanding their message.

"No ... um ...." Ms. Marcie looked at Teitelbaum for help. He just sat there smiling at her discomfort. "While we have no policy on facial hair, we feel that extreme examples of ... *facial decoration* might detract from the UniCast image in the public eye."

"You're rejecting me because of my looks?"

"No ... um ... we haven't rejected anybody. When hiring a new employee, we look at the total picture, but that picture includes ...."

After watching his new assistant struggle with Mallory for a few more minutes, Teitelbaum had had enough amusement for the day. "That's okay, Ms. Marcie. Right now, we're looking for a customer service representative who interacts with customers only on the phone. Appearance and dress don't really matter at all." He stared closely at Mallory. "Unless, of course, one's personal hygiene is such that it becomes a health menace to the other employees."

Mallory stared back, daring Teitelbaum to accuse him of a personal hygiene problem. He had showered that morning and put on clean clothes. After shaving, he had smoothed onto his face and neck an extra generous layer of Chain Mail. He knew he smelled okay and couldn't be accused of endangering anyone's health. Mallory could tell Teitelbaum didn't like him, but the rumor was that UniCast was expanding and needed new workers in all categories, quickly. The rumor was correct. He was hired. Teitelbaum had just been testing Ms. Marcie to see how she would deal with this smartass applicant who Teitelbaum already suspected was a tough nut.

Teitelbaum was becoming increasingly frustrated. Mallory seemed always one step ahead of him, successfully erasing the evidence of his wrongdoing. Mallory's excuse for being off the phone so often was now airtight, as Nell had refused to grant Teitelbaum access to the Cheer Committee records – and Mallory had destroyed them anyway. Mallory then heard Teitelbaum tell Nell that he wanted notice of the date and time of any forthcoming committee meetings. Nell replied that she'd bring that request up before the committee.

Mallory had already figured out that Nell wouldn't take any action at all unless every member of the committee approved. At committee meetings, she put off "until later" discussion of any idea that anybody might object to. Later never came. As a result, they spent their time carefully considering inconsequential minutia, such as which personal events in the life of the employees should be celebrated with an event, a luncheon, or a card. The only other subject of conversation was Bob's constant harping on his idea that the committee should place a small American flag on a little stand on each employee's desk. Nell's rote response was they couldn't afford it. Nobody else seemed to like Bob or to be interested in his plan. There was never any vote on his idea. Nell would simply turn to another topic.

Bob took each one of these defeats hard, staring down at the table with a sour mouth, the tanned furrows of his weathered face running due south. Mallory was beginning to appreciate Nell's policy of just ignoring stupid ideas. But, at one meeting, Bob jerked his head up and stared hard at Mallory. "You, Snakebeard. You don't look like the kind of guy who goes along with these sissified objections to a man's ideas. What do you say to my flag idea?"

Mallory froze. He knew nothing at all about what the little flags and stands would cost. He had no idea how much money the committee had to spend. He knew he liked to keep his own desk clear for snacks. Rose had once given him a fancy fountain pen as a gift, but the only thing he had ever used it for was spearing through plastic bags and food wrappers. He wore the point out that way before he ever got any ink in it. He didn't want a cheap little flag in a cheap holder cluttering up his desk. But he realized that Bob was the only other man on this committee of seven.

"Yeah," he nodded, leaving his mouth open to signal he had more to say. "Yeah, maybe those flags will put a little backbone in the staff."

Nell wasn't the type to roll her eyes, but Kathie, sitting right next to her, rolled enough for two. "There are two hundred and sixteen employees in this building. How many of them do you think want more crap on their desks?"

"Don't say crap. The American flag is not crap." Bob's face had the self-satisfied look of a man who had come up with one statement that was irrefutably correct.

Kathie shook her head, breathing out slowly in exasperation. "The American flag is not crap, but these cheap little flags in their cheap little stands are just going to get in everybody's way and end up broken and thrown in the trash."

"How do we know they're cheap? How do we know they'll fall apart?" Mallory actually agreed 100% with Kathie, but he was sure the right thing to do was stand up for the only other man on the committee.

"Okay, I know what we have to do." Nell suddenly interrupted, using a flat but overbearing tone that silenced the others. "Mr. Mallory, we can't make this decision without facts. I'm asking you to research the cost and quality of the flags we would need. I repeat, I don't think we have the budget for it, but I'm asking you to find out for sure so we can all agree on how to proceed."

# Chapter 13: Bullets, Peach Cake and Chin Braids

Mallory stopped at Guns-R-Us on the way home to buy bullets.

"Sorry, sir." Gus, the owner, didn't seem like he was sorry. "We're all out of cartridges for that type of gun."

"When will you have them in?"

"It might be a while. They're on backorder. Probably be a few weeks."

"Weeks? Can't I get them online?"

"Yeah, maybe. But you never know what you're getting on the internet. Half of that stuff's from China. You put some of those defective Chinese cartridges in that gun, it could blow up in your face. I'd advise you to just wait for the right ones to arrive. I have your number. I'll call you when they come in."

Mallory walked back to his car. He wasn't as disappointed as he could have been. His father had kept two rifles on that rack in his bedroom, and he realized now that it wasn't just a matter of sticking any old bullet in any old gun. There was a lot more to it than that. He'd never gone shooting with his father, and so he'd never learned this stuff. A surge of long-delayed admiration for the man passed through him, but it was quickly followed by a hollow feeling of guilt for not getting to know him better. He'd never sought out his father after the divorce, even when he was in his mid-twenties and living on his own. He'd always told himself he didn't know what to say. His father didn't call him either. Then his father remarried and had two stepsons who were just little kids. His father had obviously been busy with his new family. Then he died five years ago. They hadn't had any contact in the last few years before he died. But Mallory felt his father would be proud of the man he had become.

A Black man flashed past his window just as he was opening his car door in the parking lot. He immediately conjured up the image of his rifle in the trunk. But the man turned and flashed a smile. He realized it was Thomas. Mallory called after him.

"Thomas!"

"Hey ... *Kevin*," Thomas came back toward him. "Sorry if I frightened you."

"Oh, you didn't frighten me, Thomas. But I want to say something to you. Come here." Thomas obeyed. "Listen, you have to be more careful. There's a lot of hoodlums hanging around, even in this parking lot."

"I never saw it, Mr. Mallory. Sorry, I can't just call you *Kevin*. Never seen it, but my mother said she heard a lot of commotion in the parking lot one night a few weeks ago. Some of the other neighbors heard it, too. You be careful yourself."

"I can take care of myself."

"Uh, okay." But Thomas looked worried for him. Mallory was touched that this young man cared.

"Thomas. No secrets between us. Okay?"

"Sure, man."

"The ferret," he said. "The one that smelled so bad. I took it to the shelter the night before the party."

"Ah," Thomas nodded his head slowly. "I was wondering what happened to it."

"But you didn't ask me about the ferret then?"

"That lady, your friend, she gave me the evil eye when I said something about ferrets."

"Nell's an animal lover."

"Ah, I see." Thomas hesitated. "She worked real hard cleaning up your place that night. She still your girlfriend?" Thomas held his eyes.

"I want her to be my girlfriend. It's not working out like I planned." Mallory felt an incredible sense of relief as he said these words. Thomas just seemed to draw the truth out of him. He didn't know why. Thomas was too young to remind him of his father, too old to be a substitute son, too Black to be a substitute brother. He was like no one Mallory had ever met before. It was so easy just to tell him what actually happened.

"She likes you." Thomas smiled, and nodded knowingly.

"Did she say that?"

"No. But what kind of woman cleans up like that after a guy if she don't like him?"

"You don't know Nell. She's a neat freak. She can't stand any kind of mess, anywhere."

"A *neat freak*." Thomas pursed his lips as he drew the syllables out. Then his eyes lit up. "Good thing you got rid of that stinky-ass ferret."

\* \* \*   \* \* \*

Still in the parking lot, shaking his head, Thomas warned him that his mother was coming to see him about setting up some kind of citizen's security patrol. He seemed resigned to this foolishness, but to Mallory this plan constituted an emergency – because he knew he'd be asked to volunteer. As soon as he finished talking to Thomas, he got back in his car and drove immediately to the Dough and Go, where he stayed until it closed at eight that night. Spike waited on him there. Trying to stretch out his time in the diner, Mallory told him more hoodlum stories. He told him about the ruckus in the parking lot of his apartment complex that Ava had described to him. He mentioned that the neighbors were forming a Neighborhood Watch.

"It's funny," Spike talked to the air as he put Mallory's plate down in front of him. "We live right near Glenwood Apartments, and we've never had any trouble."

"You'd better start a Watch now, before it's too late."

The last thing Mallory wanted to do was join a Neighborhood Watch. He didn't need to join a bunch of people sitting around whining about their fears, making him sign up to a schedule of patrols that might infringe on his free time, making him write reports. A real man wouldn't put up with such a fuddy-duddy bureaucracy run by stay-at-homes with nothing better to do than dream up jobs for him to do. A real man would be vigilant, arm himself and serve as a deterrent just by his fearsome presence. He was determined not to join any neighborhood group.

But then Ava came over that night with a peach cake she had made just for him. It was still warm. The bright yellow peaches lay on top covered with a brown glaze he was sure was cinnamon sugar. Ava was a tall woman, large without being fat, with a serene smile and black, wavy hair cut just below the ears. Mallory didn't take the cake from her hands, and she looked for any kind of surface to put the cake on; but then she just took it upon herself to march right past Mallory's unmade bed into the kitchen, where she quietly made room for her dish among the food wrappers piled up all over the counter. Mallory felt like she was torturing him by shoving the cake in his face and then taking it away.

"Well!" she said, brushing her hands together as she came back out of the kitchen. "I hope you enjoy that peach cake. Peaches are so good this year."

"Thank you."

"I won't take too much of your time. I think Thomas already told you we are thinking of starting up a Neighborhood Watch for the complex. There've been so many stories going around about what they call gangbangers, even in our parking lot."

"I've heard that," Mallory reluctantly admitted.

"We thought we'd get six or seven people together to, you know, look into it. See if there is anything to these rumors."

"You mean research?"

"Yes, I think I do. You know, contact the police, see what the crime statistics are." Ava paused, lowered her voice to a more confidential tone. "I don't know if Thomas told you, but we won't be here for long. We're just here waiting for our new house to be finished. But Thomas will be here when we leave, and we thought we should try and help while we're here."

"So, you want people to get crime statistics, things like that?"

"Yes."

Mallory liked Ava, but he knew she had the wrong idea about

everything. They didn't need statistics about crime to prove what he had seen with his own eyes. And wasn't it proof enough that he had bought a rifle?

He didn't invite Ava to sit down because it never occurred to him to think about another person's comfort. There was no place to sit anyway except on the sofa bed and his computer bench. He wished she would leave so he could take a taste of that peach cake. He had trouble focusing on what she was saying. She was talking about having a meeting at her apartment. He wondered if she would serve food there. He found himself nodding as this pleasant lady talked and talked while the peach cake went cold back in the kitchen. After what seemed like at least a half hour, she moved toward the door.

"Next Thursday then, at seven," he heard her saying.

"Fine. Fine."

"And you'll contact the police department before then and see if they have any statistics about the increasing crime in our neighborhood?" She opened the door. "Thank you for volunteering, Mr. Mallory." Then she was gone.

\* \* \*  \* \* \*

It was October, and the temperature could be almost anything on any day. One frosty morning Mallory stepped out of his apartment and was almost to his car when he realized he was freezing in his short-sleeved shirt. He turned back and put on the sweatshirt he had worn ever since college. The elbows were frayed, and it was much tighter than it used to be, but it was still his favorite piece of clothing. Rose had bought him a lined nylon jacket once, but it was white and tight, and his mother said it made him look like a penguin.

Mallory ordinarily didn't mind looking shabby in his clothes. In fact, an important part of his persona was being visually offensive. His ragged sweatshirt, too-tight waistband, and the snake-like braid growing out of his goatee caused the average person to shy away from him. That was exactly the effect he wanted. He wanted to send a message loud and clear that he was not trying to please you and don't you think of asking any favors. This plan worked pretty well with almost everyone. Nell was a recent exception, as was Thomas and his family. He had started to feel uncomfortable when he was around them in his usual offensive garb. He had worn his best pair of shorts and a clean, pressed short-sleeved buttoned-down shirt to the party. Those clothes did fit in, but he had still felt uncomfortable there. When he wore his ragged sweatshirt to work that cold October morning, he felt like himself again.

"Have you made any progress on the American flag pricing?" Nell asked as she leaned into his cubicle that morning. He didn't pay much attention to her question because he was so startled that she had initiated a conversation with him. She must like him, he thought. Or, at least, she wasn't permanently repulsed by what happened at his place after the party.

"Have you made any progress on the American flag pricing?" she repeated.

"No." Mallory was amazed at how satisfying it was to tell her the simple truth. It was not a good thing that he had ignored his task for the committee; but Nell had seen a lot worse from him, and maybe one more failure, this time a small, repairable one, wouldn't hurt him too much in her eyes.

Nell screwed up her mouth. "Well, we're being honest, at least." She still stood there, and he couldn't think of anything to say.

"Kevin." He liked that she used his first name. And she spoke in a softer tone, as if it was her problem too, and they would solve it without letting anyone else in on it. "It really should be pretty easy. Just go online and google 'American flags desktop' and you can come up with the answer in a few minutes."

Mallory could have come up with a hundred excuses, but it felt like the easiest thing would be to tell the truth. "I know, but Teitelbaum's after me. You know we're not supposed to use the server like that. They can check my searches much easier than my Customer Service phone."

Nell slowly shook her head. "Everybody knows we can't afford 216 of those stupid flags."

"I'll look it up at home tonight. I promise."

"No. It's really not worth going to any trouble at all. I can do it in a minute on my computer here."

"This whole flag idea – it's completely stupid."

"Of course – but you sided with him." She seemed more disappointed than angry.

*I'm sorry*. The thought popped into his head, but it was against his philosophy to apologize. Instead, he watched her turn and go back to her cubicle.

He left for the bathroom. On his way back, she put a hand out and waved him into her cubicle. "It's done," she said. "Three thousand, six hundred and forty-four dollars for the cheapest flags. More than our entire budget for the holiday party."

"Good. That ought to squelch it."

"Yeah." Then she looked up at his face. Her own face was suddenly suffused with something like wonder. "You cut off your braid! You cut off that creepy braid!"

# Chapter 14: Rules of Attraction

He had to have her, and the website didn't give him any clue about how to get her. He still checked in with Manly Man, but the idea there seemed to be that the woman would always be chasing him. He still visited his porn site, and in fact renewed his subscription, but now it seemed to be recycling videos he had seen before. Neither of these sites seemed to be oriented toward helping him get a *particular* woman, but that's what he wanted now. He even told his mother about Nell. Of course, he lied about her age and her looks and said they were already dating hot and heavy. His mother listened to it all, but her only comment was "I miss Rose, your old girlfriend."

Nell was on his side in his fight against Teitelbaum. "I heard something you might want to know. Teitelbaum's looking for someone with an Indian accent, but he's trying to be quiet about it," she whispered to him at the entrance to his cubicle one day. Nell didn't say she knew Mallory was Apu Krishna, but she obviously had heard Apu dealing with customers over their shared cubicle wall.

Mallory explained to her why Teitelbaum was trying to be quiet about it. From his long experience with employers who were having personnel problems, he knew that middle managers were expected to squelch any problems from customers or employees before they came to the attention of the higher-ups. The last thing Teitelbaum wanted was for Starganoff to hear there was a problem he couldn't handle himself.

"I know you are Apu." Nell's tone was resigned rather than accusatory. "I don't know why you do that."

Mallory met her eyes. "I don't really know, either. Boredom, I guess."

Nell compressed her lips like she was swallowing down a harsh judgment. Then she met his eyes. He was surprised to see her smile sadly. "This job truly is boring, I guess."

"But you never complain. And you do it right."

"I think it's everyone's duty ...." she began. But then her features shifted. "Thank you." Was her voice tremulous? He watched her more closely. "Thank you for noticing. Not many people do." She looked up at him in a way she had never done before. Her hazel eyes were steady, soaking up his attention. For a moment she was much more than his flat-heeled, flat-eyed, flat-voiced critic. Her face was transformed for a moment into something much more tentative and girlish.

"I cut off my chin braid because I thought you didn't like it."

He thought she would at least meet his eyes. But she looked like she was weighing her words, consumed by her own bureaucratic need to accurately and appropriately respond. "That is true. I did not like that braid. Actually, I don't like facial hair at all on men."

He fingered what was left of his goatee. What was she trying to say?

"Do you want me to cut the rest of it off?"

"I don't think that's really any of my business." She was back to her flat, schoolteacher voice again.

"Do you think I'm attractive, Nell?"

She looked back at her screen, pursed her lips. He waited.

"I don't limit myself to attractive men."

\* \* \*   \* \* \*

His doorbell rang that night as soon as he got back from the Dough and Go. Mallory jumped happily to open it because he expected it to be Thomas. But it was Ava, and she wasn't bringing any food.

"Hi, Mr. Mallory." He stepped back from her looming presence in the door, but still kept his hand on the knob. Ava held herself back from entering his apartment. Good. He had sort of promised he would gather statistics on crime in their neighborhood, and he assumed she was there to talk about that. He definitely didn't want to talk about that. Ava smiled. "We have good news about our Neighborhood Watch idea."

"What is it?" He could tell she wanted to come in and chat. He liked Ava, but he kept his hold on the door because he wanted to keep this meeting short.

"Alright. Edison – that's my husband, Thomas's father – he talked to the police. They have a community outreach unit, and they're coming to talk to us about crime in the neighborhood." Ava smiled. "Edison thinks we're all worrying about nothing. But the police, they're happy to come. So they're coming Thursday night to talk to us all. You'll be there, right?"

"Sure." He couldn't think of an excuse.

"Have you got any crime statistics from the police yet?"

This was the question he had been fearing. "I got some … uh … raw data from the county. I'm working on creating a spread-sheet, but it might take a while." He had no idea how to get the information, or if it even existed. He didn't know how to make a spreadsheet.

Personally, Mallory thought that setting up a neighborhood meeting was the wrong way to go. The last thing he wanted was to be forced to sit and listen to everybody's stupid opinions. Quick action was what was needed in the face of danger. He felt so much safer already with the 30-30 in the trunk of his car. If he could get Thomas to carry a gun too, that would be all the safety the neigh-borhood would need. He didn't press this idea on Ava right away. She and her husband were just too stodgy and old school.

"If you'd like to come over about an hour early, you can have dinner with us first."

"Oh, yes, yes. Yeah. Great idea. I'll be there."

"They gave us the name of the officer who will be there. He's our neighborhood patrol officer, Officer Selby."

\* \* \*  \* \* \*

Mallory shaved off the rest of his goatee that night. The next night he went out to the mall and bought two new shirts. They both had collars. One was a vivid white with a colorful print. He wore that one to work the following day. Nell said he looked different. That was all she said.

He resigned himself to going to the meetings of the Employee Cheer Committee. Nell had done the research which showed that they could not afford Bob's idea of putting little American flag stands on everybody's desk. Mallory then presented the cost estimate to the committee.

"Those tiny flags will cost more than our entire holiday party fund. And they'll probably cut into our budget for the Cheerboree, too," Nell responded.

Bob pushed forward anyway. "These flags will do more for morale than the holiday party and the Cheerboree combined. I vote for the flags." He looked over at Mallory for support. Nell and Kathie and Jennifer looked over at him also, but their looks were more like daggers.

He was starting to understand why Nell had asked him to research the cost of the flags when everyone already knew that the cost would be prohibitive. It was to avoid a vote. Even though the flag idea would have lost then by a 5-2 vote, Nell didn't want a vote – because she never wanted there to be an actual vote. Nell wanted everybody to be happy.

Mallory was thrilled to be able to give her what she wanted. "Bob and I," he announced in a voice of authority, "are going to have a man to man talk about those flags after this meeting."

Nell picked up the cue. "Okay. Let's talk about the holiday party." There was no more talk about the flags.

He stayed in the breakroom with Bob after the rest of the committee left. "What's the Cheerboree?" Mallory began.

"Cheerboree? Oh, that's one of those outdoor, team-building, supposedly fun days. They had 25 people last year, me not included, out of 216."

"Look, Bob, drop the flag thing, and I promise you can run the Cheerboree next spring."

Mallory stood in Nell's cubicle entrance afterwards. He told her Bob had dropped the flag idea. He didn't mention the Cheerboree.

"I see you shaved off the rest of your goatee," she surprised him by saying.

"Um, I did."

"I'm not a fan of facial hair."

"You said that before." He tilted his head so she could get a better look at his chin.

"Okay. What do you want me to say? I like it."

"Thank you." He waited. "Isn't there anything else you want to thank me for?"

"No. Oh, yes, thank you for getting Bob to drop his flag thing. That was a big help to the committee."

"I knew that's what you wanted."

She sat back and folded her hands in her lap, looking up at him wide eyed like an awed little kid who had just been told Santa would be good to her. Mallory was thrilled with himself. He had taught her to be grateful. He had taught her to trust him. She was breathing deeply, her gaze not quite meeting his. She opened her mouth as if to say something, but then stopped. She was reaching out for something from him, he was sure. She didn't even realize what she needed yet, he was sure. But he could sense the ice melting, their friendship growing.

# Chapter 15: Kluxers and Pirates

A real man doesn't put up with anxiety. Yet Mallory felt anxious on a couple of fronts. Now that Nell was into him, he really didn't want to lose his job. Teitelbaum was thus more of a threat to him now. And if things went any further with Nell, he'd have to get Bunbury out of his apartment somehow. And he didn't know if he wanted to reveal the real end to the ferret story to Thomas. But most worrisome of all was Ava's upcoming Neighborhood Watch meeting with the planned guest appearance by Officer Selby.

Action was the recommended antidote for anxiety. The night before the meeting at Ava's, Mallory stopped at the drugstore and bought two different bottles of hair dye. He tried the brown first, and when that didn't darken his red hair enough, he added a little black. He did it in the tiny sink in his bathroom, leaving swaths of dark stain on the porcelain sink and plastic wall tiles that he didn't have time to clean up. His head was really too big for the sink, and so he didn't completely cover the red with the brown. He tried to make up for this by going extra heavy with the black in back, but the overall result was a kind of muddy reddish brown with heavy dark swirls throughout and a big black patch on the back. He also bought a pair of non-prescription reading glasses, the weakest ones he could find.

When Thomas opened the door the night of the Neighborhood Watch meeting, his eyes went wide. "What the fuck, Mr. Mallory?"

"Oh, you recognized me?"

"Yeah. You're here for dinner?" Thomas held his hands out like he was warding him off. "Just maybe stand here for a minute. I'll tell my Ma you're here."

Ava and Edison didn't recognize him at first. That was a good test. If they didn't recognize him right away, what were the chances Officer Selby would? But Mallory was having trouble seeing through the reading glasses and couldn't exactly gauge their expressions. The whole family seemed to gradually warm up to him, though. But as they all kept talking, a sudden fear hit him that they might ask him why he had changed his appearance. He hadn't planned for such a discussion. Mallory's lifelong talent for lying himself out of any situation was lately being threatened by the hard facts that Thomas, and Ava, and Edison – and even Nell – knew about him. He felt hemmed in by these facts now. Would he have to come up with a story that would jibe with *everything* he had told *everyone*? He was distracted the whole meal by trying to come up with a story. The food tasted good, though he couldn't actually see what he was eating.

The people who showed up were basically the same people who had been at the party a few weeks before. Two of the women apparently didn't recognize him from then. He didn't try to clear that up. He caught his breath when the door knocker banged with the assertive rap of the police.

"My name is Corporal Jim Selby. I've been on the police force for four years, the last two in this precinct. I'm glad you asked me to come talk to you tonight. It's alert and aware citizens like you who help keep crime down as low as it is in this area."

"We've been hearing a lot of commotion in the parking lot of this apartment complex," someone interrupted. "Have you made any arrests there?"

"No. I checked the stats before I left. No reports coming from your parking lot. This whole area seems to be pretty clean."

"People are seeing a lot of young men, mostly wearing hoodies, hanging around this complex and running through the alleys in Glenwood."

"It's not a crime to wear a hoodie." Selby answered the question no one asked. He had obviously been asked questions about people wearing hoodies before. Everybody in the room knew that *hoodies* was white code for young Black men. Selby seemed a little tired of it.

Mallory was waiting for a chance to slip quietly out of the

room. Selby had done a double take on first catching sight of him, but he had been quickly distracted by Ava, who pulled him over by the arm to introduce him to the group. Mallory sat in a chair in the back, leaning against the glass balcony doors, head down. He couldn't remember exactly what he'd told Thomas about the fate of the ferret, but he knew it wouldn't match what he had told Selby. He was terrified that Selby would mention his arrest.

"What about these Ku Kluxers? Somebody said they saw one just last week," Ava interjected. Mallory looked straight down at the floor. His heart was pounding.

He couldn't help himself. "There was no Ku Kluxer! There was no Ku Kluxer!" Everyone turned back to look at him. He didn't know exactly why he said that. But at least it was the truth. Mallory's face now changed from freckled, pasty white to beet red, adding to his disguise.

Selby stared at him in the silence that followed. Mallory tried to look back down at the floor. Selby cleared his throat, bring everyone's attention back to the front. "Miss Ava," he said quietly. "We did get a call about that. I can tell you without a doubt that that report was not well founded." Selby had definitely recognized him now. Mallory bowed his head in despair.

"We briefly apprehended the person who was the subject of that complaint. He was not a member of the Ku Klux Klan or any other hate group. He was not pretending to be a member of the Ku Klux Klan or any other hate group. He was simply an individual who, for reasons I do not understand, happened to be wearing a white plastic bag on his head at the time." Thomas and his father laughed. Selby glanced again at Mallory before shrugging his shoulders at the crowd. "In my job, you see all kinds of emotionally disturbed individuals. But we checked this one out thoroughly and determined that he is not a current danger to anyone."

Mallory felt a rush of anger. *Emotionally disturbed?* And how could Selby not recognize what was happening in the neighborhood? As much as he feared Selby would expose him, he could not hold himself back. "But what about these hoodlums in hoodies roaming the streets, stirring up trouble? Why don't you tell us the plain truth? The best protection is a gun."

"That's not the truth," Selby quickly responded. "Statistically speaking, buying a gun doubles the chances someone in your family will be shot, either by accident or suicide, or by another family member."

"That wouldn't be true if people know what they're doing," Mallory shot back. He remembered the smirk on Officer Selby's face when he was arrested. Mallory had planned to keep a low profile at this meeting, but Selby was smirking at him again now, and he couldn't stand it.

"Knowing your way around guns helps a lot," Selby acknowledged. "But does anybody here think Mr. Plastic Bag Head Man would make this community safer by carrying a gun?"

People in the room laughed. Selby stared hard at Mallory as he said that. Mallory dropped his head again, defeated. The group was already amused by Selby's story of the antics of Mr. Plastic Bag Head Man. The police, he decided, had more than one way to intimidate you, and they were pulling out all the stops to intimidate him right now. He was irritated by Selby's easy comfort in speaking to the neighbors, the way they were hanging on his every word. The police had it easy, and they obviously didn't want to hear the neighbors' evidence of crimes. Selby got paid overtime for coming to this meeting and intimidating him when he should be out chasing hoodlums. Meanwhile, Selby's chief was probably out sucking up to the county executive, who was probably sucking up to higher politicians who themselves were sucking up to Algonquin J. Tycoon himself.

Mallory fumed in his chair the rest of the meeting and didn't meet Selby's eyes when he left. Thomas came immediately to his side.

"You alright, Mr. Mallory?"

"Yeah. I'm fine." Mallory glanced up. Thomas was just too young and inexperienced to understand the complications of the real world. "I think it's the hair dye. I must have got some of it in my eyes."

\* \* \*  \* \* \*

Mallory sat at the bar in the Pirate's Den with Bob from the Cheer Committee. He rarely visited bars because he thought bars were a rip off, but this was a special occasion. He was doing a favor for Nell.

"I don't know what to do about Bob," she confided to him one day in the break room. "He's still angry about the American flag thing. Now he's against every idea we come up with for the holiday party."

"He's only one vote." Mallory couldn't understand why she wanted the goodwill of this malcontent so badly.

"Yeah, he's a malcontent, but he can cause trouble. We're supposed to be the Cheer Committee. We're not supposed to make people unhappy."

"Maybe you're part of the problem. You want to make even the lunatics happy. You can't stand being criticized by anyone."

Nell opened her mouth and exhaled without quite gritting her teeth. "I like everybody to be happy. That's how I am, Kevin."

He nodded. He understood now. She did not think like him at all. Watching her closely over the past few weeks, he saw she had her own little world that worked smoothly as far as it went. He had made some adjustments on account of her. He had stopped hoping that the holiday party be a dress-as-your-favorite-movie-star night. It hadn't been such a great idea anyway. Now that he went to the meetings and got a close look at some of his female coworkers, he didn't want to see any of them in Shakira outfits.

"Okay." He reminded himself what they had been talking about. "I'll take Bob on a field trip. I'll make sure he misses the meeting."

"You could do that? That would be wonderful, Kevin."

The Pirate's Den was one of the possible venues for the holiday party. The bartender was a huge white man in pirate garb, including a gold earring, a purple bandanna kerchief and black eyepatch. "Ahoy, mateys. What'll ya have?"

"Um ...." Bob had done all the talking on the drive from Uni-Cast. He had bored Mallory by rattling off all the details he was going to demand from the staff there. "I'll need all the details, the seating capability, the group menu, the exact price per person, the cost of any side dishes or desserts, how each attendee's drink bill would be handled separately, whether there would be a group tip, and whether those who did not drink would have their tip amounts proportionately decreased." Even though it was only a ten-minute ride from the UniCast building, Mallory had lost track of all these details by the time they reached the Pirate's Den. Apparently, so had Bob. "Um, I guess we want a couple of drinks," he told the fearsome pirate.

"Drinks it is!" The pirate's voice was three times too loud for the occasion. "And what type of drinks will ye have, mateys?"

"Two beers, please. Molson," Mallory quickly shot back. He used to drink Molson when he went to parties. He hoped they still made Molson.

"Eh, Kevin. I like a hard drink every now and again," Bob objected. "Make mine a Dewars single malt, double."

Mallory was appalled. When he bribed Bob into coming on this trip by promising he'd buy the drinks, he hadn't planned on paying for scotch. All he had to do was keep Bob out of the workplace for 45 minutes, the length of the committee meeting. It wasn't supposed to cost him a fortune – but Bob quickly finished his drink in two long gulps and started looking around for the bartender.

Mallory feared that half his disposable income for the week could disappear before the 45 minutes was up. He dragged out of his pocket the list of questions Nell had given him to ask. It included everything Bob had mentioned, plus scores of others, including the high and low prices of the available entrees, whether the salads would be served as part of the meal or separately, whether the seating arrangement would allow each person to talk to every other person, if there was a heating unit directly above the tables, whether there was a secure coat check and how much of a tip would the coat check attendants expect, whether the décor was appropriately bright for a holiday party, whether the tables were long or would have to be pushed together awkwardly, how close to the door would the party be, how clean were the women's bathrooms.

Mallory never had any intention of asking any of these questions. His only goal was to keep Bob out of the Cheer Committee meeting that was going on right then. And Bob also apparently forgot all about the questions once he tasted his scotch. His thin, rutted face quickly grew so red it looked like the surface of Mars, if Mars really had canals. He ordered another double. Mallory panicked and looked for help. There was only the fearsome pirate, who was standing with his back to the cash register, giving them the evil eye. He caught a glimpse of a waitress about to pass by. She also had dark hair and pirate garb, which mostly consisted of a bandanna, a huge earring and a ruffled white blouse. She stopped dead in her tracks when he caught her eye. He was used to this reaction ever since he had dyed his hair, but he tried to smile and wave her over.

"I don't serve at the bar. I'll get the bartender's attention for you." They could both see the bartender was staring right at them without moving.

"No. I need to talk to somebody about planning a Christmas party."

"Oh." Her attitude changed instantly. Her lips curved into a smile. She had beautiful creamy skin. Mallory was not used to women who looked this good paying any attention to him. Of course, he knew it was his mention of renting the place for a party that interested her. She was clearly interested in getting his business. Mallory figured she must be the owner's mistress. She motioned him over to an empty table under a gigantic model of a galleon hanging from the ceiling. It was one of many pirate-themed objects hanging on the walls and from the ceiling. Bob stayed behind at the bar.

She asked if he wanted another beer while they talked. He

didn't really, but he wanted to see her hop up and get it for him. "What date are we talking about?" she asked, once she had set him up with a second beer. Mallory had to pull out his notes from Nell. He spread them on the table and started looking for the date. "Oh, I see it there." She pointed at the notes. "November 23$^{rd}$? That's before Thanksgiving. Isn't that a little early for a holiday party?"

"We want to have the holiday party early enough to avoid the rush of holiday parties." Mallory mouthed the words Nell had told him. Nell had pushed it back a little earlier every year in the hope of getting better attendance. It didn't matter to him what the date was. He had no intention of going. But he liked being treated so nicely by this pretty woman. He suddenly realized he was in a position of power over her. He'd always wondered what that would feel like.

"It's the Cheer Committee," he said. "They're a little strange. But they'll do what I say. They want all these questions answered." He pushed all of Nell's notes across the table toward her. "What's your name, anyway?"

"Leila. I'm the day shift manager." Her brow creased in a frown as she tried to read all the notes. Mallory didn't like that look on her face. He pulled the notes back to his side of the table. "Don't worry about that stuff. We expect about 50 people. The committee's kind of picky about food, but I know you can't be too choosy around holiday time."

She bristled. "We have very good food here. We can handle as many as 100 guests."

He wasn't getting anywhere with her. What did he have to do to get that cheerful, subservient look back on her face? While Leila sat silent, he overheard Bob order another double at the bar. Only decisive action could save this situation. "Okay, Leila, I don't really have much time today. Why don't you just go ahead and book us for November 23$^{rd}$?"

The smile came back to her face. She jumped up. "Let me get you some copies of the menu to take with you. We require a $20 deposit per person, 30 days in advance. Food orders should be put in 24 hours in advance." He watched her bounce out of the chair and go toward a back room, her loose black pirate skirt swaying as she walked. Bob was already making short work of the latest double. Leila came back and stood beside his chair, pointing out menu items that were available for large parties. He didn't pay much attention to what she was saying. He was looking at her long, slim fingers, and noticing she did not have a wedding ring on. But he had to get out of that place before Bob drank him bankrupt. And he had already lost his dominance over Leila as soon as he committed to the deal. She seemed all business now. She wasn't even looking in his eyes. But as he turned to get up, she put her hand on his shoulder. "Oh. Take these with you." She gave him the marked-up menus with her other hand. "I can tell it will be a pleasure doing business with you, Mr. Mallory."

\*\*\* \*\*\*

Nell was adamant. "The Cheer Committee cannot pay for alcoholic beverages."

"But he drank sixty dollars' worth of scotch in fifteen minutes." Mallory had watched Bob shamble back into the UniCast office after their trip to the Pirate's Den, amazed that he was going to try to work in that condition. But Nell told him Bob always walked that way. Mallory was excused for being away from his desk because he was on official Cheer Committee business, but neither the Committee nor UniCast was going to pay for the scotch.

"I'm truly sorry about the bill for Bob's drinking. I had no idea that would happen. The committee just can't pay for that." But Nell's adamant tone suddenly changed. "We ... I ... really thank you." Nell swiveled her chair directly towards him. "With Bob gone, the committee agreed on everything. Everybody was happy." She looked up at him. "You know that's important to me. I can't thank you enough. I'll find a way to make it up to you."

Mallory had a very good idea how she could make it up to him. But he couldn't tell her that. As Manly Man often explained, there were intricate rules that required dancing around the real meaning of a budding sexual relationship. And there was an additional problem now. Leila's brief touch on his shoulder had reminded him how it felt to be actually wanted by a woman. And, so far, Nell had not even hinted at that.

"You should go out with me," he suddenly blurted out.

Nell froze, her eyes went unfocused. Her face turned red. "I ... I have a rule about not dating people from work."

This was what happened, he knew, when you told a woman exactly what you wanted. Always a mistake. "If you don't like me, you can just tell me."

She pursed her lips, looked down at her desk. He could hear her take a couple of sighing breaths. "I don't really know you, Kevin. Maybe we'll get to know each other through the committee."

"Maybe we can get to know each other by going out on a date."

"I told you. I don't .... My cat sitter leaves at five o'clock. I can't go out after then."

"Bring your cat along."

"I have three cats and two dogs."

"Don't act like an old maid."

She still stared forward, took an exasperated breath. "I assure you I am not an old maid. Just because I don't always... *emote* ... like other people, doesn't mean ...."

"It doesn't mean anything. I know you're not like other people."

# Chapter 16: Booty

Teitelbaum sent around an announcement that management would now listen in on one out of every 25 customer assistance calls made by selected employees. Employees whose phone calls were being monitored would be chosen "randomly" and would not be told when it was happening, the memo said.

"*Randomly*. That means me," he said to Nell.

She didn't disagree. "But, one in twenty-five. That's only about two calls a day they'll be listening to," she offered.

"There's no customer call I ever took that Teitelbaum would be happy with."

Mallory tried for half a day to play it straight with customers. Some of them were nice, but most of them either hadn't paid their bill, didn't understand what cable service package they had bought, couldn't explain what was wrong, didn't know what a screen or a remote or a modem was, or had forgotten to turn on their TV. He wanted to keep his job now, but he felt like he was going to crack.

"Customer Service, Representative Johnathan Teitelbaum here," he answered the next caller. "How may I help you? And don't make it anything stupid."

Nell jumped out of her cubicle and stood staring at him. "You're doing it again, Kevin? Don't you care about your job at all?"

He was shaking, whether from fear or anger he couldn't tell. "I got to get out of this place. Cover for me, will you, Nell?" He didn't wait for an answer. He left the building and ran to his car. He didn't know where he wanted to go. The Dough and Go was too far. He found himself driving toward the Pirate's Den. He had slicked down his multi-colored hair with gel to get that smooth appearance that women liked. The same giant pirate bartender nodded to him and spoke something into the back room. Soon Leila came out, wearing a short blue business skirt and a plain white blouse this time, though she still wore that giant earring. She flashed him a conspiratorial smile that instantly erased all the frustrations he had been feeling at UniCast. It seemed that some kind of pirate magic had called him to this place where he belonged.

"Here to talk about November 23$^{rd}$?" she sang out, motioning him to a table to sit down. "Pete, a Molson over here." She caught his eye. "Compliments of the house."

She certainly had a thing for him. He put his hands flat down on the table in the hopes she'd touch him, but she didn't. He picked up his beer with one hand but left the other one flat. "Have you come to any decisions on the menu?" She raised her eyebrows. "Our holiday reservations are filling up fast."

He was confused. Was she thinking of him just as a customer? In any case, he had to have just a little more of those smiling eyes. "I, um, I'm pretty sure we're going to sign with you guys." Her smile grew even more brilliant, giving him that same stirring feeling in his chest that he had felt the last time. "Yeah. We're going to do it. Fifty people."

"Have your co-workers signed up for what menu items they want?"

He didn't know what she was talking about. "Yes."

"Do you have that with you?"

"Um, no. Some people are still trying to decide."

She nodded. "Okay, that's normal. But we definitely have 50 people for November 23$^{rd}$, right? Now, there's a lot of demand for restaurants that time of year. To hold the reservation, I'll need a $300 deposit by next week."

"Three hundred dollars ... next week." He looked helplessly into her eyes. "Sure. Next week." Those words lit up that gorgeous, wide smile again, so it must have been the right thing to say. He looked around, confused. He couldn't remember why he had come. He wondered if he was being ripped off. But she seemed like a nice woman. They weren't all nice, he knew.

"You seem distracted, Mr. Mallory. Are you having a bad day?"

He couldn't deny it.

"Why don't you just relax. I'll get Pete to bring you another beer. I'll go and put you on the calendar."

"Don't go." As she went to stand up, he reached out a hand vaguely in her direction. He hoped she didn't see it shaking. He knew he had come here for something he needed, but he wasn't sure what it was. He wasn't sure she could give it to him. But when she took his shaking hand and calmed it before putting it back on the table, his heart poured out waves of silent gratitude. Then she turned around and left like nothing had happened. He was afraid she'd make him sign something when she came back. He was afraid to drink the beer Pete then put on his table. He was afraid of all the changes he was going through.

# Chapter 17: Pirates, Hoodlums and True Love

He stayed in the Pirate's Den another half hour to try to recover his composure. He finished the free beer Leila had provided him. Leila had come back to his table, but he wasn't sure what they talked about. She didn't touch him again, and he began to think she was trying to sell him something. At one point she got up from their table and seemed to be refereeing an argument between two of the waitresses. Then she came back and gave him that beautiful smile.

"That manager over at the Pirate's Den," he mentioned to Nell later. "She's real friendly." He was standing in her cubicle doorway. He was still in a bit of a daze, and he thought talking to Nell might calm him down.

"What's that in your hand?"

He looked to see. It was a cardboard file folder with "Pirate Den" printed on the front. He didn't remember ever seeing it before. Nell must have seen the surprise in his eyes, because she gently took the folder from him and opened it on her lap. He waited while she paged through it.

"Kevin," she started, her tone sounding somewhere between encouraging and exasperated. "It looks like you signed papers promising to pay a $300 deposit to the Pirate's Den by next Monday to firm up a reservation for 50 people for November 23rd. The Cheer Committee hasn't authorized that."

"I don't remember doing that. She was so nice."

"I think you were tricked by that woman. You've been drinking too, haven't you?"

"Yeah." He was starting to feel he might have screwed up.

"So, while I've been covering for you with Teitelbaum, because I thought you were upset, you've been out drinking and flirting and signing papers you had no business signing."

"Flirting?"

"I bet she's pretty and smiled at you a lot. Maybe she even touched you while you were talking?"

He stared at Nell in disbelief. "How the hell did you know that."

"You have that dazed look that men get. You totally lost track of what you were doing."

Staring at Nell now, he was coming out of his daze. The effect of the beer was wearing off, too. It seemed that Nell was right. Leila had made a fool of him. That cunning siren of the Pirate's Den had tricked him into thinking she was interested in him, playing on his loneliness, and even conjuring up little reflexive thrills of anticipation in his soul. It was a classic, crafty female trick. He was surprised that Nell knew what had happened to him. He was surprised that she cared. That gave him a good feeling, and it was not anything like the feelings Leila had summoned up with her pirate witchcraft. He also noticed that Nell was telling him basically the same thing Manly Man was always preaching.

"I lost control," he admitted. To Mallory's surprise, saying this to her wasn't any more painful that admitting it on an anonymous Manly Man post. He had read a lot of stories on the Manly website about female sorcery like Leila's. He had thought it would never work on him. But he decided right then he wouldn't post this particular story. It was not that he felt shame. Shame was not allowed on the website anyway. It was just that Nell was a better audience than the internet.

"We have to get out of this mess right away," Nell broke eye contact as she spoke in a suddenly businesslike tone. "The committee hasn't agreed to any of this. We have to call that woman and cancel the agreement you signed." She stopped and looked at him. "Who should do it?"

She was giving him a chance to solve the problem he had created. It was clear that would be the manly thing to do. And now that Nell had put things back into perspective, he felt he could face up to that pirate sorceress – or, at least, call her on the phone, where he would not have to see that smile, or that sparkling earring. He told Nell he would do it himself. He liked the look she gave him then.

As it happened, Leila wasn't seductive or intimidating at all over the phone. When he explained that there had been a shake-up in the committee and the new members would have to vote again on the locale for the holiday party, Leila responded cheerfully. "Sure, no problem. Just remember the deadlines on that paper I gave you, if you still want to party here."

\*\*\* \*\*\*

Nell never mentioned the Pirate's Den fiasco to the committee. It was a wonderful feeling to know that she had his back. And he didn't get in any trouble for his recent lapse into Indian-speak on the Customer Assistance line. He stopped doing that entirely and reverted to his strategy of dragging out the calls as long as he could. He and Nell were friends now, and they sometimes ate lunch together in the break room. He learned how to use the committee's coffee machine and sometimes even made coffee for her.

His feelings for Nell grew gradually stronger. He would appear at her cubicle doorway every day at their authorized break time, eager to get to know this woman and tell her a little more about himself. But she usually invited Kathie along on breaks. Kathie followed the lives of movie stars fanatically and rarely took time to talk. She did pay attention to him one day.

"Great idea, getting rid of that goatee and that snake thing you used to have hanging down."

"Oh."

"But it looks like somebody splattered paint on your hair."

He wasn't used to being criticized, except by his bosses. He was grateful that Nell didn't laugh. In fact, she scowled at Kathie when she said that. That helped steady him. With Nell there, he could put up a defense, instead of storming out of the room.

"It was an early try at a Halloween costume that didn't work out."

"What were you going as: Red River Mudslide?"

Nell put her hands flat on the table. "I'm not comfortable. I'm not comfortable, Kathie, with this kind of derogatory talk."

"It was just a joke, Nell," Kathie insisted.

"Hurtful jokes are never welcome."

Mallory looked from one to the other. He actually thought Kathie's comment was funny, but he didn't dare smile now.

*** ***

Mallory grew to expect to see Thomas run across the parking lot and bounce up the stairs late every afternoon. Thomas had told him he made the 25-mile-long trip to the university track twice a week; but he didn't have the gas money to make it every day, so he ran around the neighborhood on the other days. He told Mallory his 800-meter times were starting to attract the attention of the State track coach. He had asked Mallory if he would go with him to the track to time him someday. Mallory thought he might like to see him tearing around the track, but he was too embarrassed to tell Thomas he didn't know how to use the stopwatch app on his phone.

Mallory loved to watch as Thomas bounced up the steps to the landing. He waited for him on the landing this day, but he was disappointed to see that Thomas just stood at the bottom of the steps, breathing hard. But the young man was smiling, as usual.

"I'm telling you, it's dangerous on these streets with all these hoodlums running around. You ought to stay off these streets. Or at least carry a gun."

"I told you, Mr. Mallory. You can't run sprints with a gun in your pocket."

"What if I ride along behind you in my car with my gun?"

"A gun! No. You don't have a gun, do you?"

Mallory had been about to brag about his rifle, but Thomas's alarm changed his mind. "No."

Thomas quickly ran up the steps and sat down next to Mallory. Mallory could smell his sweat, but even his sweat smelled clean.

"I went to Community Technical College, too."

"You did?" Thomas raised his eyebrows, then turned and seemed to look down toward the bottom of the steps, nodding wisely, but apparently at a loss for what to say next. "Did you play any sports there?" he said finally.

"I did some intramural bowling."

"Good. Good, man." Thomas just kept nodding, not really looking at him. Mallory had to remind himself that he needed to straighten things out with Thomas.

"I'm in love with Nell, the woman I brought to your party."

This got Thomas's full attention. "She's your woman for real?"

"For real. I never felt a bond this strong with anybody. Nobody ever felt a bond this strong."

Thomas looked like he didn't know what to say. But Mallory felt he had enough love inside himself to fill the silence, enough to fill all the silences in the world.

"We have a special bond. We're *simpatico*. Do you know what that word means?"

Thomas just glared at him without answering.

"You're too young to know this feeling. But when a mature, adult woman turns her attention to you, and underneath all her beauty and intelligence and kindness on the surface this undercurrent of passion starts to flow – there's no power on earth that can stop it."

Thomas seemed unimpressed. "She told me you don't live here. Says you're just house sitting for a dude named Bunbury."

"Oh. I have to lie sometimes. You know. Women. You have to lie to them sometimes."

"You do? Hmm. Just women?"

"Yeah. You have to make yourself look good for them sometimes. I told her I owned a house when I first met her. I forgot I had said that. Then when she came here, I just had to Bunbury it."

"There's no Bunbury? Never was?"

"Right."

"How 'bout that ferret?"

"Oh, you talked to Nell about ferrets, too?" He then told Thomas the whole, true story of what happened that night.

Thomas let out a real belly laugh. "You're Mr. Plastic Bag Head Man!"

# Chapter 18: Chicken Salad

Thomas told him he had two girlfriends, and his mother didn't approve. "But you know how it is, with school and track and all, I don't have time for just one girl."

"I know what you mean." Mallory had firsthand experience of how just one girlfriend could eat up your time, and your energy, and your money. His old girlfriend, Rose, had wanted him to go shopping with her, even furniture shopping. She wanted him to run with her. She asked him to pay for a set of flatware once. Nell would be different. She had her own life, her own friends, her own values. Her own flatware. They would be together, but not in the same rut as other couples. Each time they met it would be as passionate strangers, learning each other all over again, falling in love again, flying high above the crowds of ordinary people.

He invited Thomas into his apartment. Thomas apparently saw the humorous side of Mallory's misadventures as Bunbury and Plastic Bag Head Man. Mallory had to rush ahead of him into the room to turn off the porn site that was his default tab. The browser then defaulted to Manly Man. He explained to Thomas some of the finer points of the Manly Man philosophy, but he also explained that you had to think for yourself, that Manly Man could not always tell you exactly how to run your life. For example, Manly Man preached that you should not commit to a woman until she had surrendered to you her body, or her money, or at least her soul.

"Which one of those did you get?" Thomas teased. His smile showed Mallory he didn't have to answer at all. But Mallory wanted to answer.

"Manly Man is not always right. Nell and I can connect on a deep psychological level without involving any of those things."

"So, nothing?" Thomas laughed. Mallory laughed too. He was sure of the deep connection he was building with Nell. He could now laugh at the Manly Scale of Relationship Progress. He was beyond Manly.

\* \* \* \* \* \*

Nell told him she'd hide from the Cheer Committee all his misadventures with Leila at the Pirate's Den. "You cancelled the reservation. That's enough," she told him on the morning before their meeting. "No harm was really done. There's no point in getting anyone upset. Oh, wait! What about Bob? He was there the first time."

"There's no way Bob remembers anything but those double Dewars he was downing." Mallory smiled at his own turn of phrase. Nell just nodded.

"We do have a proposal for the holiday party from The Pirate's Den," she explained to the committee. "Thanks to the efforts of Kevin and Bob, we have a copy of their menu and their prices for a party on November 23rd."

"Will they have chicken salad sandwiches?" Jennifer interrupted before Nell had even passed out the menu.

"Well, let's see what the menu says. Yes, they are offering chicken salad."

"Is the chicken salad like, with those big chunks of chicken salad, or is it like that shredded goop that tastes mostly like mayonnaise?"

"Um, well, it actually says 'pirate-sized chunks of chicken salad.'"

"I guess that means big chunks."

"I think it does."

"Do they give you a choice of different types of bread? I like my chicken salad on croissants. Can you get it on a croissant?"

Kathie looked up from her iPad. "Why don't you just look at the menu and see? Wait, I can get it up on my iPad." She swiped at her screen while everybody watched. "Nope. Nope. They have white, whole wheat, rye, pumpernickel, something called 'Pirate's Dough,' but I don't see croissants."

"I like my chicken salad on a croissant."

"Let's everybody take a look at the menu," Nell interrupted the chicken salad conversation. "And, of course, we can check out other places. But it's getting awfully late, even for a November party. We haven't even decided who can come."

"Let's do it like last year," Kathie looked up again from her tablet. "Limit it to people who work on this floor."

"That's how many?"

"I remember from last year. That's 137 people."

"The number now might be a little more or a little less," Nell observed. "I think some people might have transferred out of state or moved to the second floor since then."

As much as he hated to do it, Mallory thought he owed it to Nell to contribute to the committee something that he knew was important. "There's no way 137 people can fit in the Pirate's Den."

"Well, not everybody comes." Nell's voice was even. The other members of the committee stayed quiet.

"If it's a lot more than 100, I don't think the Pirate's Den can handle it."

"It's not going to be a lot more than 100."

"How many came last year?" Mallory persisted.

"We had the exact number in our records. But our records have apparently been lost." Nell stared at him.

Bob's head popped up. "Twenty-two. I remember because we had 78 tote bags left over last year."

"What about this name, *Pirate's Den*?" Jennifer interrupted. "Pirates were criminals. I hope there's not a lot of violent imagery like swords, and walking the plank. I don't think that kind of thing is appropriate for an office holiday party."

"Do they serve vegan meals? It doesn't sound like they do," Valerie, another committee member, spoke up.

"We can do what we did last year," Nell responded quickly. "If they don't serve vegan meals, we'll make arrangements to order a vegan carryout for you from Veg-2-U so you can bring it in."

"Why can't the whole party be at the Veg-2-U? Then I wouldn't have to be singled out."

\*\*\* \*\*\*

Mallory thought it was wonderful that Nell was backing him up so strongly at UniCast, and on the committee – and very professionally, without the slightest hint that she was doing it because of any smoldering passion between them. He patiently waited during their morning conversations for her to ask him about his plans, his dreams, his fears, maybe even his flaws. But when she finally risked delving into his personal life, she did it in front of the whole Cheer Committee.

"It has come to my attention that Kevin, a member of this committee, has a close friend who is very ill. Kevin has been most kind to Mr. Bunbury. He has been taking care of his apartment, and he even looked after his pet ferret for a while. I would like to recommend that the committee send a get-well card to Mr. Bunbury, wishing him a speedy recovery, and that the ferret remains healthy and well and ready to welcome his beloved master back."

"Here, here!" said Bob, with a wink toward Mallory, and the motion passed unanimously.

Mallory's hopes that they would forget about it were dashed when Nell appeared in his cubicle that very afternoon. "Kevin, do you have any words you can suggest that we write on the card for Mr. Bunbury?"

"I don't think a get-well card would be appropriate now. I just got word that Bunbury has been transferred to a hospice."

"Oh." Nell was shaken – but not enough, he noticed, to step forward and touch him, or give him a hug. He needed to step up his game.

"I have to go visit him tonight."

"That must be tough. I'm sorry."

"Would you go with me? I don't have anybody, you know, that close."

"I ... I don't know if that would be appropriate. I'm a total stranger to him. That would be pretty intrusive for me to come in there."

"I guess you're right." He stared down at his hands. "I guess I'm not as brave as I sometimes pretend to be. I can do this alone, but ...."

"I recognize you're going through a very tough time, and if the committee can help ...."

"I wish there were somebody .... Nell, do you think you can meet me afterwards? I normally don't drink, but I think I'm going to need one tonight. And someone to talk to."

"My cat sitter leaves at five o'clock. I can't go out after then."

"Bring your cat along."

"I have three cats and two dogs. Remember?"

He put his face in his hands and sighed deeply. He went on in a tiny voice. "What if I can get somebody to watch them? I just know I'm going to need a little normal, *live* companionship tonight."

"You know somebody who could watch them? Would they really know how to take care of animals?"

Mallory nodded. Nell took a few anxious breaths. Then she put on a little resigned smile. "Oh, okay, Kevin. I know you're hurting. If you can get somebody to cat sit, I can come out for maybe an hour or two."

*** ***

Thomas was not happy with the proposal. "I've got to run today. I got to keep on schedule."

"You can run to Nell's house. I'll give you $25."

"It'll be almost dark by then."

"I'll be honest, Thomas. It's not going well with Nell. I think she's overwhelmed by the yearnings I've aroused. I'm afraid she might shy away, not just from me, but from life itself, if I don't bring her out of her shell. She's already got the three cats and two dogs."

"That is bad. But I can't ...."

"Please, do your friend this big favor. I'll make it $100. I've got the cash right here."

# Chapter 19: Scotched

He gave Thomas Nell's address. That was the one useful thing he had fished from the Cheer Committee files before he threw them away. He had gone to see the house from the outside a few days before. She lived in an old, wooden duplex built on a road that used to be in a small town but that had long ago been absorbed by suburbia. It was only a mile and a half from his house. He knew from their very first conversation that she was a renter, but the house looked like it was in good condition. The white paint was bright and the chain link fence was not rusting or falling apart. There were some flowerpots on the stoop, but the grass seemed to be pretty much downtrodden by the dogs, who had come out and made a quick end to his surveillance.

He hadn't planned to spend cash on Thomas. He had at first been planning to ask Thomas to do the cat sitting as a favor, but then he decided he didn't want Thomas to feel like he could come over and ask for a favor himself. This would break his life-long habit of making sure he never had to go out of his way for anyone. But now he was short of cash. He didn't like the look on Thomas's face when he first offered him $25. He didn't know what that look meant, but he had maybe overcompensated by then offering him $100. That was all the cash he had. He'd have to use a credit card with Nell tonight.

He got out the Windex and cleaned out his efficiency as best he could. He knew he needed a bottle of Hennessy and knew he couldn't afford it, so he closed his eyes and handed the liquor store clerk his credit card blindly.

"Those scratches on your face have healed up pretty good," the impertinent clerk noted. "You don't want them scratches on your face. You want them on your back."

"Heh, heh." Mallory tried to act patronizing. He wanted to come off as a man too sophisticated to engage in this crude banter. But the man's comment did fire up his fantasies of his communion with Nell morphing from the intellectual and spiritual to something on a lower plane. He remembered she had gotten a little silly on Hennessy before. Now she knew him even better. They had each other's backs at work now. The next step was obvious.

They were going to meet at 7:30 in a bar in the same strip mall as the Dough and Go. He decided to eat his dinner at the Dough and Go and hang there until then. His friend Spike was working the tables for his father that evening.

"How's it hanging, Kevin? Getting any action with that new look?" Mallory enjoyed Spike joshing him like the old friend he was. But Spike's words seemed crude now that he and Nell were connecting on a higher level.

"Women seem to like the new look." Mallory couldn't help but boast.

"Attaboy."

Spike left the menu on the table and turned to go. Mallory realized that Spike wasn't really concerned about his love life. He wasn't like Thomas, who also joked around about Mallory's love life – but who actually seemed to care. Mallory decided to change the subject when Spike came back for his order.

"We had a neighborhood watch meeting about all the hoodlums running around our streets."

"Oh yeah? Other people seen 'em, too? Did you want fries or mashed with that?"

"Mashed. What? Yeah, other people saw them. My neighbors were being harassed right in our parking lot."

"Sounds like trouble," Spike mumbled as he gathered up the menu. "Maybe get yourself a gun." But Mallory could tell he didn't mean it. He felt betrayed. Wasn't it Spike who had first told him about the gangs of hoodlums running around in the alley behind the restaurant? Why was he not taking him seriously now? Mallory thought about this over his meal of fried chicken and mashed potatoes. He decided that Spike was jealous. Spike talked a lot about girls but had never mentioned having a serious girlfriend. He could probably sense that Mallory's new looks were attracting the attention of the opposite sex. More than that, he was probably yearning for a deep connection like Mallory was hoping to continue to build with Nell this very evening.

Mallory thought it best not to talk to Nell too much until after she had a drink. He was expecting her to stay quiet and in awe of his ordeal with Bunbury. He was disappointed she wore the same clothes she had worn to work that day, a blue straight skirt and a white blouse with blue trim, an outfit that struck almost a nautical theme. At least the skirt was above her knees. He had chosen a high-top in the corner so he could watch her slide herself onto the seat, but he had to sit down first and couldn't watch.

"Hennessy," he told the waiter.

"We don't have Hennessy, sir."

"Two Dewars."

"Not for me. I think I'll just have a glass of water," Nell contradicted him.

He got her attention with his supplicating eyes. "Nell, I know *I* really need a drink. Won't you drink with me, friend? We are friends, aren't we, Nell?"

"Of course. Okay. Maybe just one."

"Two doubles, waiter." He ignored her look of annoyance at his ordering doubles.

"I have a get-well card from the Cheer Committee." She searched in her purse and brought it out. "I confess, it's just one of a collection of generic cards we keep for these occasions. But we thought maybe you could personalize it and give it to your friend."

"Oh, thank you so much. Maybe I can put some words on there, change it into sort of a *goodbye* card."

"Yeah. I guess." He saw that Nell's mood was properly subdued. And then the drinks came. He waited to say anything until she had drunk half of hers. He noticed again that, although she said she rarely drank alcohol, she seemed to like it a lot.

"They have good pizza here," he offered.

"I already ate, and I shouldn't," she said quickly. "I really shouldn't," she said with less conviction. She looked at him, tilting her head questioningly. "But okay, if you feel you need to eat, I could eat maybe one piece." Her face looked softer, as if she didn't need to keep up her usual aura of self-control.

She had now let him discover two little weaknesses, food and drink. His usual instinct would be to calculate how to take advantage of this, but he felt different this time. He felt sorry that Nell was not living up to her own self-image of complete self-control. She was not quite as strong as she tried to act at work. He wanted to tell her this was not a problem. If there were these two small weaknesses, he realized there were probably many more. But this did not discourage him at all. It just made him interested in finding out more about her.

Mallory had recently given up on the idea that Nell was suppressing a strong natural desire to submit to him. He now gave up on the idea of seducing her tonight. He hadn't had any specific plan anyway. She was more stand-offish than he had expected, considering his heart-wrenching circumstances. She didn't ask him how he was feeling after visiting his friend in the hospice. She didn't ask any questions about Bunbury at all. She didn't even say his friend's name. He decided she was with him tonight only because she was a solid citizen and because he had arranged for a cat sitter for these two hours.

"I don't want to talk about my friend's situation right now," he said as the pizza was delivered. "Tell me about yourself." This was a Manly trick, but he really wanted to know more about her, especially her flaws. But even as he said this, he knew that nothing she said would change his mind about her essential goodness.

She seemed relieved not to have to talk about Bunbury. She was loosening up, smiling a little. He thought she was going to tell him the story of her life.

"I'm worried about my cats. I never leave them alone at night."

"Thomas is a very reliable guy."

"I know. I met him when you passed out in your friend's

142

apartment and we had to clean it up. I know he's a good guy, but ... I don't think my dogs and cats have ever seen a Black man before. I'm afraid they might be freaked out."

"Thomas is very good with animals." Mallory had no idea about this.

"Oh, that makes me feel better."

Mallory had been hoping for more basic information. Had she ever been married? Did she have any children? Where did she work before UniCast? But Nell talked only about Kiki and Koko and Florence, and her two dogs, Galahad and Brute. He was glad she was still drinking and didn't notice that he wasn't paying attention to her animal stories. He was disgusted that this first-class woman was lavishing all her love and attention on these rodents. He reminded himself never to tell her the true story of the ferret.

Nell ate three pieces of pizza and got a little silly during her second double scotch. "This stuff is good!"

Mallory had never drunk scotch before, but he had seen effect it had on Bob at the Pirate's Den. He could feel the effect of the whiskey after one double, but he was trying to stay sober. He was determined not to pass out on Nell again. Nell noticed he was drinking water.

"Oh, I shouldn't have drunk another one." Nell snapped out of her reverie of cats and dogs. "I feel woozy. Ooh. There's no way I can drive in this condition."

"I have to leave now." Mallory improvised. Mallory had never had a plan, but this was working out better than any plan. His hope of starting their love affair tonight had just been given new life. "It's been a really sad day. But I only had one drink. I can be your designated driver. I'll take you home."

"What about my car?"

"Thomas and I can come get your car and bring it back to you later."

"I don't like strangers driving my car."

"Then leave it here, and I'll drive you to pick it up tomorrow morning." The thought of getting involved in her life tomorrow was exhilarating. He looked around. "I'm sorry, but I really need to get away from this crowd, this noise, right now."

\* \* \*   \* \* \*

Nell had been loosey goosey in the restaurant, but she sat up stiffly in his passenger seat. "We have a fundraiser at my church once a month. The kids will clean your car, inside and out, for $20."

Mallory couldn't see why she said that. He thought she looked nervous. "Everything will be okay," he told her. "I have a gun."

They drove in silence for the next few minutes. Mallory was pleased they felt comfortable enough with each other to drive all the way to her house without a lot of chit chat. Thomas met them at the door, and before they even got inside Nell began interrogating him about the well-being of the cats. Mallory stood behind her, still in the doorway. Thomas seemed to be avoiding eye contact with him.

"Have they all eaten?"

"Yes."

"Koko is kind of aggressive. I hope you fed him separately from Kiki and Florence."

"Yes, Ma'am. Like you said. Separate bowls, separate times."

"Did you give Brute his Valium?"

"Yes, Ma'am, like you said."

"Did you make sure he swallowed it?"

"Yes."

"Did you give them their together time?"

"All together."

"Did Florence participate? I worry that she's depressed."

"Un, yeah, Florence was right in there fussing with the rest of them."

"They were fighting?"

"Not really fighting. Just a little hissing and stuff. A little growling."

"Oh, dear. I shouldn't have left them alone. I knew this was a mistake. I won't do this again."

At these words, Thomas looked at Mallory and rolled his eyes. They both then watched as Nell waded into her pets. Her walk was still wobbly from the scotch. It looked like she was trying to crouch down so they could all surround her; but suddenly Galahad, the bigger dog, an Irish Setter, jumped up in joy and knocked her to the ground.

Thomas made a sign to Mallory that this was his big chance, then stepped aside so Mallory could do the rescue. Mallory rushed toward Nell's fallen figure, but the little dog, Brute, growled at him. Mallory turned around and looked back toward Thomas. Thomas pantomimed for him to go on. Perhaps to emphasize his point, Thomas turned and walked out the door, leaving him alone with Nell. Mallory tried to edge around Brute, but the dog, which was heavyset but not much taller than the cats, kept facing him, growling, then jumping away when he came close.

"He won't hurt you," Nell reassured him. She was sitting up by this time. Her skirt had slid up above her knees, but she didn't seem to notice. She had a dreamy smile on her face. She reached out and grabbed Brute by the collar and clumsily pulled him to her side. Mallory edged closer to her. He was afraid to try to squat down into the mess of writhing animals, so he just bent over and put out his hand. Nell just stared at it. She seemed afraid to let go of Brute's collar. Galahad, the big Irish Setter, started growling at him.

"Sit!" Nell suddenly commanded. Galahad backed off a few steps and sat down. "No, I mean you, Kevin."

Mallory eased his bulk down next to her. The dogs then seemed to accept that he meant no harm to their mistress. She put her hand on top of his, which was flat on the carpet. Then she put some weight on it.

"That last drink must have hit me just now. The only way I can get up .... I'm gonna have to grab on and sort of climb up your back, if that's okay with you."

"I can lift you up." He knew he couldn't lift her up. He often had trouble just getting himself up off the floor.

"No." She scooted over behind him. "I know this is way too *personal*. But, here, turn your back to me. Just let me grab onto your shoulders."

He did as he was told. He felt her hands dig into his flesh as she yanked herself upright. Then she was on her knees behind him. She put her hands on top of his shoulders and pushed herself up. He felt her knees pressing against his back as she sought her balance. It was the first time they had ever really touched. He had known this day would come.

She scooted the cats away and put the dogs outside. They immediately started barking, and Galahad stood on his hind legs and stared at them through the glass pane in the door, whining. She came back toward Mallory, who was working his way up off the floor, pulling himself up by the sofa cushions. "I'd help you, but I think we'd both fall down."

"I can get up." He maneuvered his way up until he sank down comfortably on the sofa. "Come sit beside me." She had touched him first. She must have felt the heat growing between them.

"I don't think so," she said. "I'm going to bed. You said you wanted to be alone."

# Chapter 20: Burglary Tools

Mallory's phone rang on his way back to his place. His old car didn't have Bluetooth, so he had to wrestle his phone out of his pocket to see who it was. Mallory didn't mind talking on his cell phone while he was driving because he knew he was an excellent driver who wouldn't get distracted. But when he looked at the phone, he saw it was Thomas. He knew he'd be there in a few minutes anyway, so he didn't pick up.

No one answered the door at Thomas's apartment. He worried then that maybe Thomas had been hit by a car and taken to the hospital. Mallory had feared hospitals ever since he had once been charged $578 when he went there for a cold. But any bill this time would be Thomas's problem. He tapped to return the call.

"Howard Central Police, Corporal Selby speaking."

Mallory dropped the phone, and it bounced off the sofa and onto the carpet. He heard Selby repeat his greeting in a tinny voice from the floor. Was this some kind of cop trick to put the blame on him for something that went wrong in the neighborhood? How was Thomas involved in this? But Selby had his number, and probably his address and rap sheet, right in front of him on his monitor. Hanging up would just make Mallory look guilty.

"I didn't call the police. I'm returning a call from Thomas ...."

"Last name?"

"I don't know his last name. He called me from this phone."

"Yeah. You're his one call." Mallory then heard him turn and talk to someone else. "You called *this guy*? Yeah, I know he's your neighbor. He's also Mr. Plastic Bag Head Man. Don't you have parents or something?"

"Hello?" It was Thomas's voice now. "Mr. Mallory? Yeah, I was arrested on my way running back from Nell's house."

"What for?"

"Running While Black."

Mallory was puzzled. "Is that really a crime?"

"Officially it's a 9904." There was a pause while he could hear Thomas consulting in a low voice with Corporal Shelby. "9904, Pedestrian in Right of Way; 76532, Nuisance; 43221, Resisting Arrest; 39127, Possession of Burglary Tools."

"Burglary tool? What burglary tool?"

"I was carrying a cat leash."

"Jeez. What am I supposed to do?"

"They're gonna hold me without bail because of resisting arrest. They're taking me to a judge in the morning. Find my father. Tell him to get me a lawyer by then."

Mallory was incensed. He knew Thomas was not a criminal. Nothing in his life had ever been as clear to him as that. He knew he had to act. He insisted that Thomas get Corporal Selby back on the phone.

"Selby here. What do you want, Mr. Mallory?"

"You know Thomas is a good kid. Why are you doing this to him?"

"I'm not doing anything. I'm just the desk officer tonight. Officer Dempsey arrested him and wrote up the charges. Some people around here call him Officer Hardass."

"That's not funny."

"I can't change the charges. Your man here needs a lawyer, and some substantial citizen from the community to vouch for him. Not you."

"I was never charged with a crime for that ferret thing."

"Whatever happened to that ferret, anyway?"

"He ... escaped."

"How convenient."

"What can I do to get the kid out?"

"Get him a lawyer, like we both just told you."

\* \* \*   \* \* \*

"60427. Case of Thomas Wright."

A sheriff's deputy brought Thomas into the courtroom in

handcuffs. His left eye was swollen almost entirely shut and there was a nasty looking cut on his forehead. Mallory gulped and almost ran out of the room. But Thomas met him with his usual engaging grin, and Mallory found the courage to stand his ground at the counsel table.

"Your Honor, not only should you let this young man out on bail, but you should dismiss the charges entirely. A cat leash is not a burglary tool. This young man is a college student. He has good, middle-class parents. His father always wears a shirt and tie, even on weekends. He's on the verge of getting a track scholarship to State next fall. He needs to practice. That's plenty of excuse for running on the roads of this county. I didn't know that was a crime anyway. You know, the officer who arrested him is known as Officer Hardass. That should be enough to tell you this whole arrest is a disgusting, shameful sham."

"Attorney Mallory, I haven't seen you in this courtroom before."

"I'm new here, Your Honor. Just moved in from Allegheny County yesterday. I'd hardly set up my office yet when I got a call from his parents."

"I guess that explains your dress. Welcome to the Howard County Courts, Mr. Mallory. But I don't think you understand this proceeding. The case against Mr. Wright is not before me."

"Well, who is it before?"

"No, I mean this case here, today, is just about whether Mr. Wright is entitled to bail. The State has moved that he be held without bail because of the serious nature of the charges."

"That's ridiculous. He needs to go to his classes. He needs to do his track practices. He's a great kid. I've known him since he was a baby."

"I thought you said you just moved to this county."

"His family is from Allegheny County also. We all grew up there together."

"Alright, Mr. Mallory. Alright. And you have a point. I notice the police report is extremely vague on the factual basis for these charges. There's nothing here to justify the denial of bail. Bail is set at $1,000."

Thomas jumped up. "But I haven't got $1,000."

"I think you'll be able to post it. Please explain to your client how this works, Mr. Mallory."

"Will do."

Mallory had no idea how bail worked. The judge, the prosecutor and Thomas were all looking at him. He stood there with his mouth open, at a complete loss. His legs began trembling. But, just as he was about to make something up, the judge called the next case and the lawyer for the next defendant moved to the counsel table and practically pushed him out of the way.

They took Thomas right back to the holding cell anyway. Mallory wandered out the back door of the courtroom, hoping maybe to see a sign for a bail office. There were 20 or 30 people milling around in the hallways, most of whom looked like they knew what they were doing. Mallory hadn't been able to find Thomas's parents. They weren't answering their phones. Thomas had told him they were going somewhere for a few days, but he couldn't remember where. He said they took little trips together a lot. Mallory wandered down the hallway, squinting at the tiny signs on every door.

Corporal Selby caught up to him and touched his arm. "Good job there at the bail hearing, *Attorney* Mallory."

Mallory guessed *Attorney* was a better title than *Mr. Plastic Bag Head Man*. But he cringed. Was Selby being sarcastic? Had he just committed a crime by pretending to be a lawyer? But Selby pulled him over to the side. "I've seen worse lawyers. You did a pretty good job for your man in there. Just between you and me, it's a bullshit charge anyway."

"What do you mean?"

Selby pulled him a little more to the side, until they each had a shoulder against the wall.

"The arresting officer, Dempsey. He's a rough character."

Mallory's eyes grew wide. "What do you mean?"

"I can tell you this. Your client's not the first Black man he's arrested who's shown up in court beat to shit."

Mallory had a sudden vision of Dempsey waiting for him in the parking lot. But he reminded himself that he was white. He was safe. He had to get Thomas out. He didn't really know what bail was. In all the TV shows he'd watched about tough bail bondsmen, the criminal had already skipped town.

"Do you know how you get bail?" Mallory ventured.

"You don't know how to post bond?"

He didn't know if bail and bond were the same thing. He didn't know how to get either one. There was no correct answer to Selby's question.

"Like I said in court, I'm new in this county." Mallory felt like he was slowly sinking. "Can you tell me where the ...um... *guy* has his office?"

"I don't know any bondsmen." Selby seemed helpful, not suspicious. "But I know somebody who does."

The bail bondsman wanted 10% of the bond in cash.

"A hundred dollars. When do I get that back?"

"You don't."

Mallory didn't have $100 in his pocket anyway. He had used up all his cash buying scotch for Nell and paying Thomas to look after Nell's dogs. Then he realized Thomas must still have the $100 he paid him. Selby had told him all of Thomas's belongings had been seized. He went back to see Selby again.

"Can you get me the money out of his wallet so he can make bail?"

"Nope. It's all locked up. Every inmate's property is seized for safekeeping. Nobody can touch that money, except the inmate himself." Selby raised his thick eyebrows slightly. "Unless, of course, his *attorney* signs it out."

\* \* \* \* \* \*

Thomas hugged Mallory right at the door of the detention

center. He didn't mind that Mallory had forged his name, putting up his Honda Civic as collateral to the bail bondsman. Mallory had called UniCast that morning with the excuse that he had a court date. He made it to work by the middle of the afternoon. He couldn't wait to tell Nell the story of Thomas's arrest and his own heroic role in his release. But Nell approached him first, practically jumping him in the break room.

"Have you seen my cat leash, the yellow one?"

"A lot happened last night."

"I know. Believe me, I'm never going to drink so much again."

"I mean after you got home. Thomas was arrested on the way back from your house."

"Oh my God. Fast work! I haven't even reported that cat leash stolen yet."

"It's got nothing to do with your cat leash. I mean, the cat leash was involved a little. He had it in his pocket when he was arrested."

"I never should have allowed people like that in my house."

"What do you mean, 'people like that?'"

"I mean ... strangers."

"He didn't steal your cat leash. He had it in his pocket and forgot about it. Why would a nineteen-year-old college student with no cat want a cat leash?"

"Why did they arrest him, then?"

"They thought he was one of those hoodlums that have been running around the neighborhood lately. But he's not one of them. He's a professional runner. That's why he was on the road."

"Well, they wouldn't know that just by seeing him run, would they? And they probably saw the cat leash."

"They didn't see the cat leash. All they saw was Thomas running."

"You know, I was put off last night when you said you had a gun. But I'm starting to think it makes sense."

This conversation was supposed to be the heroic story of Mallory rescuing his friend from jail. Obviously, Nell was too upset by losing her cat leash to concentrate on anything else right now. He'd have to wait to tell her. He had the insight now to gauge her moods and wait for the proper opening. She was more complicated than he'd realized. He was learning to adjust, acting maturely for maybe the first time in his life. She had taught him that.

# Chapter 21: Neatness Counts

The thought of Nell sitting in her cubicle, right behind his partition, hour after hour, day after day, made it hard for him to concentrate. For a few days, he tried to distract himself by picking one customer and actually trying to help. He succeeded on the very first day, but by the second day he realized how boring the actual job was. Compared to that, even the committee work looked interesting. After the last meeting, Nell had suggested diplomatically that he excuse himself from planning the holiday party and instead try to come up with a plan for the Cheerboree.

Cheerboree was the annual outdoor team building event held once a year for all UniCast employees in the state. Mallory did not like outdoor activities. He did not want to do mandatory bonding activities with fellow workers. He opposed all forms of enforced gaiety. But Nell wanted him to do it, so he went ahead and looked on the internet for outdoor team-building companies and bookmarked the ones showing the prettiest women.

Teitelbaum now stood and watched over him in his cubicle at least once a day. Mallory's new tactic was to bore the hell out of him. That was pretty easy. He pretended he was a little hard of hearing and asked the customer to repeat almost everything they said. Then he repeated it to them very fast and asked them to confirm that his information was correct. If they hesitated at all to confirm, he made them repeat the process. Although this rigamarole might have caused Teitelbaum to question his intelligence, he couldn't be fired for being stupid. To be doubly sure of his job security, Mallory had filed a complaint with Starganoff that Teitelbaum was harassing him. Now, Teitelbaum had to weigh his actions carefully. Every time he criticized Mallory, there was a chance he'd hurt himself more than his recalcitrant employee.

On the day of Thomas's bail hearing, he'd noticed that all the male attorneys wore suits, shirts, and ties; so he decided to buy those things for Thomas's actual trial. The tie was a problem. He bought a beautiful yellow one with tiny green fish, but he got into an argument with the salesman who was trying to teach him to tie it, and they ended up facing each other, hands gripping each other's shoulders as in the beginning of a Sumo wrestling match. He settled for a clip-on bow tie. He charged everything on his credit card. The suit cost so much he decided he might as well wear it to work every day. To save money on a haircut, he borrowed a pair of scissors from Ava and cut off most of his lava-colored hair. Nell said he looked nice. "That shirt. It fits." He didn't care what anyone else thought. She did mention that most men did not wear sneakers with suits.

When Thomas's parents came home, they were so grateful he had gotten Thomas out on bail they stuffed him with peach cobbler and apple pie for almost a week. Edison, Thomas's father, said he would pay whatever it cost to get the best criminal lawyer in town for the actual trial. Mallory told Edison that he would be wasting his money by doing that. He could do the job himself. In fact, being an attorney had been so easy he had been thinking of asking Officer Selby to send him a few more clients.

"Mom, Dad, let him do it. He's pretty good."

Mallory knew then he was in love with Thomas – in a manly way, of course. He wanted nothing more than to save this kind young man, a man who'd cleaned up his room, and his puke, when he'd made such a fool of himself after the party. A man who knew about Bunbury and didn't condemn him for it.

"Son, that makes no sense. You're charged with serious crimes. We need the best criminal lawyer." Edison looked over at Mallory to see if he was offended.

"But I believe in your son," Mallory defended himself. "I don't think he would do any of those crimes he was charged with in a million years."

"Me neither. But that don't make me an expert criminal lawyer."

"Dad. Wait. I already made some calls. The cheapest one of those fancy downtown lawyers wants $5,000 cash just to step into the courtroom."

"God! Still, son, we can get a home equity loan on the house ...."

"We don't even own a house right now."

\*\*\* \*\*\*

Wearing his new suit, Mallory started visiting the police station at night, always asking for Corporal Selby. It was three days before Selby was available.

"What's up, Counselor?"

"I need some detective work. I need evidence Thomas is innocent."

"Um, I'm the police. We don't do detective work for defendants."

"You've got to help me prove he's not guilty."

"Didn't you hear me?" Selby gave him a look like he was dealing with Mr. Plastic Bag Head Man again. "I can't do that." They were in the reception area in front of the high desk of the sergeant. Selby quietly pinched the cloth of Mallory's shirt right at the point where it covered his protuberant belly and quietly pulled him over to the edge of the room.

"Do you have any idea what you're doing?" Selby whispered harshly.

"I think I'm quite good at lawyering. You said so yourself."

"That was just a bail hearing. Your Thomas could go to jail for up to four years. He'd be a convicted felon for the rest of his life. I told you: Dempsey's a brute. What are you seeing on the body camera footage?"

"What's body camera footage?"

"Every cop in this county has to wear a body camera. The prosecutor has the footage. They have to give it to you if you ask for it."

"Great idea! I'll ask for it."

\* \* \*   \* \* \*

The snippy woman in the prosecutor's office said they wouldn't *give* him anything. He could watch the video and take notes if he wanted. They put him at an empty desk and told him not to touch the controls on the computer. The video showed the inside of a car cruising through a bright and sunny landscape of concrete and asphalt. It was obviously hours before the time Thomas was arrested in the near darkness.

The prosecutor's office hadn't told him anything in advance. He had no idea how much footage there was. Just in case, he had visited the Dough and Go beforehand and bought enough cinnamon buns and donuts and coffee to last eight hours. He hadn't been stocking up at the Dough as often lately. He noticed that Nell usually ate just a small sandwich and a piece of fruit for lunch. He tried that one day, but it was really hard. He admired Nell's sticking to her diet, though he wished she would dress so he could see more of her figure. He was hoping to get rid of his own paunch somehow.

He unwrapped one of the Dough's signature buns first. The smell of cinnamon permeated the air. He knew he didn't have to pay any attention to the video for the first couple of hours. He unwrapped the paper and rolled it open on top of the blotter on the desk. Sticky glops of sugar and cinnamon fell on the paper. He took his time eating the first one, then swiped up the remaining glops with his fingers. It was so good he had to have his coffee immediately. He put the plastic cup right on the blotter, squirted in some cream from a disposable container, dumped in two packets of sugar. He thought he was being as careful as anybody could who had to eat such a large amount of food in such a small space.

Fifteen minutes later, the snippy woman returned and stood looking over his shoulder. He had finished the first bun and was in the middle of an éclair. Some of the goop had escaped the paper and was seeping into the blotter. Also, there were tiny, white grains over the entire desk surface, as Mallory hadn't been too accurate in pouring his second packet of sugar. Meanwhile, on the video, Officer Dempsey was still sitting in his cruiser in the park, eating his lunch. The woman sighed, then disappeared.

She came back a few minutes later. "Here." She handed him a video stick. "Here's the part you need. Ten minutes before the arrest, the arrest, and ending at the station. We're giving it to you as a courtesy. Please go, and take it home."

# Chapter 22: Standards Fall

Bob hounded the other members of the Cheer Committee for weeks about the holiday party, and at the last minute he won one small victory. People had been very reluctant to sign up for the November 23$^{rd}$ occasion, using as an excuse that they had to be home to prepare for Thanksgiving, and so the early sign-up total was very low. Nell refused to consider moving the date to December. By the time of these discussions, it was too late anyway. They had committed to the Pirate's Den, reserving space for 25 for the 23rd. Seventeen had signed up so far. Seven from the Committee and ten "outsiders," as Nell privately referred to them.

Nell had argued from the beginning that they needed to give people an incentive to come.

"An open bar," was Bob's perennial reply.

"Christmas decorations," Jennifer pleaded.

"A half day off from work," Mallory suggested. This was a very popular idea, but Teitelbaum vetoed it right away.

The winning idea was the chair's. "Tote bags!" Nell proclaimed. "Not those boring, scruffy ones from last year. Tote bags with some special symbol or artwork. You know, to express the joy the committee is trying to spread."

"It'll cost us money," Mallory warned.

"They're very cheap," Kathie chimed in. "I've seen them on Etsy for as cheap as two dollars."

"Aargh," Mallory grumbled. He was thinking about the credit card bill that was coming for all his new clothes, and for his bar tab.

"I don't think anybody in America needs yet another tote bag," Bob complained.

Nell, as always, was centered and steady. She didn't respond to Mallory's grumbling, didn't even look at him. She turned to Bob. "People love tote bags. A giveaway tote bag will add another incentive for people to come." She stared at Bob until he looked away.

"All right. All right," Bob muttered. "But I'll go for that on one condition. The American flag has to be on those tote bags."

Nell sighed, looked at the others. "Okay, Bob. We'll put the American flag on the tote bags. All agreed?"

"I disagree." When Mallory spoke up, ruining Nell's push for a consensus, she let out an exasperated sigh. Mallory knew she would never proceed unless everyone agreed. "I'll go along with Bob's flag design on one side of the bag. But I want to design the other side."

"That sounds fair," Kathie interjected before Bob could object. The rest of the committee, except for Bob, nodded in agreement. "What kind of design are you thinking of, Mr. Mallory?"

"I don't know. Something maybe … environmental."

"That sounds good. I'll show you the website. You can get, like, outlines of green trees on a beige background."

"I'm thinking of something not so passive, something more active and awe-inspiring."

"You can get silhouettes of moose, deer, bears, whatever," Kathie offered.

Bob perked up. "I got it! An American eagle."

"No." Mallory was suddenly decisive. "I'll get together with Kathie. We'll think of something to put on the other side."

After the meeting he went to Kathie's cubicle and told her he wanted a ferret.

Kathie shook her head. "No, you don't." But when he insisted he did, she sighed and began scanning the 500 possible designs available on the website. "They have bobcats and lynx, but no ferrets." She seemed happy about that.

"Open that other window. There's a place where you can import your own images."

"I can't spend all day on this. I have to get back to my customers."

\* \* \* \* \* \*

Mallory wasn't happy with the way the bags turned out. Kathie had been rushing him that day after the committee meeting, and he hadn't been able to find a suitable picture of a ferret that he could copy and download. So he pulled up a painting app and did his best to draw a picture of a ferret, making as close an approximation to his former pet as he could.

"It's looks like a cartoon," Kathie laughed. The drawing certainly didn't resemble the threatening little beady-eyed animal that had scratched his face. "It's okay, though." She clicked a few keys. Now she seemed even more hurried. "I'll just put this in as a placeholder. See if you can find a real illustration by tomorrow."

Mallory promptly forgot all about the project until the bags arrived a week later, complete with Mallory's crude drawing of a ferret on the back side.

The American flag/ferret totes turned out to be popular. People who weren't even going to the party started to buy them ahead of time, and Kathie's first order of 50 sold out a week before the 23rd. She quickly put in a rush order for 100 more. Nell sent memo after memo to the entire staff, reminding them they could get the totes free if they came to the party. She called Leila at the Pirate's Den and told her to change the reservation to 100, but Leila told her it was too late. Nell then put out an email to the staff, saying the committee had underestimated interest in the holiday party and could not guarantee that everyone who wanted to sign up could be accommodated. The new tote bags arrived two days before the party, but Kathie sold only three of those. The novelty had worn off.

\*\*\* \*\*\*

Mallory and Bob carried two cardboard boxes full of tote bags into the Pirate's Den on the day of the party. Leila approached them wearing a frilly white pirate blouse and a dark slit skirt. She had a plastic scabbard and sword belted around her waist. Mallory drank in her dark eyes and carmine lips, breathed the exotic scent of the perfume oozing out of her waterfall of glossy dark hair. But he told himself he was not tempted, that he had learned from Nell the value of a deeper relationship. Leila handed him a folder but otherwise paid him little attention. He wasn't surprised she didn't flirt with him. He felt he was now exuding a special male pheromone, one that subtly announced to women who approached him that he was not available because he was connected to a special woman in a much deeper way.

The tables reserved for the holiday party were arranged along an inside wall and took up only about a quarter of the restaurant. Two waiters, one male and one female, were standing against the wall, both wearing pirate garb and holding iPads in their hands. Nell told them not to start taking orders because more people were going to arrive. The tables were set for 25, but there were a lot of empty seats. Leila asked Mallory what they planned to do with the boxes, which were sitting on the last table. He looked over at Nell. She was counting chairs and people. Seventeen people had shown up, including all seven members of the Employee Cheer Committee and ten outsiders. Kathie had already pulled out a small pile of tote bags and was giving them out to everybody who was there. There were a lot left over. Nell walked over to where Leila, Mallory and Bob were standing.

Somebody had to state the obvious. "There's going to be a lot of leftover bags," Mallory offered.

Leila put her hands on her hips. "The main courses that were pre-ordered are almost done. People should be ordering any drinks or appetizers they need right now. Do you really need this last table? If you'll get the boxes off it, I can get rid of it for you."

"I got an idea." Bob was excited. "We can hang these extra bags along the wall. People will love seeing a line of flags. And if there are any outsiders who come late, we can just hand 'em one."

"You can't put any nails or anything into the wall," Leila said quickly.

But Nell was interested in the idea. "What if we string a cord from that coatrack in the corner to, um, the wheel of that giant plastic cannon hanging on the wall? Then we can just hang the bags on the string." Leila reluctantly agreed. She obviously wanted to get that extra table to use for the other patrons who were swarming into the bar for their pre-Thanksgiving alcohol fix.

Although Mallory was not proud of his artwork, he still insisted that the ferret side of the bags be given the same exposure as the flag side. Bob was aghast at the idea of alternating flags and ferrets – until Mallory offered to buy him a drink if he'd let it go.

The waiters were finally allowed to take drink orders. Mallory believed he had become a connoisseur of alcoholic drinks. He had learned from his last experience with Bob at the Pirate's Den that a double of scotch would get Bob out of his hair for the rest of the night. But scotch had a bad effect on Nell. After two Dewars doubles, she had cut short their rendezvous at the pizza place and refused to speak to him in the car, paying attention only to her cats and dogs when they arrived at her place. The correct aphrodisiac for Nell was Hennessy. That was the drink she'd had at Thomas's parents' party, and it had left her laughing and silly and open to him.

Bob downed the scotch Mallory bought him and wandered off to the bar before the waiters even brought out any of the appetizers. But Nell drank only slowly at first. She seemed to think she needed to tell the waiters where to put the tiny plates. Leila had refused Nell's request for seventeen separate checks for the drinks and appetizers, so Nell had taken over the responsibility of counting who ate what and who drank what. She briefly disappeared back to her car and came back with a clipboard and told everybody to write down every appetizer and drink they were taking. But she was distracted from supervising that process when the Veg-2-U delivery woman arrived and was intercepted by Leila just at the giant, round, glass porthole that served as the door to the restaurant. Nell came over to supervise.

"You can't do this," Leila hissed at Nell.

Nell seemed shaken. "We, um, I thought ...."

Mallory stood back as far as he could from this confrontation.

Leila was a little taller than Nell in her heels. With one knee cocked out the slit in her skirt, she blocked the delivery woman. Mallory had no sympathy for Valerie, the committee member who had ordered the vegan meal. But he admired Nell for standing up for her principles. Nell was never satisfied until every person she was dealing with was happy. But when Leila said delivering outside food to the restaurant violated the county health code, Nell's resolve seemed to melt. Her face fell.

Mallory returned to the bar to get another drink, and he picked up a second one for Nell. He found her back at the tables. She had finished her first drink. She was now looking frantically at the clipboard. The first three people had written down carefully the name and price of the appetizer they had ordered, as well as their drinks. But there was an illegible signature on the fourth line. Nell was demanding to know whose it was.

"How do we know?" somebody complained. "We can't see it. Pass the clipboard around so we can see the signature." They began passing it around, but the first woman to get it knocked it into the next woman's martini glass, and her Cosmo Lite fairly jumped out of the glass and soaked the bottom half of the sheet. "It's okay. It's okay. We can still read it," the first woman insisted, though she seemed to stare at it very closely before concluding, "No, it's not me. I know I ordered a sloe gin, and ... I think I can find it here. Yeah, here it is. Number fourteen, sloe gin. That's me. So, it's not me you're looking for. Should I pass it on?"

"Yes." Nell's voice seemed to be growing weak. Mallory handed her the second drink. By this time, everyone's drinks were kicking in, and people were talking louder.

"Some of these people must have used a roller ball pen," the second woman observed. "It's a little smeared. I can't read the last few names."

Nell's built-up exasperation exploded. "Hey, it's simple!" This got everyone's attention, including the waiters, who stopped in their tracks. The bartender stared at the group with his one squinting pirate eye. "Is the signature on line number four your signature?" Nell continued, moderating her tone. "Yes or no."

"Well. No." The woman's voice was icy. "But I can't see how anyone's going to read all ...."

"Thank you. Please pass the clipboard to the next person."

Just then one of the outsiders across the table grabbed the clipboard. He put it down between his drink and his appetizer, got a cigarette lighter out of his pocket, held it over the paper and started to read all the names out loud, deliberately mispronouncing each one. Everyone but Nell started to laugh. Another outsider grabbed the clipboard, tore the paper off and threw it back. Someone started chanting "Burn it! Burn it!" The bartender put one hand on the bar and leaped over it in his race to the table. Leila suddenly appeared out of nowhere, grabbed the paper and the cigarette lighter and clicked away quickly on her high heels, her sword swinging in erratic arcs at her side. Everyone seemed awestruck by the pirate crew's quick action, and table went quiet for a moment.

Nell seemed paralyzed. Mallory took her drink hand and moved it slowly up to her lips. She took a big gulp. "Ah! Thank you," she said. She put her hand on his chest as if to steady herself. The playful, bold Nell was coming out of her shell, he was sure. But Leila came back with fire in her eyes.

"Come look at this. This is unacceptable." She led them to the front door where, standing on the sidewalk, staring at them from behind the thick plate glass, Valerie was eating her vegan lunch out of a paper bag. Apparently, the Veg-2-U carryout was very environmentally friendly and did not include disposable cutlery, because Valerie was using her bare hands to shove gobs of chickpea salad into her mouth.

"It looks like she's on the public right of way," newly minted attorney Mallory opined.

"I'm calling the bartender if you don't get rid of her this instant."

Nell looked up at him – for guidance, he was sure. She seemed a little dizzy. On the other side of the glass door, Valerie was starting to draw the attention of people on the sidewalk. But then there was a loud crash inside the restaurant, followed by a lot of screaming. All three of them forgot about Valerie and rushed back. All the holiday partyers were either standing up or trying to get enough room to stand up. There was a tremendous rattling of dishes and plates. People at the next table were getting up and wiping their hands on their clothes. The pirate cannon had fallen and shattered their entire table. The men at that table stood around, looking stunned. All the women were frantically clutching their pocketbooks or searching for them. When Mallory and Nell and Leila got close, they saw Bob lying on his back on the floor, tangled in cord and covered with flags, wrestling with the coat rack.

"What happened? Did he have a seizure?" Nell pressed the first person she saw for an answer.

"No. He decided to wrap himself in the flag. All the flags on the line. He grabbed one end of the cord off the coat rack and wrapped it around himself and started twisting. He was trying to get the American-flag side in front. But, you see ...."

Bob was still lying on the floor, ferret side up. The bartender reached down and helped him pull himself to his feet. One of the other partyers helped him untangle the lines and bags. Someone else said he'd take him home. Then the whole party was invited to leave. Nell exasperated Mallory by offering to help clean up.

"You're in no shape to do anything," Leila said. "Go home." But then she stopped them at the door. "Somebody has to pay for this." The pirate bartender appeared behind her, looking larger than he had ever looked before.

Nell was steadying herself with her arm around his waist. Mallory felt Nell's whole body stiffen when Leila made her demand. His instincts told him what a manly man would do.

"Here's my credit card. I'll take care of it. Put all the damages on this card." But before he let Leila fully grab it out of his fingers, he added one condition. "No, one more thing. Give us each another round to go." He felt Nell breathe deeply and relax against him.

\* \* \*    \* \* \*

"We're supposed to be back at work soon. They only gave us two hours off for the party," Nell told Mallory as they approached his car in the Pirate parking lot. Nell was far too drunk to drive. She had agreed to go back to the UniCast offices in Mallory's car. But Mallory's actual plan was different.

"I saw Bunbury last night."

"Oh. How is he doing?"

"Better. He might be out soon."

"Out *soon*? Of a *hospice*?"

"Yeah. He wants me to pick up some things from his apartment. His will, and papers and stuff. I promised I'd do it today. Mind if we swing by there?"

"Sure. Okay." She sounded appropriately breezy, just like a woman who had been slugging down cognac for the last two hours. Mallory had planned on killing off Bunbury, but what could you do?

He had forgotten how unpredictable she was when she was high. She was giggling now. He noticed she had stopped complaining about the holiday party fiasco the minute he put all the damages on his own credit card. He worried now that the bill could be in the thousands of dollars. His search for a true love connection was costing him many times more than he had ever spent on his porn site and Manly Man put together.

One of his new expenses was the entire bottle of Hennessy he'd bought the night before and put on his kitchen counter. But this additional dent in his credit card would be well worth it for the effect it would have on Nell. When they arrived at his place, she said she didn't want any, but he poured her a double shot anyway and put it on a little side table next to the sofa bed. They sat together on it, the only comfortable place in his apartment. She was still laughing about the party. He put his arm around her

167

shoulders, but she shook it off with a laugh. But then she drank a little more and started to lean into him. He dared to put his arm around her again. She let it stay there this time. He was really excited.

"What, are you breathing heavy, Big Boy?" she teased.

"Yes." He took her hand and kissed it.

"You don't understand," she said. "I'm not ... *good* at this."

He leaned in to kiss her. She flinched but let him do it, pressing back briefly with closed lips before turning her head. She giggled for a second, then let out a deep sigh. She turned completely away from him and reached for her drink. He was disappointed to see her pick up her glass and put it to her lips without drinking, as if establishing a barrier against any more kissing.

"You tricked me just now," she said from behind her protective glass. "I mean, you're a good committee member, but I don't want to kiss you."

"You did."

"You got me drunk. I thought you'd have the decency to leave me alone, physically."

"I want to be decent with you." Mallory said it automatically, without thinking, but he realized at that instant that it was true. His good intentions would win her over in the end, he was sure. He had hope. He had seen a lot of movies where the first kiss had been a lot more disastrous than theirs.

"I am interested in you," she admitted. "But not in that way. You seem to be changing. For the better, maybe." She tilted her glass like she was toasting him, but still held it up between them like a shield.

Mallory was quietly ecstatic. She *saw* him. She *noticed* him. He wondered if he should tell her now about getting Thomas released on bail, and the great plans he had for winning the trial. There was so much more to him than she knew. But this was not the time. She was drunk, and not really open to hearing more about him at that moment. She started on her drink again, drained it and asked him for a refill. His heart raced.

Mallory knew the alcohol would enhance her feelings of gratitude toward him. He knew she was repressing her romantic feelings only because of her strict code of conduct. She had once told him that she would never date a person she worked with. But he knew that was how half the romances in the world had started.

"I do like your liquor." Nell was slurring her words. When he got up to get her another, she suddenly lay back flat across the sofa bed, arms akimbo, legs spread wide open. By the time he came back with the drink in his hands, she had blacked out. He put the drink aside and edged his way onto the sofa beside her. He waited to see if she would come to. She didn't. He touched her face, her arm, her leg, but got no reaction. He rearranged her on the sofa.

He leaned over her and pushed her skirt up as far as he could. She reacted no more than a dead body would. He knelt next to the bed, pushed a hand up each side of her legs, then her hips, searching for the elastic of her panties, reaching much farther than he had expected would be necessary, then grabbed them and tugged them off. He was disappointed in how large and white they were.

# Chapter 23: Running While Black

Mallory wore his new suit everywhere, every day, for three weeks, until Kathie told him he had to get it cleaned. He threw it in the washing machine in the basement of his apartment complex. It lost a little of its soft weave, but it still looked better than half the suits the lawyers in District Court were wearing the day Thomas's case came to trial.

Mallory had insisted that Thomas and his parents arrive a half hour before the trial was scheduled. He wanted to see how trials were done before he did one himself. Edison and Ava were stone silent. Thomas had told him they were furious at him for insisting that Mallory be his attorney. "They're not mad at you," he told Mallory that morning. "They know you'll do the best you can. They just want a fancy, high-priced lawyer, that's all."

"I won your case at the bail hearing, didn't I?"

"I know. I know. They're just old. They don't know what they're doing. Don't worry about it."

Mallory sat them in the front row of the courtroom so the District Attorney could see that he had a suit on and was ready to do battle. The judge hadn't appeared yet. Mallory recognized Baxter Armstrong, the prosecutor from the bail hearing, sitting at one of the tables up front. Armstrong did a double take, not at Mallory's suit but at Thomas, whose new suit was sleeker than any of the others in the courtroom. The suit had been Ava and Edison's idea, but Mallory saw it already had an effect.

"May I talk to you in the conference room, counselor?" Mallory thought Armstrong was using that title to be sarcastic, so he didn't respond. "Mr. Mallory, I think it's in your client's interest that we have a conference together before this trial starts."

"Oh. Sure, okay." Mallory followed Armstrong through a side door to the courtroom. He didn't look back at Thomas or his parents because he had no idea what to tell them. The room was tiny, with a long wooden table and a few leather-covered chairs that looked like they had been used up in some other lifetime and were now in a way station on their way to the dump.

"Let's talk about a plea bargain." Armstrong started abruptly. "I've seen the body camera footage. I know our case is not perfect. I think I can offer you a deal that will let your client walk home today a free man."

Mallory knew he had forgotten something. He hadn't looked at the body camera footage. He had no idea what it showed. This didn't bother him as much as it might some lawyers. Mallory firmly believed that not knowing the facts of any situation did not disqualify him from having a strong opinion about it.

"It had better be a good deal." He made his voice firm.

Armstrong looked at him evenly. "You won't find a better deal anywhere than this." Mallory didn't say anything, and this actually did seem to unnerve Armstrong a little. He rattled out the terms of the deal. "We'll drop Nuisance. We'll drop Pedestrian in Right of Way. We'll drop Possession of Burglary Tools. If your client pleads guilty to Resisting Arrest, we will recommend a sentence of time served, and he walks out of this court today a free man."

"Time served?"

"He was already held in detention for twelve hours. That will be his whole sentence. He walks out of the courtroom today a free man."

"Sounds pretty good. I'll take the deal."

"Ahem. Don't you need to talk to your client?"

"Oh. Yeah, of course."

"Go talk to your client. I'll push this case back to this afternoon's docket."

\* \* \* \* \* \*

Edison's reaction was so loud Ava insisted they carry on the rest of the conversation at home. Mallory had taken only half a day off for court leave, but he was carried along so strongly by the sweep of events that he soon found himself arguing with Ava and Edison and Thomas in their living room. Thomas was on his side, at least at first. "Dad, if we take the deal, *I'll go free*. But I can get a four-year sentence if I turn down the deal and then get convicted."

"But you're innocent, son." His face and his whole body seemed somehow sharper, like he was coming out of the slightly overweight bureaucratic cocoon he had been living in.

"Yeah," Ava added. "You did nothing wrong, Thomas. The video shows that."

"People see what they want to see, Mama. I don't want to go to jail."

Edison was becoming more agitated and was moving his torso forward and back in the chair like a football player anxious to get off the bench. "If you take this deal, Thomas. You'll be a convicted felon for the rest of your life. Nobody will care that you served only one day jail time. Your life will be ruined."

"Maybe you're right, Dad." Mallory was distressed to see Thomas weakening. If he didn't take the deal and they went to trial, he'd have to take a whole day of leave time from work. "But I'm just scared of that long jail time," Thomas admitted.

"Running scared is no way to run your life, son." Edison gave Mallory a frightening glance and suddenly leaned his powerful body toward him. "What do you think about that video, Attorney Mallory? Does it show Thomas resisting arrest?"

Mallory froze. A dead silence came over the room. "Um, why don't we all look at the video again. Together. See if we can gain any insight that way."

They were silent while Thomas dragged out a huge laptop and put it on the dining room table. He pulled the thumb drive out of a drawer in an ancient mahogany china cabinet. Mallory really wished he had looked at the footage before. He didn't know anything about Pedestrian in Right of Way, much less Nuisance and Resisting Arrest. He was pretty sure, though, that a cat leash was not a burglary tool. He didn't have a clue as to how to advise these good people. He wondered for just an instant if he should use his credit card to get Thomas a real lawyer.

The flickering startup screen reminded him of his porn site, which reminded him of Nell. Prim and proper as she pretended to be at work, she'd been loose and loopy in his apartment after the holiday party, totally at the mercy of his credit card and his cognac. He'd taught her how to loosen her inhibitions, but she still seemed to be dodging the deep commitment he craved.

Thomas had seen the video enough times to know where to start. It first showed the inside of a police car driving along a road next to a field at twilight. The car slowed as it approached Thomas, who was running on the narrow shoulder. The car slowed and followed him for probably a couple hundred yards. "That's Pedestrian in Right of Way, I guess," Thomas narrated. "But except for one or two steps, my feet were never in the traffic lane." In the video, Thomas could be seen glancing back over his shoulder at the car as it continued to follow him. Suddenly the siren went off and a revolving red light colored the entire scene. Thomas's shoulders visibly tensed up. He quickened his pace for a few yards, then gradually slowed to a stop and turned toward the car.

Thomas put both hands up in the air as he faced the car. He was not wearing a hoodie, Mallory noticed. The camera view changed as the officer got out of his car and walked around toward Thomas, but when it returned to the scene Thomas was still frozen in position, with his hands still in the air. The camera then showed a claustrophobic view of Thomas's sweatsuit as the officer patted him down for weapons.

"What are you doing on this road, near nighttime?" the officer asked.

"Um, running home from a cat sitting gig."

"Don't be smart, boy. What is this thing in your pocket?"

"A cat leash."

"I said don't be smart."

"That's what it is."

Suddenly, a dark object in the officer's hand crossed the screen and hit Thomas in the face. Thomas staggered backwards, then crumpled to the ground, groaning in obvious pain. "That'll teach you to run from me, boy."

# Chapter 24: A New Lawyer in Town

"I'm here to demand that you drop all charges against my son." Edison had insisted on attending Mallory's next meeting with Baxter Armstrong, the prosecutor. "This was a vicious, unprovoked attack on this unarmed young boy who had committed no crime, and who was obeying the policeman, standing still, with his hands in the air."

"He was acting suspiciously, and he had a suspicious bulge in his pocket that might have been a weapon." Armstrong's voice seemed threatening.

"The cat leash? Now it's a weapon? In the charges, you claimed it was a burglary tool. Do you think you can get away with this? We have the video. I work in the county office building. You think every person there won't see it when I get there tomorrow morning?"

Mallory thought he could learn something from Edison. Mallory prided himself on being an expert at arguing, but his specialty was defense. His particular strength was in making up facts that would confuse and confound his antagonists. But this case was totally different. They were on the offense now, thanks to Edison's strong arguments. And he didn't have to make up any facts, thanks to the video. Still, he thought he had to contribute something.

"And I'm filing suit this afternoon for ten million dollars against you, Officer Dempsey, the police department, the county, and the judge, for harassment, racial profiling and, um, police brutality."

"Give me a minute." Armstrong held his hand up to stop the conversation. His face dropped, his eyes searched the top of his desk as if he would find something to say there. He then stood up quickly and walked toward the door. "I'll be right back."

"Except Officer Selby. I'm not suing him," Mallory added to the prosecutor's back as he left the room.

"Do you really think we should sue for money?" Edison's heavy gaze intimidated Mallory. "I work for the county. I don't know how much of a fuss I want to make. If we can just get the charges dropped ...."

"I was bluffing. I just made that up."

"Maybe you'd better check with me before you make any more threats."

The prosecutor was back in ten minutes. "Okay, I just talked to Chief. It took some time. I had to show him the video. Assuming my supervisor agrees, we will drop all charges against your son. And to make sure this event doesn't harm Thomas in his future career, we'll expunge all records of his arrest."

"No, you won't," Edison shocked Mallory by interrupting. "The arrest happened, and the video happened, and I'm not letting you just erase the whole thing."

There was a short silence in the room. Mallory's idea of suing had obviously taken hold in Edison's mind. Prosecutor Armstrong ducked his head as if he saw the lawsuit coming and was trying to make sure it wouldn't hit him. "Your lawsuit," he said then, "doesn't really involve the prosecutor's office. As I'm sure you know, Mr. Mallory, the county attorney will have to handle any civil suit. All we can do here in the prosecutor's office is drop all the criminal charges. And that's exactly what we will do. Assuming my supervisor agrees, and I think he will, we will drop the charges and will keep the arrest records, and the video, if that's what you want. That's honestly all we can do in this office today."

\* \* \* \* \* \*

"Maybe we really shouldn't sue," Ava said. She, Edison, Thomas and Mallory were back in their apartment right after the charges were dismissed. "The police are part of the county government. We'd be suing the county government. You could lose your job."

"They can't fire me for that," Edison spoke abruptly.

"Maybe not, but they can stop promoting you. You'll be up for head of your division when Schenley retires next year," Ava persisted.

"Can't we just sue Officer Dempsey, and leave the county out of it?" Thomas looked over at Mallory.

"You never sue just one cop. You sue all the way up to the top." Mallory's information came entirely from news flashes he had seen on his iPad or headlines he'd briefly scanned over the years about this type of lawsuit.

"Yeah, no sense suing just Dempsey. He won't have any money worth suing for," Edison added. Mallory hadn't thought of that. "I say we go big. Sue all the way up the chain of command." Thomas nodded yes. Ava shrugged. Mallory had already given his opinion.

"Good," Edison nodded. "But Mr. Mallory, are you sure you're the right lawyer for the job? These lawsuits are a huge undertaking. Depositions can go on for weeks, if not months. They'll file all sorts of motions. I know you have a full-time job. Are you sure you have the time and energy to take this on?"

"Dad, I know you want a different kind of lawyer. But I don't. He got me out on bail when you were out of town. Today, he got all the charges dismissed. He's good, and he's my friend."

Mallory had never read anything about any lawsuits except headlines saying one was started and other headlines saying somebody had recovered millions. He had no idea how long it would take. He had never heard of a deposition. But his confidence was zooming after he had gotten Thomas completely cleared of the criminal charges. He assured Edison and Ava and Thomas that he was fully capable of filing a multi-million-dollar lawsuit. But what moved Mallory most was the feeling that Thomas truly admired him. The kid was really bright. He had outstanding insight for someone his age and color.

# Chapter 25: The Value of a Good Suit

"Kevin? Kevin Mallory?" He cringed and pushed his grocery cart quickly up the aisle and away from the sound of that familiar voice, but he heard the determined click of high heels close behind. He tried to take a quick left turn, but that escape route was blocked by a five-foot mayonnaise display. His old girlfriend had him cornered.

"Kevin, it *is* you! You look so different." Rose was staring at him, seemingly too surprised to go on. Mallory had counted on never seeing her again, but he was trapped.

"Rose."

"You look good. Your clothes are so different. And have you lost weight?"

He had to admit she looked good, too. She hadn't faded as much as he would have expected. She was wearing a sleek purple dress with gold buttons – a little too fancy for grocery shopping, he thought. Of course, he had no room to complain about that. He was grocery shopping wearing his suit. She brushed her dark hair back as she greeted him, exposing tiny white earrings. She stepped closer to him, arousing him, as she had obviously intended.

"Have I lost weight?" he echoed her. "Maybe."

"What's with the suit?" She stepped back and looked him up and down. He liked her doing that.

"I've been, um, doing law. Got a couple lawsuits going on."

"You're a *lawyer* now? You hadn't even started law school when ...." Her sculpted brows furrowed with interest.

"Double time. You know, online and in-person both."

"Oh."

\*\*\* \*\*\*

The evening after they first met, Mallory took Rose to the

bar she recommended. "Gin martini, straight up, extra dry, extra dirty."

"Uh, Heineken."

"I like this place because they make my martinis exactly the right way." She caught his eye and put her hand on his arm. He took her hand and placed it on his leg. She smiled and let it stay there for a minute. His heart rate shot up. When they left, she was wobbly on her heels and clung to his arm. They went back to her apartment. That night was the beginning of the most magical period of his life. They had unbelievable sex that first night. She seemed to crave his physical domination. She begged for exactly what she wanted, without any shame. He followed her detailed instructions precisely, proud that, through his obedience, he had found the secret to unlocking her deep instinctive urges.

He moved in a week later. A few of her particularities bothered him at first. She was convinced there was only one right way to do anything. And she would explain to him in great detail the reasons why this was so. The shampoo had to be on the right and the conditioner on the left in the shower caddy. The bathroom mat had to be lined up precisely with the borders of the floor tiles. The shades had to be lowered exactly two-thirds and exactly at dusk. He had brought only a few items from his room with him, but most of them she found deficient. Her fastidiousness in the apartment stood in stark contrast to her wild behavior in bed. He couldn't figure out the connection. But he followed her directions to the letter.

"Don't use those flour sack dishtowels. They leave streaks on the plates. Microfiber towels are the only ones that do it right." His trip to the grocery store taught him a lot. "Don't buy Barilla spaghetti. Barilla spaghetti boxes have larger windows than San Giorgio's. They let in light that might degrade the pasta sooner." He made a mental note about that. He had never been into food preparation, but he learned that celery must be cut in three-eighth-inch segments. "Any longer and they get fibrous, any shorter and their flavor gets lost." He made the mistake of buying a bottle of cloves and putting them in the last slot on her complicated spice rack. "No, they need to be in alphabetical order. Put them between the caraway and the coriander."

"But there's no slot between carraway and coriander."

"Move everything from coriander on down one slot and change all the labels."

"But there's over 50 slots. Why didn't you just leave the clove spot open when you ran out of cloves?"

"That's not the right way to do it. If you don't constantly re-alphabetize, you waste space."

Rose hadn't griped too much when he told her he decided against the Starbucks job. "You don't want to take just any job," she explained. "You need a job that will qualify you for jobs of more and more responsibility."

The last thing Mallory had wanted was a job of more responsibility. He signed up as an Uber driver. This gave him an excellent opportunity to describe to his passengers how the Algonquin J. Tycoons of Uber were ripping off all its drivers, and to explain to them the real meaning of the Me Too and Black Lives Matter movements. His ratings began to fall, and they fell faster as the back floor of his car filled up with Dough and Go wrappers. After he was fired, he decided he'd rather just stay home and watch crime shows and YouTube. When Rose came home from work each evening, he'd make up some job he had applied for, usually "management associate." He was pretty sure nobody really knew what that meant. Rose was invariably supportive. And he had learned the right way to buy groceries.

Living with her, he had found himself moving in the same rhythms as when he was living with his mother. He had to be careful to do every chore in precisely the right way. The right way was always Rose's way. But Mallory didn't mind. He had no opinions about these trivialities that women thought were so important. He didn't mind doing them robotically in any way she asked, just as he had done for his mother.

But there was a huge difference between Rose and his mother.

Performing exactly as required by his mother was a negative thing. He moved in lockstep with his mother, but mostly just to keep out of her way. The result was a net of zero. It seemed like he was doing all this work for the sole purpose of being invisible to her. But his pattern with Rose had a completely different result. His complaisance made him real to her, excited her. She actually wanted him.

Mallory found Rose's abiding faith in him inspiring. He was beginning to believe in himself and in their life together. He was beginning to believe he would never have to work again. He didn't see any reason why life could not go on forever like this. But it turned out that Rose had an opinion about that, too.

"Three months," she informed him one evening as he devoured her chicken pot pie at the dinner table.

He looked up. "It took you three months to make this?"

"I'm talking about you. In this economy, a man with an AA degree should be able to find a decent job in three months."

"But, Rose, I'm trying." He wondered if he should try. But he didn't like her putting this pressure on him. Why was she suddenly trying to control every aspect of his life?

"Men of your age and education will succeed in getting a job within three months, if they are really trying."

"How do you know this?"

"I have a friend who works at the Bureau of Labor Statistics. I've discussed your employment situation with her a couple of times."

"So that's where you get your advice on your love life – the Bureau of Labor Statistics?"

"You've never mentioned the word *love* before. You still have two weeks left. If you don't have a job by then, I can't have you living here anymore."

She cut him off sexually a few nights later. The next morning, he subscribed to a deep porn site and charged it to her credit card. When she found out, he apologized so profusely they fell into bed again. But the next morning she packed his suitcase and put it by the apartment door. When he woke up two hours later and saw the suitcase, he told himself it was his ticket to freedom.

He called his mother and asked if he could move back into her basement. He began driving for Lyft and keeping his opinions to himself. His mother got him a job as a counter person at a dry cleaner she had used for twenty years. But, within a few months, they told him business was slow and they'd have to lay him off. He threatened to sue them for their noxious dry cleaning fluids. They laid him off anyway. He found a series of jobs, including one as an actual management associate, but he didn't feel that any of them compensated him enough for his valuable time.

He sat in his mother's basement at night, watching YouTube and porn. Memories of his nights with Rose bothered him a lot. He couldn't figure out what went wrong. Then, while searching for the answer on Google, he discovered Manly Man. Manly Man explained that real women are genetically programmed to submit to a dominant male; but, like children, they are easily distracted by shiny objects and bright colors and don't always appreciate it when a real man has come upon the scene. Rose had been entirely, and appropriately, submissive to him, he reasoned. Therefore, there must have been a shiny object. Probably in the form of another man. A trendier, better dressed, flashier man. Mallory generally didn't like to compare himself to other men, but he was sure he would have given Rose a better life than this flashy no-good. It was her loss. He decided to move on. It was a waste of time to pine for a woman who was gone. Besides, he knew the skills he had learned from Rose would attract women to him like flies.

\*\*\* \*\*\*

He would never have predicted that, years later, his old flame Rose would be the first woman attracted to the new Mallory. He definitely felt that vibe, right there in the supermarket aisle. Maybe it was the suit.

"Yeah," he said now as casually as possible. "I have a good

182

job. I have my own apartment." He didn't mention Nell, whose image was fading quickly from his mind at that point in the conversation. Rose's curious eyes stimulated a long-buried dream that he could have her again. And who was to say a man of his caliber didn't deserve two lovers, one for the body and one for the soul?

"That's nice, Kevin. Maybe I underestimated you."

"You did."

Rose didn't like being told she was wrong about anything. "Oh. Well. I have things to do." She turned to go. Mallory grabbed the top rung of her shopping cart. But she yanked it free, glaring at him. "Don't kid yourself. We're *so* over."

So, why was she teasing him again? "You should come see my place."

"I'm glad you're doing better. I really am." She stopped backing away.

Mallory remembered how thrilled he'd been those first few nights they connected in bed. He knew you can't teach an old dog new tricks, but he thought her old tricks would still be better than his porn site. And he was more mature now. He could control his need for sex now. He could control it enough to scheme how to get it. And he wanted it. Just on the side. Until he could get Nell to love him. "You don't have a boyfriend now, do you?" It was a guess, and her silence was enough of an answer. "I have HBO Plus, and an 80-inch TV screen. I drink cognac now."

She didn't meet his eyes. "Maybe some other time." She turned away again, then turned back, her eyes steady. "I don't have time to fool around anymore. You know what I mean?"

\*\*\* \*\*\*

Mallory had learned there wasn't that much to being a lawyer. Wearing a suit seemed to be the most important thing, and he had found out from Kathie that taking it to the dry cleaners was the best way to keep it looking snappy. But when he took it to the dry cleaners, he learned that it would be 48 hours before he got it back. So, he bought another suit on his credit card so he'd have one to wear every day.

He hadn't had the nerve to check his credit card bill. He was terrified that the damage bill from the Pirate's Den would be in the thousands of dollars. Another $800 for another suit didn't seem like much compared to that. And another couple of $150-dollar bottles of cognac seemed like chicken feed compared to those other items. Smaller items didn't even seem worth worrying about, so he started putting his Dough & Go meals and all the rest of his purchases on his credit card also. Although he was starting to doubt that he could afford even the minimum monthly payment right now, he knew there was a financial bonanza waiting for him in his lawsuit for Thomas.

He had no idea how to file a lawsuit, so he put the actual mechanics of doing it out of his mind for a couple of weeks. But, one evening, Thomas knocked on his door.

"Dad wants me to ask how the lawsuit is coming."

"Did he release the video to the press?" Mallory was pretty sure this was how a lawsuit started.

"No. He gave it back to you. Remember?"

"Oh, right." He didn't remember what he had done with it. "I'm ready to release it to the news media tomorrow."

"About that, Mr. Mallory." Thomas's tone was hesitant. "If this gets on social media, I'll be like, a famous figure. Famous for being beaten. For the rest of my life, maybe. That's not how I'd like to be known."

"You would get that track scholarship right away," Mallory guessed. "I heard they're giving out athletic scholarships out to people who never played the sport."

"That's something different. I don't want to be a professional victim for the rest of my life. My parents aren't big on that either."

"Releasing stuff to the media. That's the usual way these things get started."

"My father says most lawsuits are quiet. Nobody hears about them unless somebody gets millions."

"Hmm." Mallory realized this was probably true. "I can do it the old-fashioned, quiet way, if that's what you and your family really want."

"We do."

"Maybe we should just threaten a lawsuit. See how much money they offer us."

But Thomas's face registered deep disappointment. "We wouldn't need you for that, Mr. Mallory. My father and mother could do that all by themselves, just with the video. We want more than money. We want to make a change in that police department. At least we want them to get rid of that bully, Dempsey."

"Yeah. Yeah. Of course." For the first time since the idea of a lawsuit was first discussed, Mallory felt fear about what he was getting into. He didn't mind dealing with the prosecutors, and he relished the idea of suing the county government, but he was terrified of the police. What if Dempsey, or the whole police department, found out that he was Mr. Plastic Bag Head Man? Could they still bring charges against him for his ferret escapade?

And he realized he was in somewhat over his head with this lawsuit. "I need help," he mumbled to himself. But then he was shocked to see that Thomas had heard him. "These lawsuits need a lot of research," he quickly added. "I've been so busy at work, I haven't had time to be as thorough as I'd intended." He saw Thomas's jaw set. He looked like he had just been let down by his friend. Mallory couldn't bear that look. He had to try to help. But he had no idea how to.

"I'm ... not very good at this legal research business," he confessed to his friend.

Thomas nodded but stood staring past him. "You tricked us."

Mallory searched his conscience. "I didn't think it was a trick. I thought I could do it."

Thomas dropped his head and sighed. Mallory wished he would look him in the eye. He asked him to.

"A lot of you is just bullshit," Thomas finally said. "You'll tell folk anything makes you look good."

Mallory was always willing to lie to make himself look good, and he felt justified in doing that. He had been on defense his whole life. He had never been given a fair shake ever since the day his father left. He was constantly being cheated. Lying his way out of difficulties was his way of evening the score. Reprimands, insults, demotions, firings – they were all water off a duck's back to him. But Thomas had genuinely looked up to him. Thomas had always given him the benefit of the doubt. He wasn't being cheated by Thomas or his family. His lies to them had been offensive lies, in every sense of the word. He owed them a little more honesty.

"I've been having trouble researching this suit. I might have to get some legal help on it." He hesitated. "This case might be a little over my head." He dropped his hands to his side, dropped his head, hoping to avoid seeing Thomas's reaction.

But when he looked up, Thomas surprised him. "My father doesn't really trust you, Mr. Mallory, but I do."

"Really? Do you really want me on the case?"

"You're my man."

Mallory couldn't figure out why Thomas liked him. "Why do you trust my opinion over your father's? He's a really smart guy."

Thomas shook his head in almost a shiver, a movement that passed down through his whole body. "That's what I been told my whole life. Every one of his ideas is better than mine. I'm almost twenty. I need to make my own decisions. Them being out of town when I was arrested, and me hooking up with you – that was the best thing I ever did."

Of course, it was the most natural thing in the world for Thomas to think of him as a hero. Who else could have cut through the red tape and the legal mumbo jumbo to get him out so quickly? Who else could have shown him how to bring a woman to his apartment and get her high enough she wouldn't remember what she did there?

"Maybe I can help you work on the case." Thomas was almost pleading now. Mallory's problem, however, was he had no

186

idea at all how to proceed. "I'm good on the internet. Maybe I can look up stuff for you."

"I don't know ...."

"I can go on the court sites and get copies of the papers in police brutality cases like mine."

Mallory tried to hide his surprise. "Well, I guess that's one way to go. People have done that sometimes," he guessed. "Why don't you find a couple of those old cases. That way you can get some ideas of how you might want to go with your case."

"Why don't we do it right now?"

# Chapter 26: The Missing Panties

Nell put her hands flat on the table and sighed deeply before she started. "I have to report to the Employee Cheer Committee that we are banned from having any more parties at the Pirate's Den. And they sent us a bill for all the drinks we ordered – I'm still not convinced their appetizer count is correct – and for replacing the cannon and refinishing the sixteen-foot oak table the cannon fell on, and for lost revenue when the group at that other table walked out."

"That lost revenue business, that's bullshit," Bob contributed. "They're just padding the bill."

"Maybe so, but that's just the bad news. The good news is that Kevin Mallory has already paid the entire bill, as a gift to the Committee." Bob's mouth dropped open. Kathie dropped her iPad in shock.

"I wouldn't have paid a penny," Valerie complained. "They don't serve any decent vegan food. I should sue them for not letting me in."

Nell ignored Valerie's complaint. "Mr. Mallory has paid the bill. The Committee is free and clear of debt. I think we owe Mr. Mallory a vote of thanks." Nell indicated how this was to be done by clapping. A few of the members clapped vigorously. Valerie sat on her hands.

Nell glanced across the table at Mallory. She had been avoiding speaking to him in the week since the party. He wasn't surprised at that. He had driven her home after she passed out in his apartment. He had steered her to her bed and left her lying there with her clothes on. Her cats had rushed at her, and Koko, the beautiful black and white one, had sat on her face. He shooed off Koko and unscrewed a large lampshade and put it over her head to keep the cat away. He knew she must have been surprised at that when she woke up. It was the kind of thing she might have asked him about the next time they met, but she was apparently too embarrassed to ask about that. And she was probably even more embarrassed to ask why she had found her panties neatly folded up inside her pocketbook.

"Now that the holiday season is over ...." Nell began.

"It's still December," Bob corrected her.

"But the holiday season is over, as far as the Cheer Committee is concerned. It's never too early to start planning ahead. We need to start planning for the Cheerboree."

Mallory had learned that the Cheerboree was an outdoor event that featured a picnic lunch and team-building activities. Although Nell seemed very excited about planning it, there was a lot of dissent on the committee. Most of the discussion was based on last year's experience. Kathie complained that she had been bitten by a bug and said she would not go unless the place would be sprayed for insects before they arrived. Valerie said she wouldn't go to any place that had been contaminated by insecticides. Bob asked if they could bring their own coolers. Everyone knew that meant liquor. Mallory was fantasizing that the team-building activities would bring him into close physical contact with the female workers. He decided he would ask Bob about that after the meeting. Nell suggested they figure out a menu that would please everybody, then have each committee member bring enough of one dish to feed the expected 45 to 50 attendees. There was a question about which dishes would cost the most to prepare, and whether UniCast would pay them for the ingredients. This veered off into an argument about the menu itself. Bob kept insisting he would bring his own meal in a cooler. Nell couldn't get the committee to focus on when the Cheerboree would be held. She seemed to have trouble focusing herself.

"Alright. Let's put off all the Cheerboree discussions until a later meeting. And let's end this meeting now. Thank you all for coming. I'd like to speak to Mr. Mallory alone."

A few of the members waited behind and patted him on the shoulder before they left the room. Mallory drank in this approval, but the delay seemed to be frustrating to Nell. He knew she needed to talk to him in private. He knew she was nervous about it. Good.

It was killing him that she was still resisting their mutual attraction. If she was yearning for him like he was yearning for her, she was hiding it well. But he had learned that women are taught by their own matriarchal society to repress even their most basic needs. It was time to awaken her soul. "You said I was more interesting now, with my new hair, and new suit, and all."

Her expression relaxed a little. "That's true. You do seem to be trying harder. I should validate that." He didn't want to be validated. He wanted to be loved. He was desperate for that. But her next words let him keep hope that he had at least rocked her world. "Kevin, I want to talk to you about what happened between us in your friend Bunbury's apartment after the holiday party."

"You don't remember?"

"I remember you tried to kiss me, and I didn't respond. Then I remember I passed out."

"That's about what happened."

"What do you mean, *about* what happened?"

"That's what happened."

"Then you took me home."

"I did."

She, of course, didn't want to talk about the panties in her pocketbook. But she couldn't accuse him without bringing up that particular fact. And she was too ashamed to do that.

He hadn't done anything to her. Having sex with a limp, passed-out body had never been one of his fantasies. He had originally planned to use the panties later that night as an aide to his internet pleasure; but the panties were brand new, pure white, and he decided he didn't want to do anything to ruin them. In the end, he hadn't done anything except slip them into her pocketbook.

Over the past week, he had enjoyed her blushes, her downcast eyes, her shying away from every opportunity to talk to him. She obviously wasn't sure what they had done. It would be to his

190

advantage that she think they might be lovers.

But her embarrassed silence had gone on for too long. He needed to treat her gently now, as any new lover would. She was obviously on edge, but she wasn't saying anything. He decided he would have to be the one to break the ice.

"There's nothing wrong, you know, if a man and a woman ...."

Nell blushed a deeper red. She was breathing hard. Her mouth hung open. "Tell me we didn't."

"You were so sweet."

Her jaw was clenched now, but her face was still red. "I don't remember it. I'm pretty sure I had no intention of doing anything. Sometimes I drink too much."

# Chapter 27: A False Persona

Within a few days, Thomas had printed out and brought to him copies of papers filed in seven different police brutality cases. Mallory did the best he could with the information. He picked the only case in which the police hadn't actually killed the plaintiff, skipped over all the legal rigamarole in the beginning and the end, and corrected the statement of facts in pencil so they were closer to what happened to Thomas. Thomas suggested they use his name and Officer Dempsey's name instead of the names already on the papers.

"I think we have to send them to the court or something."

"Yeah," Thomas agreed. "I think it's called filing the case." Thomas filed the case himself. He told Mallory later he had gone to the wrong court two times, but the people were very nice to him and sent him in the right direction. He found out he had to deliver a copy to Officer Dempsey and to the County Executive, and he did that too. Mallory decided the filing job must be pretty simple, since Thomas had done it.

Mallory's cell phone rang while he was dealing with a UniCast customer. He clicked the customer off and answered his personal phone.

"Hold for County Attorney Finkelman," a brusque, authoritative female voice commanded him. Mallory hung up. The phone rang again, and again he was told to hold for County Attorney Finkelman. He hung up again. The phone rang again, from the same number. This time a man's voice spoke up cheerily. "Mallory? Kevin Mallory? Glad to get a hold of you. I'm Ned Finkelman, County Attorney. Can we talk for a second about *Wright v. Dempsey, et. al.?*"

"What?"

"The alleged police brutality case you filed yesterday."

"Yeah. But the guy I was dealing with was named Armstrong."

"He's the prosecutor who handles criminal cases. I'm the County Attorney who handles civil cases. You know the difference between a criminal case and a civil case, don't you?"

"Of course. We want at least three million dollars."

"Then why did you sue for one million?"

"Um ... that must have been a typo."

"Is it also a typo that your client has three different names?"

"Of course, a first name, a middle name and a last name."

"It doesn't appear to me that you know what you're doing. What is your bar number, anyway? I didn't see it on the papers you filed."

"It's ... it's ... pending."

"Your name doesn't appear on the master attorney roster. You know that practicing law without a license is a felony in this state."

Mallory figured Finkelman was bluffing. Why would this high and mighty County Attorney guy bother to check the state master list of attorneys – if there even was such a thing as a master list? He hung up. Why should he give Finkelman any better treatment than he gave to his UniCast customers every day?

Thomas was chafing at the restrictions his parents were putting on the lawsuit. He had told them he could get the video to go viral and be picked up by all the media.

"It would be the most effective thing to get a good settlement, but they won't let me do it," he complained bitterly to Mallory that night. "They say the worse thing I can do to my career is to become famous as a victim – but I don't believe that anymore."

"Yeah, I see what you mean. Look what happened to George Floyd. He got killed when he brought that lawsuit."

"Huh?"

Thomas shook his head. His shoulders slumped. The look on his face couldn't have been any sadder. He hesitated like he was trying to hold something in, but he couldn't, and his disappointment just poured out.

"You're not really a lawyer, are you, Mr. Mallory?"

Mallory was utterly crushed by the force of Thomas's disillusion. Of course, he had lied to Thomas and his family over and over, just as he had lied his way out of every difficult situation throughout his entire life. But he had lied to Thomas honorably, to help the young man who was the only person on earth who believed in him. Lying was his way of helping Thomas; it was the only thing he did really well.

"I don't care that you screwed the case up." Thomas went on even as Mallory cringed at every word. "I care that you lied, to me. I thought we were friends."

"We are friends, aren't we? I did lie. That's what I do. I'm a scummy friend. I don't deserve to be your friend. But that's what I want, more than anything else in the world. To be your friend."

"Who are you, really?"

No one had ever asked that question of Mallory before. He had no idea how to answer. He knew he was a lifelong avoider of consequences, a violator of common standards of decency, a person who disliked all of mankind and deliberately lived inside his own head so as not to have to try to understand anybody else. He had always been proud of that stance. But he wasn't proud now.

"I don't know. I don't know who I am."

# Chapter 28: Just Trying to Help

Mallory entered a season of penance. He tried to rethink his relationship with Nell. He had obviously read too much into her complimenting his haircut and his suit. She hadn't really kissed him, not with any passion, even when she was drunk. She seemed devastated by the idea that they had made love. She was just not into him romantically. He had to face that. But he still loved her.

He had been wrong to let her think they had sex, but he couldn't think of any way to fix that now. Confessing that he stole her underpants while she was passed out would end their relationship forever – and possibly land him in jail. He figured the best thing to do was to put off his fantasy of a smoldering romance and start to act as a faithful colleague and friend.

"I owe you one." He stood in the opening to Nell's cubicle the morning following his conversation with Thomas.

Nell's face was lined with suspicion. "What are you talking about?"

"I owe you one. Let's leave it at that." The tension in her face seemed to lessen a little, so he went on. "If there's any way I can help you on the committee, or on the Cheerboree, or in your work here, just let me know, and I'll help as much as I can."

She seemed to sense that he wanted a truce. "Thank you." When he didn't immediately respond, she moved to fill in the silence. "And thank you again for taking care of that Pirate's Den ... thing. How much did they charge you, anyway?"

"Sixteen hundred dollars."

"What! For drinks and appetizers?"

"They charged for the other table, too. The table the cannon fell on. All their food and drinks. Then they added lost profit on drinks the cannon table would have bought if they hadn't all run out."

"Those people really are pirates."

"That's okay. I decided it was worth it if I could be a solid committee member, and a good friend to you."

"Thank you." The silence that they both observed after these words seemed like the beginning of a truce, a truce between friends, friends who had maybe gone too far one drunken afternoon but had too much respect for each other to let it get in their way.

Mallory threw himself into planning for the Cheerboree. For the next few weeks, he entertained himself by stalking the cubicles of the committee members, asking their ideas about dates and locations, not to mention team-building activities and the food and the guest list. He soon realized that Nell's idea of getting every committee member to agree on every aspect of the event was going to be hard to achieve. The fitness types were never going to agree with the couch potatoes, the vegans were never going to agree with the barbeque types, the Lyme-diseasers were never going to agree with the pesticide phobics, and nobody wanted to pay more than $15 for a full day of food and professionally supervised activities. And then of course there was Bob.

Mallory spent two full days drawing up a matrix with committee members' names on one axis and activities and food on the other, hoping to come up with a brilliant solution. He left Bob out of the matrix entirely, but he came up with the idea of appeasing him by having everyone sing the Star Spangled Banner at the start of the day. But as hard as he manipulated the chart, and as often as he talked to the various opposing sides, he could not come up with a consensus broad enough to be pleasing to Nell.

"We can talk it out at the meetings," she insisted. "We have plenty of time."

"Most of these team-building companies say they're already booking for events this coming spring."

"We have plenty of time. We'll talk it out."

Mallory saw his chance to really do a favor for Nell. He looked at his matrix again and crossed off anyone who disagreed on anything with more than one other person. He scratched out Bob. He scratched the Star Spangled Banner. He contacted the

196

team-building companies and scratched off those that required people to fly on a zip line or swing on high ropes. He talked to a state park ranger who recommended an area where they had never had a problem with bugs. He found out where to rent volleyball nets and cornhole and horseshoe games. He contacted caterers and eliminated any that served kale.

He reserved everything for the following April 27th. He calculated they could break even if they got 75 people to go. UniCast traditionally allowed people time off for the Cheerboree, and there were 500 employees in the metro area, so this number seemed possible. He went to check out the committee's records to find out how many people had gone to last year's Cheerboree, but then he remembered he had thrown all the records out. Nell had gotten only 17 people to come to the holiday party at the Pirate's Den, but that might have been because Nell had sent that memo basically telling people not to come. He didn't have the committee's or the company's approval of any of this; but all the vendors were telling him he had to book now, so he used his credit card for all of the deposits. He decided this would be his Christmas present to Nell.

*** ***

"Your Honor, I am Ned Finkelman, County Attorney for Pembroke County."

"I know who you are, Mr. Finkelman." The judge seemed aggravated already. It was after normal court hours. The County Attorney had requested an emergency hearing on his Motion to Dismiss Thomas's case. Mallory had been notified on his cell phone by the judge's clerk, who told him where and when to show up. He had asked the clerk if his clients had to come to the hearing also, and he had breathed a sigh of relief when she said no. He didn't know if Thomas had told his mother and father that he wasn't really an attorney. He had been afraid to ask.

"This is supposed to be a hearing on a motion." The judge

still seemed impatient. "But there is no motion, at least not in my file."

"Your Honor, these are extraordinary circumstances."

"They'd better be."

"Your Honor, we anticipated having a Motion to Dismiss filed by now, and we were working on that, but that's when the extraordinary circumstances came up. I've been busy researching those circumstances. It appears, Your Honor, it appears that Mr. Kevin Mallory, who has entered his appearance on behalf of the plaintiff, Thomas Wright, is not an attorney. Mr. Mallory has thus not only committed a felony by filing this case, but it has come to my attention that he previously represented Mr. Wright in his bail hearing also."

"And I won that hearing, too." Mallory contributed.

"I advise you not to say anything," the judge quickly intoned. "I assume you are going to be charged with a criminal act. You have the right to remain silent."

"Your Honor, I was brought here under false pretenses."

"Hm. That may be correct. All the more reason to keep your trap shut. What's the real point of this hearing, Mr. Finkelman?"

That question was answered when the back doors of the courtroom opened and Baxter Armstrong, the prosecutor Mallory had dealt with before, entered carrying a manila file. "The prosecutor is here to formally serve the charges of felony practicing law without a license on Mr. Mallory," Finkelman explained. Armstrong handed Mallory the entire file.

"The penalty is up to two years in prison and a $10,000 fine," Armstrong explained.

"This is a complete setup," Mallory complained.

"Your Honor, we had to act quickly in this matter," Armstrong continued. "Mr. Mallory is not only a non-attorney, but he has also filed the most confusing, illogical, factually self-contradictory and rambling civil rights complaint that I have ever seen. Our office thought it would be a disservice to the family – his clients, the people he's supposed to be representing – to let him go one inch further on this case."

"He's just jealous that I beat him at the bail hearing," Mallory persisted.

The judge pounded his gavel. "Enough. Mr. Mallory may be guilty, or he may be innocent. That's for another court to decide on another day." The judge then stared directly at Finkelman. "But the court is very concerned that it has been used by Mr. Finkelman as a ruse to get Mr. Mallory here, to serve him with the charges. This is a deliberate abuse of the court's time. The court does not take this kind of shenanigans lightly. Mr. Finkelman, this court hereby finds you in contempt and orders you to pay a $50 fine. Court is adjourned."

# Chapter 29: Escalade to Somewhere

Mallory was sure they didn't have much of a case against him because, after the charges were announced, he was released on his own recognizance, without having to post any bail money. No bail money – while even Thomas, who was totally innocent in his case, had been required to post $1,000 bail. The judge had seemed much angrier at that County Attorney Finkelman than at him; and when he fined that pretentious bastard $50, Mallory felt like he had won that hearing.

Thomas didn't agree. "Didn't you read the papers they gave you? It says you could go to jail for up to two years."

"Oh, that's nonsense. You should have seen that judge's face, Thomas."

"It says here you have a right to get your own attorney. I think you should get one."

"How can I afford an attorney? I live in an efficiency apartment. I've been buying everything with credit cards."

"I thought I saw you drive up yesterday in a Cadillac Escalade."

"Leased. On my credit card. I can't pass for a lawyer driving a ten-year-old Camry."

"Don't you get it? You can never pass for a lawyer. They've already caught you faking it."

"Oh, I'm sure there's some way out." Even though he was deathly afraid of the police, Mallory was not afraid of either the prosecutor or the county attorney. He knew he could handle anybody who wore a suit and attacked him only with words.

"Look, Mr. Mallory, I'm going to have to tell my parents that you aren't a lawyer. It's got to come out anyway."

"You haven't told them already?" The realization that Thomas was covering up for him, even to his parents, melted Mallory's heart. "You should tell them, Thomas. And tell them I agree you should get a real lawyer for your civil suit."

"They're not really aiming to make a federal case out of it."

"Maybe they're right. What do I know?"

\* \* \* \* \* \*

He picked up Rose in his Escalade and took her to a Sunday brunch. He knew he was being unfaithful to Nell, but he couldn't seem to get Nell's attention lately. Nell seemed to want only a platonic relationship. And his encounter with Rose in the supermarket had awakened certain erotic memories. He wasn't sure he could resist her now. And she was obviously intrigued by his suit.

"Ooo, you seem to be doing better for yourself," she cooed as she climbed up into the shiny black SUV in her high heels. She kept her exposed knees primly together but slanted her whole body toward him. Thomas had convinced him not to use the Escalade to impersonate a lawyer, but he knew now that the vehicle had other uses. She looked expectantly into his eyes. Either her skin was exceptionally clear or she was wearing a soft sheen of translucent makeup. Her lips were a natural lush rose.

"I shouldn't be meeting you. I have a soul mate."

"But you are meeting me." She smiled her response. "Is there something lacking in your relationship?" Her flirtatious note made his heart skip a beat.

"I get confused." He laid his hand on the console.

She put hers on top of his. "There's nothing wrong in doing a little exploring. Let's see how this goes."

Over brunch, Rose filled him in on some of her life since she had kicked him out two years ago. She had a boyfriend for about six months. "But I realized it wasn't going anywhere. He wasn't going anywhere. But he did have his own place." She glanced over at him when she said that.

"I have a house now."

"That's great. Can I see it?"

He decided he had to Bunbury her.

"Oh, that's so kind of you, taking care of your friend's

apartment," she said when he finished his tale. Her voice grew warm. "So, you're taking care of two places now?"

"Just temporarily. I'm staying full-time at Bunbury's apartment right now. His neighborhood's a little rough, and he's worried about break-ins. Would you like to see his place?"

She hesitated. "I'd like to see your house."

"Mine? I'm having some work done on it right now. It's a mess. But I can drive us by it on the way to Bunbury's, if you want."

\* \* \*   \* \* \*

As soon as Rose slipped off into a satisfied sleep beside him, Mallory's thoughts turned to Nell. Nell had needed multiple slugs of cognac to be induced into even halfway accepting his kiss. For Rose to go all the way, all he had needed was a good job and a house. He noticed how much more effort she put into looking pretty than Nell did. She was a shallow girl who was into looks and material things. She was selling him sex for a suit, ecstasy for an Escalade. He had convinced himself that he could wait for Nell, but Rose's female charms affected him now like one of those sweet cinnamon buns he had never been able to resist.

But she wanted to know too much. When had he started practicing law? When would his house be fixed? How was his mother? She didn't bring up the fact that she had kicked him out two years before. Manly Man had said that as women reach thirty, they develop two more needs, needs that can only be satisfied by a man. They still need to be dominated, but they also want to be impregnated – and supported for life. Rose was showing all the warning signs, but he needed her sweet cinnamon candy while waiting for his true love to realize that they were made for each other.

He had been planning on turning the Escalade back in to the dealer; but after he dropped off Rose that afternoon, he decided to keep it. He didn't admit to himself that this meant he was going to keep on seeing her. It would be wrong to plan a long-term liaison with Rose while still courting Nell. He stopped at the Dough and Go on the way home, hoping to discuss this issue with Spike. But Spike wasn't there, and Mallory instead just sat there and drank coffee and ate a big piece of chocolate cake.

\* \* \* \* \* \*

"Kevin?" Nell tilted back in her work chair with a strange look on her face like she wasn't sure she was asking the right person. "Kathie and I have been trying to schedule a girls' night out for a couple of weeks now. Friday is the only night we can both do it. I was wondering if you would mind terribly ...."

"No problem," he cut her off. "I'm free that night." He wasn't free that night. He had been planning to bed Rose that night. "I can go. I can even drive everybody. Designated driver. I have an Escalade."

"That's not what I meant. It's a *girls'* night out. I need somebody to cat sit. Just for a couple of hours. From seven to ten."

He sighed, looked away, then turned back. "Would it make you happy if I did that?"

"Yeah. It would. I promise."

"Then it would make me happy, too."

He had to admit to himself that none of Nell's pets were as ferocious as his ferret. Nell told him he had to let the dogs stay in the house while she was gone. Otherwise, she said, the cats would get lonely. Galahad, her hyperactive Irish setter, was the biggest problem, leaping erratically on the sofa whenever the cats tried to rub themselves up against him. Little Brute was some kind of squat little hound. He barked whenever a car went by on the street outside. He had a resonant bark.

The big event was the administration of Valium to Brute. Nell couldn't do it before she left because it had to be done at precisely eight o'clock. Brute backed away whenever Mallory approached him with the pill. Mallory thought this problem was easily solved. He embedded the pill in a wad of the special dog food that Nell had bought for Brute. Mallory smiled when Brute chomped at it greedily, but he was soon disappointed when Brute dropped the food on the floor, pawed it, gnawed it and licked it around the edges until everything was gone but one untouched little Valium pill sitting on the living room rug, pristine except for a wet sheen of dog saliva. Mallory picked up the pill and threw it away.

The dogs and cats did get along amazingly well. Brute didn't seem any worse for missing his Valium. Galahad seemed to be the one who really needed it, but there were no prescriptions for him. The big dog eventually settled down enough to allow Florence, the older cat, to snuggle down next to him. The cats had obviously learned to ignore Brute's barking at every single car that went by outside. Kiki wandered off somewhere behind the sofa and hardly showed her face all night.

Mallory noticed for the first time what a beautiful cat Koko was. Pitch black, with white paws, a brown and white chest and a matching underbody, he was the skinniest cat with the longest tail Mallory had ever seen. He scratched Mallory when he first tried to pet him, but Mallory still couldn't help reaching out. After the commotion about the Valium died down, Koko started edging closer, eventually letting Mallory touch him, pet him from his head to the tip of his long tail. Koko didn't purr, but he approached Mallory twice more for that treatment before the end of the night.

Nell and Kathie were both high when they arrived, Nell the higher by far.

"Oh, thank you, Kevin! This was the most wonderful favor," Kathie, the first to speak, gushed at him.

"Are they all alright? Did Galahad have a bowel movement?" Nell seemed worried still. "Did Brute get his Valium? Are the cats alright?"

Mallory assured her that all had gone according to plan.

"Thank you, Kevin." Nell was less effusive than Kathie, but Mallory could understand that she felt the weight of being responsible for the well-being of all the animals. Except for the Valium, he was pretty sure he had handled everything well. She seemed comfortable talking about her animals. He was hoping Kathie would leave soon, so he could tell her all the details, all that he had done for her.

"Kathie, you need at least one cup of my fresh ground coffee before you go," Nell practically giggled. "I was in no shape to drive, but you're not that much better."

"Okay, maybe one."

Even as she talked to Kathie, Nell began ushering him out the door. She stopped with her hand on the knob and turned to him. "You've come a long way from being that arrogant s.o.b. who used to bump his chair into my cubicle wall fifteen times a day."

"Thank you," he said numbly, edging toward her, wondering what was next. But by the time he reached her she had already ripped the door open.

# Chapter 30: Substance and Other Abuse

"I can't believe this! You already scheduled the Cheerboree for April 27th? Paid the deposits and all? Paid them yourself? What were you thinking?" Nell couldn't keep her voice down. He gestured for her to follow as he rushed toward the break room, deliberately moving so fast she couldn't follow and talk at the same time.

"I did it for you," he announced when they were alone in the break room, smiling the biggest, most generous smile he could manage. "I did all the work. I put my own money up front because the time to make reservations was running out. It's all set. I figured you didn't need any more hassles after the holiday party fiasco."

"It wasn't a fiasco. And we learned some things we can use when we plan parties in the future."

"But what about the Cheerboree. I did it all. For you. Aren't you happy?"

"This was not authorized! The Cheer Committee hadn't agreed on any of this yet."

"And they never would have all agreed on a plan. Can't you see? I did it for you, Nell. To make your life easier." Mallory realized he had to make his motivation plainer. He guessed that, Manly Man's advice to the contrary, actions don't always speak louder than words. "I love you."

"No, you don't. Don't be silly."

In all the archives of Manly Man, he had never seen directions for a situation like this. He was on his own. But he guessed that was natural for the unique man he was. He didn't fit into any specific manly category. And Nell wasn't anything like the women Manly Man discussed online. The two of them were unique individuals who had found each other. Their connection would never follow the ordinary rules. She might really believe she was brushing him off, but the seeds of respect and devotion had already been planted.

"But why April 27th? That's my birthday," she continued to complain.

"Perfect! It'll be my birthday present to you."

"You don't understand. I always take off on my birthday."

"So? Cheerboree is like a vacation day anyway, only we get paid. And we'll pretend everybody's there just for your birthday."

"Every birthday I take the day off, and I go out to lunch with my mother and my aunt."

"So? Bring them to the Cheerboree."

"Non-employees are not permitted to come. This problem you created is not so easily solved. I wish you hadn't done this. On top of everything else, you're undermining my authority in the committee."

Mallory usually took Nell's side, but he felt he was in the right this time. In the real world, friends, even lovers, had their differences. The proof of this came the very next day. Nell came to his cubicle and, in the gentlest possible voice, asked if he could cat sit again that Friday. She was having another girls' night out. She didn't mention their disagreement about the Cheerboree.

"You're a good friend," she said when he agreed.

\* \* \*   \* \* \*

The small, two-story home Nell rented was one of a line of small, irregularly placed white clapboard houses strung along a forgotten roadway bordering a patch of tall, scraggly pine woods. Some of the houses were well kept, some were decrepit. Nell's was about halfway in between. Mallory felt more like a target for crime now that he had the Escalade. He knew the hoodlums would be attracted to it. He pulled deep into her driveway, past the gravel part and into the pure dirt, just to keep it out of the way of those thieves. But then her dogs in the back yard started barking at the giant SUV like it was a monster out to eat them. They didn't stop, even when he got out and threatened them with his rifle. He couldn't stand the idea of listening to their hysterical barking all evening, so he pulled his vehicle back closer to the road.

The dogs needed their inside time, Nell explained. They needed to bond with the cats and learn how to respect inside boundaries, especially the rules about what they could and couldn't do with the furniture. She instructed Mallory on how to keep them off the kitchen table and the living room furniture, and how to tell when they needed to go to the bathroom. Unfortunately, although he spent 21 out of every 24 hours outside, Brute, once inside, decided that every single noise coming from outside was a sign of terrifying danger. This riled up hyperactive Galahad, who would make a running circle of the living room, sofa and all, causing yet another amiable scuffle with the cats.

Mallory decided it would be best if they all had a dose of Valium. He set out on that project the instant Nell and Kathie were out the door. He found a hammer in one of the kitchen drawers and ground the first pill against the countertop until it was not much more than a pile of dust. He found some packets of gourmet dog food in the refrigerator and carefully mixed in the ground Valium so thoroughly that it could not be separated from the food itself. He made another batch, and the two dogs each stupidly gulped down the whole thing down. The cats were a little harder. Florence and Kiki were pretty easily tricked with the pill-in-a-pellet-of-food trick, but Koko wasn't fooled. Mallory tried to force the cat's jaw open and shove the pellet in, but Koko scratched his face. Mallory jumped back and let go. He decided Koko didn't really need the medication, so he took Koko's dose himself. A minute later, Koko came back and rubbed affectionately against Mallory's pants leg as if thanking him, then disappeared.

The level of chaos seemed lower than the last time, though there was still some chasing around the room. Brute still jumped up at every noise outside, but his deep hound's howl was now reduced to a low growl. Mallory was mesmerized by Koko. The beautiful black-and-white cat kept returning to him for more attention. Mallory would pat his head with one hand, and Koko would then slowly walk through his caress all the way to the tip of its tail. He decided he really liked that cat. He fell asleep and was awakened only by Galahad's desperate scratching at the door to get out. He had a moment of panic imagining the giant Irish Setter taking a dump in Nell's living room, but he rushed to the door and let the dog out just in time. The commotion stirred up the rest of the animals. Mallory thought about dosing them again, but then he remembered Nell telling him she did weekly pill counts. By 10:30 it was obvious Nell was staying out later than last time. But he knew he had no right to complain. He had completely undermined her authority on the committee by making crucial decisions about the Cheerboree without consulting her. He owed her one for that.

He and all the animals were asleep again by the time Nell and Kathie arrived back at about 11:30. They weren't nearly as tipsy as the last time. Kathie strode in very comfortably and sat right down at the kitchen counter. She brushed off the remains of the Valium dust he had left at that spot. Nell didn't cross-examine him about the animals' bowel habits nearly as much as last time. The two women seemed more like old friends than silly girlish officemates.

"You did a good job here, Kevin." Nell seemed exceptionally mellow. "I owe you one."

"Don't say that. I'm not even even yet." He didn't know how much Kathie knew about his Cheerboree fiasco. Nell had sworn him to secrecy until they could figure out what to do about it. He didn't want to undermine her now in front of Kathie.

"You mean the Cheerboree thing?" Kathie looked up at him. "I personally don't think it was a bad idea. I told Nell she should just go with it."

Mallory decided he liked Kathie. Nell started to make coffee. Mallory hoped he'd be invited to stay; but as soon as the pot was perking, Nell started easing him out toward the front door. He wasn't sad. He felt he had made enough progress at working his way back into her good graces for one night. He offered to wait outside in his SUV to keep a lookout for hoodlums until Kathie left, but Nell said he had done enough, and he should just go home and get some rest.

On the way home, Mallory was startled to hear Rose's amplified voice suddenly harping at him from all eight of his Escalade's speakers. "Where have you been?"

"Like I told you. At the hospital."

"You were there until 11:45?"

"Bunbury's taken a turn for the worse."

"Oh. Okay. Sorry. Is he going to be okay?"

"Yeah. I think he finally passed the crisis point."

"What's wrong with him, anyway?"

"Um, something. Something I don't understand. Some kind of *plasia* or something. Can I come over to your place now?"

"It's late. I'm tired. I'm going to bed."

"That's what I want to do, too. Go to bed. With you. Right now."

"Is that all you want with me, really?" Her voice was suddenly thinner.

"No. No." Yes. Yes.

"It's late. Late at night, and also late in my life. Look, I'm sorry I kicked you out years ago. It just seemed like you ... weren't going anywhere. No job and all."

"That's what inspired me. To get my life in order. I owe you that."

"Oh. That's a nice thing to say, that I had something to do with your ... *improvements*."

"Everything."

Still, he couldn't talk her into having sex with him that night. He couldn't think of what else to do. The Dough and Go had long since closed. As he approached the busier streets of his neighborhood, he started worrying about those hoodlums and thugs haunting the streets. He knew he was at a much higher risk of being attacked now that he was driving a sleek, black SUV. It was just the kind of urban car those people wanted. His Escalade didn't have an actual trunk, so he carried the rifle laid across the two captains' chairs in the second row. He had tried again to buy bullets at Guns-R-Us, but Gus had turned him down again. Still, if they thought he had a gun, they would know not to mess with him.

He pulled in to the 7-11 closest to his apartment. He thought he'd buy some soda to mix with his Hennessy, get a buzz on, and search through his porn site for someone who looked like Nell. Or Rose. It didn't matter. They all looked pretty much the same down there. He got the same clerk he had seen the night of the ferret.

"Scratches again? Looks like somebody's messing with a nasty female."

This admiration felt good. "You might say that." He was actually pretty sure Koko was a male.

He mixed his drink when he got home and turned on his computer. He took a few gulps as the screen powered up. It really hadn't been that good a night. He'd earned a little credit by doing his penance for Nell, but their friendship wasn't showing any sign yet of blossoming into the romance that was their destiny. He had missed out on a delicious night of lovemaking with Rose, and he didn't know how much farther he could go with his former girl-friend anyway. Sooner or later, Rose would talk to his mother. They had always been pals back then. Then Rose would have to decide if a dead-end job at UniCast and an efficiency apartment was enough for her to open her legs for him on a regular basis. He doubted it.

He turned on the computer, but he was drinking so fast his libido couldn't catch up. He fell asleep fully dressed on the sofa bed. But he woke up three hours later with his heart pounding. It was still pitch dark outside. The scratches on his face were still stinging. His apartment was completely dark except for the little orange blip of the phone charger way across the room. He didn't remember what the orange light meant, but it seemed like he was being warned of danger from all sides. He turned over and over in his mind different ways he could handle his problems with Nell, and Rose, and even Teitelbaum. He didn't used to have problems. He tried to track back to where they started. What kept popping into his mind was the night he abandoned his ferret, Coco, at that rest stop along the interstate. Now the cat, Koko, had made friends with him, but scratched his face, too. What did it all mean?

# Chapter 31: Acting Only as a Friend

"You utter one word in this room, Mr. Mallory, and I'll have the judge revoke your recognizance." County Attorney Finkelman's face was red with anger.

"One word," Mallory replied. He had no idea what *recognizance* meant. He was convinced he could get millions for Thomas in this lawsuit, even if he couldn't officially be his lawyer anymore.

"Mr. Mallory is here at this settlement conference, not as our lawyer, but as our family friend." Thomas's father forced himself into the conversation. There had been a low-keyed but long argument in Thomas's apartment the night before. Edison and Ava had been determined that their son cut all ties with Mallory after they learned he had lied to them about being a lawyer. Mallory admitted that he'd lied, but he pointed out that he got Thomas out on bail and that he got the video that proved that he was innocent. Thomas's parents seemed unconvinced.

"But it's *my* lawsuit," Thomas had finally interjected forcefully. Both his parents seemed shocked by their son's temerity. Mallory had never seen easygoing, soft-spoken Thomas contradict his parents. Ava and Edison were large people, and solid, in every sense of the word. Mallory had the feeling they had been right in every decision they had ever made about raising their son. Thomas had obviously grown up in a world that had love and order and predictability. Mallory remembered his own childhood only as disconnected scenes of chaos and resentment.

"I'm serious, Mr. Mallory," Finkelman continued. "I'm allowing you to come into this settlement conference at Mr. Wright's insistence, just as a friend of the family. But if you speak one word, or give the plaintiffs one word of legal advice, I will have the sheriff take you off to jail immediately."

Thomas turned to him, put a comforting hand on his arm. "Don't say anything, Mr. Mallory. Don't worry. We got this."

"The first thing we want," Edison Wright began, "is for Officer Dempsey to be fired. He doesn't belong on the police force, or any place where he has control over citizens. This obviously needs to be done, and it's not negotiable."

"Well, we have a problem right there. Police officers, like all state employees, have certain procedural rights. They have the right to go before a panel of other officers before any action is taken against them. And they have the union to protect them. We can't fire an officer just like that."

"Then we have no deal. We'll proceed with the lawsuit. We'll get a real, experienced litigation lawyer. And you can expect the video of Thomas's arrest to go viral within the next 24 hours."

County Attorney Finkelman put his hand out to slow the momentum of the discussion. "No. Wait. I could talk to the County Council. This might be considered an emergency matter. Maybe in an emergency we could bypass some of the usual personnel procedures."

"So, we're now assuming that Dempsey will be immediately fired." Edison pushed the conversation forward. "Let's talk about the rest of the settlement."

\*\*\* \*\*\*

"My Dad says we can get at least $200,000, plus Dempsey being fired, if we don't release the video, and we give it back to them," Thomas said to Mallory later that night.

"That's a bad deal. Don't take it. That video is worth millions." Mallory tried to remember where he'd put it.

"And they want a confidentiality agreement. We can't say anything about the case to anybody."

"That's bullshit."

"I agree. I'd rather release that video than take the money."

"It's your case, not your father's. It's your decision. Maybe I'm not a lawyer, but I know that much."

But Mallory wanted to talk to Thomas about his own

problems. "I've been cat sitting for Nell. It's not too bad. I really like one of her cats."

"You didn't like that ferret."

"Yeah. But this cat's really pretty. And he likes me. Funny thing, he's got the same name as my old ferret, Coco. Only *K* instead of *C*."

"You gonna ask Nell for it?"

"My relationship with Nell is kind of complicated. We definitely have each other's backs. That's a really good feeling."

"No pussy, though?"

Mallory laughed. "How did you guess? It doesn't matter, though. I've got a little piece going on the side."

"You dog!"

"Old girlfriend. But I don't know how long that will last. I had to pull out all the stops to get her into my bed."

"Bunbury?"

"Bunbury, and lawyer. And a house somewhere else in Glenwood."

"When I said I had two girlfriends, I mean, they're just friends. I mean, we might get it on once in a while, but I don't have to lie to them."

"I wish I could be as honest as you. I really do. But, Thomas, if I was totally honest with women, they wouldn't come near me." Mallory noticed that Thomas didn't contradict him on this. "And I figure I'm going to jail anyway. I might as well grab as much pussy as I can while I have the chance."

"You're not going to jail, man. No way you're going to jail."

# Chapter 32: Reality Sucks

"Okay, it seems like April 27$^{th}$ is a good day for your event. It's highly unusual, though, for the Employee Cheer Committee members to make a financial commitment before getting the authorization of Accounting. But I'll recommend the committee members be reimbursed for the deposits already made." Teitelbaum seemed pretty relaxed, considering he was in the presence of both Nell and Mallory.

Nell had finally caved on the Cheerboree issue. She had to admit that Mallory had chosen a good date for most people, and that it was probably smart to lock in the vendors by paying the early deposits. Her friend Kathie was adamant that Mallory's plan was good. And Mallory had told her he would cat sit for her again if needed. She had agreed to bring up the issue to the committee on a day when Bob wasn't there, and to help Mallory and Kathie bulldoze any opposition. The committee succumbed to the pressure and approved the plan. Nell then even agreed to try to get Teitelbaum to approve reimbursement for the deposits already made.

"Who should Accounting make the check out to?" Teitelbaum was scribbling on a pad as he talked.

"Make it out to Mr. Mallory."

Teitelbaum stopped dead. But he had little choice. Mallory had printed out and brought along a copy of his credit card bill showing all the deposits paid. Mallory had blacked out all the other payments, to the Pirate's Den, the men's clothing store, Cruisin' Cadillac, Manly Man, and all the other companies he was overspending his salary on. Teitelbaum tilted the paper to see if he could read the other entries through the black marker – until Nell reminded him it might not be appropriate for an employer to scrutinize an employee's personal expenditures. Running a nervous hand through his thinning grey hair, Teitelbaum agreed again to the expenditure.

Mallory found himself committed to another cat-sitting gig at Nell's for the following Friday night. He knew Rose would be suspicious. And he didn't know if he could get away with putting Bunbury in the hospital again. But he didn't feel guilty about putting Rose off. To him, Rose was now the bad girl, the *femme fatale* trying to steal him from his virtuous true friend and ally.

Nell suggested he buy a new suit. The first one he bought was getting ragged and smelled – well, it smelled like cats. She said he didn't have to wear a suit while cat sitting. She apparently didn't realize he was never going to give up the aura of dignity a suit gave him. He called Rose and told her he was in a really contentious trial that was certain to go through to the evening on Friday. He suggested they meet Saturday instead.

"Oh, a trial! Can I come watch?"

"No, it's a sealed case. Government official accused of bribery."

"Wow. Hey, maybe we could stop over your mother's before we go out Saturday. I haven't seen her in a long time."

"Okay, but let's do it later in the evening. I think she's going out with friends earlier."

\*\*\* \*\*\*

He bought a new suit and wore it cat sitting at Nell's on Friday night. He wanted her to know he was reliable, steadfast, and dressed to the nines on every occasion. But she barely looked at him when he arrived, rushing out the door almost as he came in. The good side of that was she didn't have time to leave any of her usual detailed instructions about the animals and their current gastronomical habits. He figured he knew enough to let the dogs out when they scratched at the door. Otherwise, he decided to follow the same plan as last time, doping up everyone in the house except Koko.

He and Koko definitely had a thing going. That beautiful black and white cat again ran its whole body, from its head to the tip of its long tail, through his fingers when he first sat down. Within an hour his grey suit was covered with black and white cat hairs from the knees down. Mallory didn't mind. The other animals seemed pleasantly sedated. He called his mother and arranged for he and Rose to visit late the next evening. His mother wanted them to come earlier so she could cook dinner for them, but Mallory declined. His mother was a worse cook than Rose, even worse than Mallory himself. Besides, he figured his Bunburying with Rose would be over once they reached his mother's, so he'd get his one last lick in at her before that.

It was time he focused on Nell. He was proud of what they had accomplished together. They had Teitelbaum on the run. The manager hardly bothered either of them anymore. Mallory was now a well-known, active Cheer Committee member with an excuse to be off the phones and anywhere in the building at almost any time. Nell was more effective on the committee once he had shown her that idiots like Bob should just be ignored. They both took breaks whenever they wanted. The masking tape was still on the surveillance camera in the break room.

Every time he thought about Rose, he felt guilty. But whenever he thought about Nell, he felt good. Wasn't that proof enough? He thought a lot about that brief kiss he and Nell had shared in his apartment after the holiday party. He blamed himself for poor preparation. Even a kiss needed proper foreplay. His escapade with Rose showed that his libido, damned up by Nell's reticence, was leaking out in the wrong places. He needed to break through to Nell soon.

Koko strutted around the room and rubbed against his shins. He wondered how he could have been so mean as to abandon Coco at that rest stop out in the woods. He took another dog Valium. He stared at the cat and started to fantasize that Coco had been reincarnated as Koko just so he could make up for his past sins. Yes, that made sense. All the frazzled threads of his life were weaving themselves together again under the aura of his devotion to Nell. He fondled Koko's soft fur each time the cat walked by.

218

There seemed to be some spiritual connection between the two of them. It definitely had something to do with Coco. And it was forgiveness, he was sure.

He knew he was a better person now, a person who deserved forgiveness, and it was mostly due to Nell. He had to find some way to express that to her. He had to do it tonight. That's why he had agreed to take Rose to his mother's, so his lies would be exposed and he could make a clean break from her. His urges for Rose didn't seem as strong as they had been a few years ago anyway. He realized he craved a higher type of connection now. Koko was both a signal of forgiveness and a concrete connection with Nell. Nell had that remarkable power to show him what a decent, dynamic man he could be. He had to consummate that relationship, if only spiritually. He had to do it tonight.

Mallory, Koko and Brute were all asleep on the sofa by the time Nell and Kathie came back, long after midnight. Mallory thought the two women were acting strangely, but he put it down to his own tranquillized state. They seemed quieter, and they moved more slowly around the house than in the past; but he sensed a hushed eagerness he had never noticed before. Their glances were too sharp, their grins too suppressed for it to have been the result of Hennessy. Cocaine? But they weren't hyper, just very, very quietly alert.

Nell didn't ask him a single thing about the animals. Maybe she had faith in him by this time. She put the dogs outside with hardly a word, only briefly caressing Galahad's head when he put his nose in her crotch. She quietly shooed the cats off the furniture. Two of the cats disappeared. Koko poked his head out from behind the armchair as if to preside at the beginning of his new relationship with Nell. But Nell turned back to Kathie, who was seated at the bar. "Do you need some coffee?" There was a laugh in her offer.

"I'll take more wine if you have it. It looks like Mr. Mallory here might need some coffee, though."

"It looks like he's already had his sleep," Nell laughed. "Are you alright to leave?"

"I'd like some coffee." It was his first chance ever to stay after a cat sitting gig.

Nell made Mallory a single cup from her Keurig machine, then stood drumming her fingers on the countertop while he sipped it.

"We didn't mean to be so late." Kathie broke the silence. "We just got into a conversation ... and drank a lot of wine, and just sort of got *into it*, you know, and before we realized it, it was after midnight."

"That's alright," Mallory said. "Glad to be of service to you ladies." Meaning Nell. But the only chance he got to talk to Nell alone was a few minutes later, as she was ushering him out the door.

"Thank you, Kevin. The animals seem to like you now. Especially Koko."

"Glad to be of help." He dared to put his fingertips on her arm.

She turned her head up slightly, but not enough to meet his eyes, as if she were too tired even to complain about his touching her. "Good night." She opened the door for him to leave.

Koko appeared and dove between his legs, almost tripping him as he went out. He turned around to see where the cat went.

"Get back in here, Koko," she commanded, but Koko was gone. Then the door slammed shut before he could turn back around.

Mallory tromped off the porch in a daze. Nell had parked her car out front because his SUV was still in the driveway. He had imagined she would at least want to take another look at his shiny new Escalade. He had never washed it, but it still glittered there silently in the moonlight. He leaned back against it for strength. The bright yellow square of the living room window seemed to be taunting him. The only person he had ever cared about was inside, seemingly indifferent to his loneliness out there in the dark. He didn't understand why she didn't show the slightest spark of real interest in him, despite everything he had tried. He was just not good enough for her, and there didn't seem to be anything he could do to make himself good enough.

He turned and kicked the door of his Escalade. His foot didn't make a dent in it, and the door hardly made a sound, but it hurt so much he bent over in pain, then collapsed into a squat, then sat on the ground grasping his shoe. He thought he might have broken a toe; but as he pondered that possibility, he came to the conclusion that it didn't matter. It probably wouldn't matter to Nell if he walked with a limp for the rest of his life. She probably wouldn't even notice.

No, that was wrong. She would care if she really knew him, if she saw his sincere desire to be with her and make her life better in every way. He felt himself drawn toward the lighted window. He needed to see her, to see if he could somehow project his pain through the window, into the house, into her heart. He thought he had been making some strides by befriending her cat. But he needed more. He needed her understanding, her sympathy. But deep in his heart he knew he needed more than that. He needed the magic of love.

Through the window, Mallory then saw Nell and Kathie sitting next to each other on the sofa. Kathie hadn't drunk very much of her wine. Her half empty glass sat on the coffee table. Nell took a last drink of hers and put her glass down. Florence the cat sat on the sofa between them. The two women looked at each other; then Nell scooped up Florence with one hand and gently put her down on the floor. With her other hand she reached out and touched Kathie's face. Kathie turned towards her, eyes wide with apprehension – but with her lips already parted. They kissed tentatively, broke apart, giggled, then came together again, more and more passionately. Nell was clearly showing Kathie what to do at each step.

Mallory watched the whole thing. He felt suddenly stupid, and sick. As he opened the door to get into the car, something brushed past his ankles. He recognized Koko's black and white fur rippling in the moonlight. He reached down and touched the cat and felt him purring against his legs. Apparently, Nell had been lusting after Kathie so much she had been in too much of a hurry to retrieve the cat. Mallory's stomach churned at the idea of knocking on the door and dealing with Nell right now. He picked up Koko and tossed him onto the passenger seat of the SUV.

# Chapter 33: Friends Indeed

"So?" Rose said as they lay in bed afterwards, facing each other. He was softly stroking her skin, from hip to knee back to hip. "Are we going for coffee at your mother's now?"

Going to his mother's would be the end of his affair with Rose. He had planned it that way. And he was going to go through with that plan now, even though the earth had shifted from under his feet since he made it. Rose was the clingy type. She wanted to know everything he was thinking and doing. He knew he couldn't hide out for long behind Bunbury and his new suits. Rose would find out the truth tonight, as soon as she started talking to his mother. And he understood now what it was like to be lied to. Nell had strung him along for months. She had even kissed him. He had spent thousands of dollars just to be made a fool of by that stone cold lesbian.

Rose still worked in the accounting department for the same company she did when they lived together. When he had first moved in with her, he had just graduated from Community Technical after five years of off-and-on enrollment. He didn't think that was a big accomplishment, but Rose had always acted like it was. Now, of course, he couldn't have possibly earned a law degree in the two years since they broke up, but Rose was again giving him the benefit of the doubt. He couldn't believe how stupid she was.

"I want to talk about before," she said as she sat comfortably in the lush, high passenger seat of his Escalade. "I guess I wasn't very sympathetic about your long stint of unemployment. I guess I misjudged you."

She hadn't misjudged him. He'd really enjoyed watching TV all day, crime shows, housewife shows, especially bachelor shows, warming himself up for his little woman to come home and let him bed her even before dinner. And she enjoyed it herself; or at least she pretended to. And it made no difference to him if her cries were real or not. He had applied for some jobs, but during the interviews he hadn't been able to hide his resentment of the Algonquin J. Tycoons who earned millions by running every business they bought into the ground. His father had worked for small contractors, a lot of them, and he never had a good word to say about small contractors either. Mallory didn't have the manual skills his father had. He wasn't even sure what those skills were.

"You didn't misjudge me two years ago." He took his eyes off the road to catch her eye. "You're misjudging me now."

"What do you mean?"

She really wasn't that bright, he thought. Or maybe she was just too trusting. "This car's leased. I have to take it back soon."

"So? That's no big deal."

"I'm not a lawyer. I don't own a house. That tiny apartment we were just in, that's my apartment."

Rose's mouth dropped open. She stared down toward her pocketbook in the darkness of the car's interior, twisting the strap in her hands, untwisting it. But he was surprised by the next thing she said.

"*Everything's* fake? Even that beautiful cat? You said you were just keeping it while Bunbury was in the hospital."

"There's no hospital. There's no Bunbury."

"Oh." Her mouth dropped open and her head sagged again. She looked like a woman who had just been beaten with a belt.

"I'm sorry." Strangely, this apology, the first in Mallory's adult life, came easily. "That day I saw you in the supermarket. You looked so hot I couldn't stop myself."

"So, it's all a lie." Her voice was flat. "Even the cat? You don't even own that beautiful cat?"

"Koko? No. No. Koko is mine. All mine. You saw how much he likes me."

\* \* \*   \* \* \*

Mallory's mother was obviously glad to see Rose again, but the set of her jaw told them she was disappointed in them for not coming earlier for dinner. Delores Mallory had a round face going soft, with two grim creases drawing down the edges of her mouth. She had never remarried after Mallory's father left. She often mentioned how hard it had been to get Mallory's father to pay even minimal child support. She admitted she had no use for men. She had bonded with Rose years before when the younger woman took in Mallory, but Mallory had never been able to stand their endless chatter about useless things. At least, he thought now, this was his last night with the two of them together.

Delores seemed thrilled that he'd worn a suit, but she pointed out that it was rumpled at the crotch and needed a good cleaning. It didn't take long for her and Rose to catch up with each other's lives. They both still had the same halfway decent jobs, and both still resented the way they were treated, and neither was going to do anything about it. They were two of the reliable, faithful drones that the Algonquin Tycoons of the world exploited by the thousands to make themselves rich. And it didn't seem to bother them that things weren't fair. They'd rather just count down the years to retirement while talking endlessly, chewing the cud about relatives, or food, or a new type of curtain they'd found on sale.

Rose didn't rat him out to Delores for all the lies he had told her. His new suit was the only true thing new in his persona, and the two women chewed on that cud for twenty minutes at least. Rose was subtly trying to find out from Delores if Mallory had a real job at all. He joined this part of the conversation, admitting his job was low-paid and boring, but also mentioning his new-found prominence on the Employee Cheer Committee. Rose even acted impressed. Mostly, he just wanted to get the evening over with so he could drop off Rose, go home, and plot his revenge against Nell.

Rose looked straight ahead out the windshield on the way back to her apartment. "I like your mother," were the only words she ventured. Mallory didn't respond. There was no point. He was never getting in her pants again. Thomas had once asked him who he really was, and he hadn't been able to come up with an answer.

He knew now he was less than he had ever imagined. He'd been made a complete fool of by a lesbian, and now he was shamed by this nice, average slut.

He dropped her off on the sidewalk in front of her apartment building. After climbing out of the vehicle down to the street, she turned back. "Your apartment isn't anything to be ashamed of." She had the door almost closed. "And I really liked your cat."

\* \* \* \* \* \*

For the third time in two days, he recognized that knock at his door. He knew he could not block out Thomas from his life forever.

"I got to apologize. I let my father talk to a lawyer, a real, licensed lawyer," Thomas began. He was tracking Mallory's face for signs of disappointment. "I know. I'm sorry. Don't be angry."

"Please come in. Would you like a drink? I haven't got anything but Hennessy."

"That'll do." They sat on the opposite ends of the sofa bed.

After they each took a long swallow, Mallory spoke first. "Aren't all lawyers basically just robbers?"

"I don't think so. It's a friend of my father from his old work days. My father offered him $500 just to tell him what to expect in the settlement negotiations. My father followed his advice. The deal is almost set."

"A million dollars, right?"

"Fifty thousand. And some other stuff."

The amount sounded low to Mallory. He kept picturing the video going viral of the policeman's flashlight hitting Thomas in the face. Wasn't it worth more than 50 thou to the county to keep that video out of the public eye? But he tried to keep quiet.

"Listen," Thomas went on. "I'm telling you all what's on the table right now. Officer Dempsey gets fired. There's no confidentiality clause. We can release the video whenever we want. We get $50,000, which will pay for a year of my college whether I get the track scholarship or not."

"I could have got you more."

"Listen. It's not a done deal yet. And there's more. This last part – and this is the part I said there would be no negotiating on – I told them I want them to drop all criminal charges against you for practicing law without a license."

# Chapter 34: The Importance of Being Koko

Mallory decided to keep the Escalade. He did it for Koko. He wanted Koko to have a better life than he did. He barely made enough money to pay the minimum payments on his credit card balance, an amount that would allow him to pay off his balance in seven years – if he never bought another item on his credit card in those seven years. But he knew he was going to have to get the card out again soon. His older suit was looking threadbare, and he knew an old, worn suit was worse than no suit at all. Wearing a suit all day, every day, was what got him the respect he deserved from the committee, from other co-workers, from Edison and Ava, from Spike at the Dough and Go, from people he saw in his apartment complex parking lot. It got him more than respect from Rose. Even his mother seemed to pay a little more attention to what he was saying once he dressed that way.

Koko was the least Nell owed him for the way that dyke had strung him out and humiliated him. She appeared at his cubicle the Monday after his final cat sitting gig, asking cloyingly if he had had a nice weekend before getting to the point. "Koko hasn't been home since Friday night. You didn't see him outside the house that night, did you?"

"No. You and Kathie seem to be really, really good friends now."

"Yeah, we are."

"How long did she stay after I left Friday night?"

"That's really none of your business." She turned away.

He resumed his old habit of sliding his chair back so it would hit her cubicle wall. He began talking to committee members and claiming credit for taking charge of the Cheerboree. But he didn't mention this to Nell. He could barely look her in the eye. She had strung him along, drained his bank account, drunk his cognac, even kissed him, all so she could make lesbian love to Kathie while he babysat her cats. He had always suspected there were more lezzies around than people would admit. He just hadn't known how good they were at hiding their schemes against real men. No wonder he'd had trouble hooking up with women. He should have paid the extra $13.95 for Manly Man's tutorial on Recognizing the Lesbo.

Mallory visited her cubicle again. She looked up. He thought he saw a quiver in her lip. Nell was the kind of person who wouldn't tell you she was queer – but then would act offended that you didn't know. He'd never noticed before that she'd let her dark brown bob go frizzy. Now that her hair was longer, she was holding it back again with those tortoise shell barrettes that seemed to be saying don't even think about saying I'm pretty. She was obviously having trouble deciding if she should tell him she was gay.

He decided to make her dilemma worse. "Have you taken a pregnancy test yet?"

"What!"

"You know ... after the holiday party. What we did. I think I have the right to know if I'm going to be a father."

Nell's skin blanched, her mouth dropped open. She stared past him for a long time. Slowly recovering, she glared at him, her eyes now dark slits. "If I am pregnant," her voice became less tremulous as she spoke, "if I am pregnant, it's because you raped me."

"That's not how I remember it." He reminded himself to always keep a stock of cognac on hand. Her overindulgence in Hennessy had not only erased her memory of what had happened, but it was now also helping him create a new, false memory. He knew Nell would now rush to get a pregnancy test as well as a battery of STD tests and God knew what other infectious disease tests. She'd probably feel she had to tell Kathie to get the tests, too. He wished he could see that conversation. He was going to really enjoy pretending to be worried along with her.

And he was also going to keep Koko as compensation for all

his pain and suffering at the hands of his owner. He bought him premium cat food and a carved scratch pole and a kitty litter pan that fit inside a finished wooden box with the name "Koko" etched beautifully into the side. He bought the fanciest, softest cat bed he could find – but Koko ended up sleeping with him in his own bed anyway. He knew Koko might be a reincarnation of Coco. He suspected Koko had come into his life to give him a chance to make up for the way he had treated his old pet ferret. The loving way he brushed against him seemed to be proof that he was forgiven.

After their conversation about her possible pregnancy, Nell tried to shut him out, but the very next day she had to force herself to talk to him about the cat. She was suspicious about Koko. "I remember Koko was at the door when you were leaving that night," she started without any polite preliminaries. "Are you sure you didn't accidentally run over him on your way out? Then maybe you dumped him somewhere so I wouldn't find out? I wouldn't put it past you. Just tell me if that's the truth."

"That's not the truth."

"Maybe he jumped in that giant car of yours and is still hiding there somewhere in the back."

"He's not."

"No, I mean it's possible. He seemed to like you. He might have even followed you into your apartment and be hiding in there somewhere."

"That apartment? I don't even live there anymore. Bunbury has completely recovered, and he's back in there now. He certainly would have told me if there was a cat in there."

His next plan of revenge on Nell concerned the Cheer Committee. People were already taking him seriously there. A suit, and a credit card, and a little decisiveness had gone a long way toward the members recognizing his leadership potential. Mallory could feel the power radiating from his new pinstriped wool suit as he made his move.

"This committee sucks," he announced before everyone had

even taken their seats. The shock was so great that some of them remained standing.

"Maybe you should get off the committee, then," was Nell's immediate reply.

The standers waited a beat, then sat down in the silence, the sound of their scraping chairs embarrassingly obvious.

Mallory ignored Nell's comment. "Out of a building of 250 people, we had exactly twelve who signed up for the holiday party, outside of ourselves. What kind of leadership is that?"

"I remind you that everybody agreed on all the details of that party."

"Yeah, and *I* agreed to all the details of the Cheerboree, and I got it settled in one week, and we already have 50 people signed up."

Mallory had never seen Nell's face turn so red. She turned to Kathie, but Kathie's eyes switched back and forth between Nell and the tabletop. Nell then tried to stare him down. "I'm the one who runs this committee."

"Maybe that's a mistake."

The tense silence lasted a full minute until Valerie spoke up.

"I would like to know if the caterers for the Cheerboree will have room in their refrigerators or coolers for those of us who would like to bring their own food."

\* \* \* \* \* \*

Thomas backed up so quickly he fell down on the floor of the landing.

"Oh, it's you." Mallory lowered the rifle. "I was afraid it was Nell, coming to get my cat."

"What are you doing, man? You're going to get somebody killed."

"Don't worry. It's not loaded."

Thomas was still on the floor, still breathing heavily. "You scared the shit out of me!"

231

"I'm sorry." Mallory laid the rifle on the floor and helped Thomas up.

"Put that away, man. Somebody sees that, they're going to pull their own gun."

"Come on inside. Have a drink. I have some cognac left over."

Thomas came in but declined the drink, saying he hadn't done his running for the day. "You still chasing after that woman from work?"

"Not anymore. This is embarrassing. I'm only telling you because you're my best friend." Mallory took a sip of Hennessy. "I got rid of Nell. She led me on and led me on. Then she turned gay."

"Turned gay?"

"Yeah. Full-blown lezzie. Another woman at work."

"That right?" Thomas didn't seem surprised. "You didn't know?"

"No. She kissed me. She led me on at work. We helped each other. Why else would a woman do all that unless she wanted to be nailed? Anyway," he looked at Thomas, "she made a fool of me. Cost me a lot of money. And a lot of cognac."

Thomas looked at him, smiled, shrugged. "Women. Cost you either way."

"Yeah."

"But I gotta tell you something heavy, Mr. Mallory. My case. The settlement. The county council has to approve it. But they don't like it."

"I told you 50 thou wasn't enough."

"No. You got that wrong." Thomas's eyes sought his, communicating a need to be taken seriously. "They're okay with paying me 50 thou. They're okay with firing Dempsey. It's about you. They don't like dropping the felony charges against you."

"Well, they have to, don't they? It's already agreed." Mallory couldn't break the habit of brushing off any negative news regarding himself.

"Yeah, the lawyers agreed, but the County Council has the

final say. The Council is saying they won't get involved in an un-related criminal case. Your case. Word is they're going to turn down my settlement at their meeting next week. Then you'll have to go to trial on your case. Sorry."

# Chapter 35: Revenge

"Unfortunately, I don't think I can help you with that problem, sir. The prices are set by management here at Unicast."

"This is the second time this year you've raised the price. And I only watch five channels out of the 130 I'm paying for."

*"I know. I get a lot of calls about that."* Mallory hesitated. He realized he no longer hated his job. Of the 250 employees in the building, he was the only one who wore a suit every day, and people were starting to recognize him. Teitelbaum had asked him sarcastically if he was angling for a promotion. He told Teitelbaum he was gunning for his job. He began to think the customers were as much the victims of UniCast Cable, and the hedge fund barons who owned it, as he was.

"I'll give you something you can do," he told this customer now, his voice low. "Tell me right now you don't think it's worth it, and say you want to quit UniCast right away."

"Tell you I want to quit entirely?"

"Right. You tell me that right now and I have to refer you to a supervisor. When you get to the supervisor, tell him the same thing."

"Then what? Switch to Fios? And pay startup costs and installation fees and equipment fees and God knows what other fees all over again?"

"No. You won't have to switch. Just tell the supervisor you're going to switch. Tell him you're going to switch because you can't pay the increased fees. The supervisor will cut you a deal."

"You mean there's no set price that everybody pays?"

"There's no set price. They set it as high as they can fool people into paying, and they'll set it as low as they have to to keep your business."

"Um, okay, I guess I'll try it. Thank you. Thank you for your advice. If I get a deal, I'm going to send the company an email saying how helpful you've been. May I have your name, please?"

"Algonquin J. Tycoon."

\*\*\* \*\*\*

Mallory couldn't afford to let his credit card debt get any higher. But there were a few more necessities that had to go on that card. Koko turned out to be a very finicky eater, and he tried eight different gourmet cat foods before he found one that Koko liked. Although Koko had the run of his place, Mallory needed a cage to hide the cat at Thomas's if Nell came looking. Thomas had volunteered to hide it, but Ava had insisted the cat needed to be in a cage if it was to come in her apartment. Trying to save money, Mallory had driven out to the rest stop where he had once abandoned Coco in hopes of finding his old ferret cage, but a group of teenagers hanging around outside the bathrooms started looking suspiciously at the well-dressed man beating around in the bushes. He fled the scene and bought a new cage instead. He cut his trips to the Dough and Go to twice a week and started eating ramen noodles for dinner every Wednesday.

Mallory had always felt victimized, but he had never been able to put his finger on exactly who was stacking the deck against him. It has always seemed to be certain *types* of people who had gotten control of everything and were blocking his every avenue to happiness. It was of course the hedge-fund Algonquin J. Tycoons of the world; but it was also the women who were constantly inventing new ways to castrate men, the politicians and government officials who were constantly telling him his every gut reaction was wrong, the environmental do-gooders who cared more about a straw in a turtle's nose than his right to make a decent living. More hurtful than what they actually said was their attitude toward him. They made him feel like some dumb animal who would deserve to stay on the planet only if he agreed to be thoroughly re-trained.

Mallory was training himself to be a man nobody would mess with. The new car, the old-fashioned but expensive clothing, professionally trimmed hair, an actual brown leather attaché case instead of a backpack, a new willingness to look people in the eye on those rare occasions when they had the nerve to confront him – it all made him seem like a serious person who was not quite on the same wavelength as the common herd of UniCast employees. He wanted them to be put off, to step back. He had nothing in common with any of them now. Instead, he focused on home. He lavished his love on Koko and valued the companionship only of Thomas, the one human being he felt he could trust.

He did use his new-found significance at UniCast to cast doubt on Nell's competence to head the Employee Cheer Committee. He dropped remarks to Bob to sow some doubt about her impartiality. He even approached Kathie and hinted that Nell was too absorbed in her own personal life to run the committee well.

"Why do you say that?" Kathie shrank back, a faint blush reddening her features. Kathie obviously didn't know what Mallory knew about the two of them.

"Her personal life, her *appetites*. They're so intense, I hear. I'm not sure she can properly focus on committee business."

Kathie's face colored a deeper red. Mallory guessed that her coupling with Nell, which he had watched to its conclusion through the window of Nell's living room, had been Kathie's first adventure with another woman. Mallory had nothing against lesbians as long as they didn't pretend that men weren't essential. Kathie was not like that at all. He liked Kathie. He diagnosed her as more lonely than lezzie. And she had good instincts about how the committee should be run. He smiled even as her face flushed, because he knew he could use both her embarrassment and her instincts in his plan.

He even maneuvered himself into a sort of détente with Teitelbaum. Teitelbaum had long ago given up tracking his phone times, and Mallory's generosity in fronting the money for the Cheerboree deposits had a great effect on the supervisor's opinion. Mallory was sure he had such gravitas now he couldn't be fired for violating a few silly rules about staying on the phones. Teitelbaum seemed to be leaving him alone to wander the floor as he wished.

Mallory visited the Public Defender's office to see if he could get a free lawyer for his criminal case. He had to fill out a tedious form about his finances, then wait for an intake person to interview him to see if he was financially eligible.

"It looks like you're not going to make it," the intake specialist told him immediately upon his sitting down in the hard, wooden chair beside the worker's desk.

"What? I'm broke. Can't you see?"

"Yeah, but we can't count Escalade payments. Or bar tabs. And the $800 a month in clothing has to be disallowed. Cat food, too."

The prosecutor dragged him to a preliminary hearing where he had to plead.

"Not guilty," he interrupted the judge.

"You have the right to be represented by an attorney. Do you understand that, Mr. Mallory?"

"I do. But I'm representing myself."

"You do realize that the charge is practicing law without a license?"

"I know, and I'm good at it."

"And you want to act as your own lawyer?"

"You said I have the right to do that."

He had called one of the lawyers recommended to him by Thomas's father. That thief had wanted $5,000 just to enter his appearance in the case. And he said the first thing he would do was postpone the case. When Mallory said he didn't have any money, the robber said he could put it on his credit card. But Mallory had already maxed out his credit card. That criminal lawyer then told him to get another credit card, but Mallory had been using the same credit card his mother took out for him when he was sixteen, and he didn't want to go to all the trouble of getting another one. He decided to skip the trouble and expense of getting on the lawyer merry-go-round.

The judge ordered his continued release on his own recognizance. He advised Mallory again to get his own attorney.

"I think I can do better than these fakers, judge."

He tried to get Nell out of his mind with an orgy of good old heterosexual porn. He was working on getting rid of his Nell-sickness any way he could. Still, her image sometimes sneaked into these video fantasies, taunting him until he was spent. Manly Man didn't have any free cures for a broken heart. Broken hearts had to pay. Mallory spent another $13.99 for this specialized advice. This time, he left blank most of the eleven pages of information he was supposed to fill in about the affair. This didn't seem to matter. He had to wait 24 hours for the answer this time. *Women are like streetcars. If you miss one, there will be another one coming along right after.*

What the hell was a streetcar? How old was Manly Man, anyway? He decided revenge was the best remedy. When he got notice of his trial date, he went to the court clerk's office and had them issue a subpoena to Nell. He couldn't wait to see her reaction.

"What is this all about? What is *State v. Mallory?*" He could see she was shaken.

"A case I'm doing against the state."

"What's that got to do with me? Why does it say I have to bring the results of 'any and all pregnancy tests and tests for any and all communicable diseases?'"

He shrugged and walked away. She didn't even make eye contact with him for the next few days. He relished the idea of cross-examining Nell in court about where her panties had ended up after her drunken afternoon in his apartment. He wondered if he should subpoena Kathie, too, and ask her what happened on the last cat-sitting night. Maybe Teitelbaum, too. He thought his case was going really well.

Thomas kept trying to persuade him to get a real lawyer. "I don't want you to go to jail because of me."

"Don't worry. I'm going to do great."

"Mr. Mallory, my father's worried about you, too. You don't know the law. You don't know the rules of the court, how to present evidence, any of that stuff."

Mallory bridled. "You think your father's superior to me?"

Thomas stepped back. "No. I didn't say that."

"Listen. Just because I don't know anything, that doesn't mean I'm stupid."

Thomas stared at him, then broke eye contact. "I came here to tell you what we're doing on our case against the county. My father has hired a downtown lawyer, and he's demanding a million from the county. He's started hinting to the press that the county is covering up brutality against people of color. That county attorney guy, Finkelman, says he'll agree to half a million, but only if we sign a confidentiality agreement. My Dad wants me to sign off and take the money."

Mallory didn't need an education to know the truth. "Your Dad's part of the system, too."

Thomas closed his eyes. His jaw tightened. "Don't say that."

Mallory didn't back down.

"Oh, man!" Thomas was breathing deeply. "Don't say that." They were standing in the stairwell where they held most of their conversations. Thomas asked if he could come in. He asked for a drink of water, and they stood facing each other in Mallory's tiny kitchen. "My Dad, he worked hard his whole life, since he was fourteen. My Mom, too. No charity. No help from nobody. Now's their chance."

"You want to keep quiet your whole life? Watch that asshole Dempsey go unpunished? Maybe watch him become Chief of Police one day?"

Thomas put his glass down, put his hands to his face. "I mean, it's ... it's my case, really."

"Damn right."

Thomas was breathing slowly and heavily through his fingers. He finally looked up. "What would you do if you were me, Mr. Mallory?"

Mallory searched his soul. He could not lie to his best friend, his only friend, about something so important. "If it was me, I'd sign anything they wanted me to sign for a half million dollars." Thomas slowly nodded his head, slowly moved his gaze up to Mallory. His disappointment was registered in his face. "But it's *not* me," Mallory went on. "It's *you*. You're a better man than me already. Stay that way. Don't take their sleazy deal."

# Chapter 36: The Difficulty of Letting Go

Teitelbaum looked skeptical, but Mallory plugged on. "The customer's teenage son signed up for Gaming Madness, 24 Hip Hop, Sportza Palooza and fourteen other services. She's got a $357 a month bill. For three months."

"There's no way we can forgive a past bill. Absolutely no way."

"I know, but we're not supposed to let teenagers sign up in the first place. It was our mistake."

"I know. But rule number one is they have to pay. They received the services. They have to pay for them."

"Just listen, she just wants our Standard Service from now on, for $89 a month."

"So? Switch her."

"I told her instead we'd only charge her for Antenna Service, $47 a month."

"Why would we do that?"

"We would do that so she doesn't complain to the FCC, as she had threatened to do." Mallory lied. The customer had never mentioned the FCC. "And we would keep undercharging her until she has made up for what she lost in the three months we overcharged her."

Teitelbaum was skeptical, but Mallory could see he had been worn down in the past few months by his battles with the employees. Teitelbaum seemed to have lost his zeal for running a tight ship after the CEO of the company gave himself a $38 million bonus at the end of the fiscal year. And Teitelbaum was having medical problems that were slowing him down. His foot was swollen from an attack of gout, and he was pretty much confined to his desk. Teitelbaum had the authority to ask Accounting to check out Mallory's statements about this customer, but Mallory guessed he wouldn't bother.

"Alright," Teitelbaum conceded. "I'll forward your email to

billing and authorize them to make the changes for this customer that you requested."

"UniCast is making a special exception for you," Mallory later explained to the customer. "To make up for our overcharging you, and your inconvenience, we will change your bill, permanently, to $47 a month. You pay only $47 a month from now on, for life, but you must not call or come into our offices again, and you must never mention this deal to anyone at the company."

"Oh, thank you! Thank you! I'm going to write a letter about what great service you have given me. May I ask your name?"

Mallory smiled to himself. "Promise me you won't mention any of the dollar figures at all. And my name ... uh ... my name is ... Bung Toe."

\*\*\* \*\*\*

"Have you received the results of your tests yet?" This was the first time Mallory had spoken to Nell in days. They were in the break room.

"None of your business," Nell hissed as she turned her head away.

"What do you mean," he stage-whispered. "I have the right to know if I'm going to be a daddy or not."

"You don't have any rights, you pervert. And my lawyer told me you can't subpoena my medical records in your court case."

"You have a lawyer now? You should give me his name."

"Well, I talked to a lawyer. He said it's highly unusual. He doubted if it was legal, and ...."

"... and he told you he would look into it for you for $500. And you didn't pay."

She stared at him. "Close enough," she admitted. "Why are you torturing me?"

Because I can't have you, and it tortures me to see you with someone else.

"I don't know."

"Well, if it will make you feel any better, I can tell you I'm not pregnant."

Suddenly it occurred to him that this was not a good result. He'd rather see her tied to him by biology than free to leave his sight forever. But a positive test had always been impossible. Why was he thinking about impossible things?

"Too bad. Too bad for you. That was your last chance. I know you're a lezzie now."

"You're disgusting."

"We can talk about all this when you're on the witness stand."

"You're totally disgusting."

\* \* \* \* \* \*

The sharp words between him and Nell blotted out his pain for a moment, but the conflict never lasted long enough. The only real relief he got from his heartache was from Koko. Koko brought with him a part of Nell, a part that loved him and enjoyed his company. And, at the same time, Koko was also somehow, mysteriously, his connection to Coco and the good old days of his halcyon, pre-Nell past. Koko could calm him down. Koko's soft purring and slow prancing with his tail held high was better than Valium on those lonely late fall evenings when the darkness closed in on him. He usually waited until Koko went to bed before he turned on his computer to delve into his favorite sites. But now, he tried *not* to picture Nell when he got excited.

On one especially cold, dark evening he was surprised to get a call from Rose.

"Your mother suggested I call." Why would she start with this? This was not a good way to start a conversation with Mallory. "I just wanted to see how you were doing."

"I guess same as always. Cruddy job. Cruddy apartment. Still have that cat."

"Nice cat."

"Why did you call? You're not pregnant, are you?"

243

"No! I guess we were pretty careful."

"Yeah."

"And I wanted to say. It's not such a bad life you have. You don't have the greatest job, or the greatest apartment, but it's nothing to be ashamed of. And I know you lied to me, but you did it because you wanted me to respect you – and that's something, I guess."

"Something."

"I mean, you cared enough to make up a whole life, including that fantastic story about Bunbury, just for me."

"Yeah."

"Okay. I'm not getting much of a response from you. I'll just come right out and say it. Are you interested in getting together again? Telling the truth this time? Both of us?"

Mallory was spent, having finished his internet session for the night, so the only words she said that interested him were the last three. What truth had *Rose* been hiding? Of course, it would have been easy to hide anything from him when they were recently together. He had hardly been able to see beyond that soft brunette hair, those pert nipples, those black straps disguising themselves as clothes. As he pondered this mystery, Koko strode by, rubbing his back against his shins. He knew it was a sign.

# Chapter 37: Keeping Your Friends Close

"We have three preliminary questions we have to ask the vendors of the Cheerboree," Nell announced. "First, will the caterer provide some extra refrigerated space for Valerie's special food that she needs? Second, will Bob be allowed to place small American flags – at his own expense – on the tables after the tablecloths are on but before any dishes or utensils are set out? Third, will the massage tent be staffed by masseurs or masseuses and, if so, what will the masseuses be wearing?"

"What a sexist question!" someone yelled. "Who asked that question? Bob, I bet."

"No, actually that was Valerie also. Valerie?"

"I'd just like this to be about health and fitness." Valerie explained. "I don't want to sign up for a massage myself if there's going to be all these men around leering at all the skinny young masseuses in their Spandex."

"Oh, okay." Nell seemed suddenly tired. "We don't know the answer to any of these questions. We need to contact the vendors. Mr. Mallory, why don't you just go ahead and ask them these questions."

"Nope. I'm done."

"He did pay for all the deposits," someone chimed in. "That was nice."

"But he's already been in contact with these people. He has their phone numbers. He's the obvious person to do it," Nell insisted.

"On second thought, I'll do it. You all keep on with your meeting. I'll go and call them right now."

He left the room, grabbing a cinnamon bun on the way out, but returned not three minutes later, wiping his fingers with the handkerchief he kept in his suit's vest pocket. He spoke before even sitting down. "The answers are no, no, and standard professional attire."

"Are you sure?" Valerie persisted. "My food would only take up a teeny bit of space in their ice chest, and then I wouldn't have to carry my padded lunch box with ice around all morning."

"I don't think he even called anybody," Bob complained.

There was a tense moment of silence, interrupted only by someone complaining. "Why can't we bring our dogs? That would make it so much more fun." Everyone ignored that question, and the silence dragged on.

"I have all their phone numbers here," Mallory spoke into the stillness of the room. "If anyone feels they can get a better answer from the vendors, feel free to call them yourself."

No one apparently felt they could get a better answer from the vendors.

Nell asked him to stay behind when the meeting was over. "You're deliberately undermining me, aren't you?"

"I'm just trying to make these meetings less boring."

"If they are so boring, why don't you just quit the committee?"

"I don't know if you know this, Nell, but if you're a member of the committee, you can get all the coffee you want for five dollars a week."

Nell sniffed, turned, and walked out of the room. But every little angry exchange with her made it easier for Mallory to put his old romantic cravings in perspective. If they could make a drug that would make him entirely forget that she ever existed, he would take it. But that wasn't going to happen, and he had to see her every day. He might as well make life as miserable for her as it was for him.

Of course, Rose was now a nice distraction. She declined his first invitation that she come over for a drink. Instead, she wanted to go out to a club. They crowded into a barn-like structure set on the edge of the lake and ate tacos and burritos. Eventually, after a few Margaritas, they edged onto the dance floor, where Mallory's suit caused a few raised eyebrows and Rose's strapless dress a few lingering stares. Mallory had never had much of an idea of Nell's actual shape. Rose dressed so her shape was easier to see. He thought all women should dress that way. But the situation was a little uncomfortable. They were more than a little overdressed for this younger, sloppy-flashy-dressed crowd.

"They're keeping their distance from us," Rose shouted in his ear. "It's like we're the chaperones." But it didn't stop her from dancing. "We can go to your place now," she said a little later, holding her hand on his chest as he gasped for air. "As long as you have a good supply of that cognac."

"Whew!" she said when they arrived at his place, "I'm not as young as I used to be." She came into the kitchen and stood behind him while he mixed the drinks.

"I don't really know what to do with this kind of liquor," he confessed. "So I just pour it plain into glasses."

"It worked on me last time, didn't it?"

She took the drink he handed her and walked into the other room, kicking off her shoes in the middle of the floor. She spotted Koko and picked him up with her other hand. Koko seemed to like her. She put down her drink and stroked the cat as she interrogated him.

"Do you like your job?"

"No."

"Do you have any friends there?"

"No. I have one friend. He lives right next door. But he's Black. His whole family is Black."

"I have a lot of Black friends. At work. What's his name?"

"Thomas. I did have a friend at work, too. We were in love. But she turned out to be gay. She shit all over me. It's embarrassing."

Rose did snicker a little at that. He could take that as long as she was willing to show him what she could do in bed. Koko climbed in with them as soon as the action calmed down. He knew he was supposed to ask her about her life. He didn't really care about any part of her life that took place outside of his apartment.

"What about you, Rose? Same job?"

"Same company. Assistant Director now. The woman before me had that job for forty-seven years," she sighed. "I hope I won't be there that long."

"So, I ...uh... told you about my love life. What about yours?"

"It's like, there's a million guys out there, and you turn thirty, and they're all suddenly gone."

\* \* \* \* \* \*

The days were getting shorter. Thomas was not starting his daily run until the afternoon, often not returning until the evening, rounding the corner into the apartment complex parking lot at dusk. Mallory waited for him on the landing one evening, watching the full moon glaze the parked cars. Thomas stopped at the bottom of the stairs.

"Why don't you practice at the school track?"

"Still under construction. I need to work on my stamina," Thomas managed to say between breaths. His face was covered with sweat.

"What event do you run, anyway?"

"Eight hundred meters." He looked up at Mallory. "Everybody gets that same look on their face when I say that. Basically, it's a half mile."

"It's almost dark."

Thomas put his hands on the railing and began stretching out his legs. "So?"

"You're not afraid?"

"Afraid of what?"

"Hoodlums?"

"Oh, I see where you're going. I'd be more afraid of home-owners."

"I got some bullets for my rifle."

Thomas stopped his stretching exercises. "Why, man? You

don't need that."

"That's what everybody thinks. That asshole Gus, over at Guns-R-Us, he wouldn't sell me any bullets. I got some on the internet. Thirty percent more powerful than the Winchester Super-X slugs. Half the price."

"Made in China, I bet."

"I guess."

"You're going to blow yourself up."

"That's what Gus said. But sometimes you have to take a chance, step up and be a man to make something good happen." Thomas shook his head at the older man, but Mallory went on and explained his plan. "I'm going to be your armed escort when you run at night."

"Whoa."

"You're at risk, man. And I've got nothing better to do. I'll follow you in the Escalade, with my rifle. Nobody will mess with you. I owe that much to you."

"You don't owe me, Mr. Mallory."

"Your lawsuit. You gave up a half million dollar settlement to try to get the criminal charges against me dismissed."

"That ain't exactly what happened."

Mallory stopped listening. People were always trying to make things more complicated than they really were. His gut reaction told him Thomas was a good man in trouble. The situation cried out for courage, not fancy pants logic. Courage, an Escalade, and a 30-30.

# Chapter 38: A Jury of His Peers?

Rose surprised him. She did things with him that made him forget about the internet. But at the same time, he couldn't cut out that part of himself that still yearned for Nell. The man he now was, the suit, the haircut, the shoes, had all started as changes he had made for Nell. She had manipulated him into making all those changes, all the while taking advantage of him so she could seduce Kathie. He wasn't sure anymore if these changes had been wise manly choices.

He bought another bottle of dye and tried to change his hair color to a uniform dark brown. Rose laughed; she said it now looked *orangish* on top and black in the back. Rose didn't really seem to care what color his hair was. And the people at work still seemed impressed with his suits. He kept dressing the same way, damn the cost. He'd keep it all – the suits, the shoes, the car.

Since he no longer had Bunbury as an excuse for the way the apartment was kept, Rose required him to straighten it up to her specifications. She gave him a schedule of when he should exercise Koko and take him to the vet. She bought nutritious food for Mallory and saw that he ate it. He told himself he couldn't afford to eat out anyway.

They talked about going out on a Friday night.

"No, wait. I'm due in court Friday."

"Oh, come on. Court? You're not still pretending to be a lawyer, are you?"

"Yeah, no. It's like, my own case. I'm mean I'm charged with a crime. I might be locked up by Friday night. How about Thursday night?"

"Locked up! I want to come to this trial."

"My former girlfriend will be there. It might be ugly."

"What did she charge you with? Did you hit her? I have a right to know."

"No. Nothing like that. It's a law I broke. A technicality.

Practicing law without a license. I really am a good lawyer. But I could get two years."

"I'll see you there."

\* \* \* \* \* \*

Mallory thought he should warn Thomas. "This might be the last night I can be your escort."

"That's all right, Mr. Mallory. That big old Escalade following me down the road at ten miles an hour, emergency flashers on. It's putting me in the spotlight."

"You need protection from all those hoodlums running around this area. But my trial's tomorrow. I can't help you tomorrow. And if I'm locked up tomorrow, I won't be able to help you at all after that."

"What! You didn't tell me? I'm coming to your trial! I'm the one got you in this mess."

"I got plenty of witnesses. I subpoenaed that county attorney, Finkelman, who started all this mess. I subpoenaed the county council. I subpoenaed Nell. I got a new girlfriend and she's coming, too. If I were you, I'd stay away from the courts, after all the trouble you've been in."

"I'm coming. The only reason they're bringing this chickenshit charge is they're pissed at me."

Mallory had been served with the charges at the preliminary hearing. At the time, he had glanced over all the papers that evening while he prepared Koko's meal. He recognized the words *practicing law without a license* and *two years' imprisonment*. He meant to read the rest of it later, but he never got around to it. He spent the morning before he left for court playing with Koko and a rubber ball tied to a string. Koko did not like being left alone for too long. If he was locked up, he'd have to remember to ask Rose to take care of the cat.

\* \* \*   \* \* \*

"Where's the jury?" Mallory demanded as soon as his case was called.

The judge looked at him incredulously. "This is not a jury trial, Mr. Mallory."

"I'm an American. I have a right to a jury trial."

"Unless there's something in this file that I overlooked .... I don't see that you have filed a request for a jury trial."

"You mean I have to file a request for my constitutional right to a jury trial?"

Prosecutor Armstrong snickered, as did several people in the audience. Mallory pointed to Armstrong. "He thinks this is funny, that he denied me my right to a jury trial."

"Your Honor," Armstrong stood up. "Mr. Mallory simply did not file the request. Period."

"Who is your lawyer now?" the judged asked.

"I'm representing myself, Judge."

"Hmm. Let me get this straight. You're charged in a criminal information with practicing law without a license, and in that very case you are representing yourself as your own lawyer."

"It's still America, isn't it, Judge?"

"Mr. Mallory, Mr. Armstrong, I want to see you in my chambers."

"What's *chambers*?"

The sheriff stood up, approached Mallory, and pointed to a door. Mallory held out his wrists, but the sheriff advised him, "You don't have to be manacled, son."

Mallory noticed that the judge had a really big office and a really nice chair. Even the visitors' chairs that he and Armstrong sat in were better than anything in the whole UniCast building.

"Your Honor," Armstrong began, "what you've seen this morning is just the tip of the iceberg, as far as Mr. Mallory's shenanigans go. This man has absolutely no idea how to defend himself in this criminal case. He's subpoenaed seventeen witnesses. I can almost guarantee you he will gum up this Court's docket for at least the rest of the day. I'm requesting that you appoint an attorney to represent him."

"Your Honor, I object! Mr. Armstrong is just mad because I beat the pants off him. My record in court is 100%."

"Your record *in court*," the judge said. "How many cases have you had in court?"

"One. And I beat him bad, Judge."

The judge turned to Prosecutor Armstrong. "What kind of case was that?"

"Bail hearing, Your Honor."

"And ...?"

"He did prevail, Your Honor."

The judge sat back. "I'm wondering if this whole thing is worth it. Mr. Mallory, do you realize how expensive it is to convene a jury trial?"

"I can pay. I just got a new credit card, Judge."

The judge smiled. "I should really direct that question to Mr. Armstrong. Mr. Armstrong, is this case really worth the trouble it's going to be? I mean, he represented one person, at one bail hearing? And who was harmed?"

"I have a transcript of false statements he made to the court."

"False statements about the merits of the bail case?"

"Well, no, Your Honor. False statements only about Mr. Mallory's qualifications to practice law."

"I'm very qualified to practice law, Judge. I'm a very skilled attorney."

The judge waved Mallory's comment off and spoke to Armstrong. "Do you have any evidence of how much he charged his so-called client?"

"He did not charge anything, Your Honor."

"Again, is this case worth the trouble and expense of a jury trial?"

"Judge," Mallory interrupted, "Thomas didn't do anything, and I got a video of Dempsey smashing him in the face with his flashlight."

The judge turned to Mallory. "I have no idea who these people are who you're talking about."

"They're just pissed at me because the county has to pay Thomas a half million dollars."

The judge turned to the prosecutor. "Is there some kind of civil case involved relating to this prosecution?"

"Um, yes, Your Honor. The person he is referring to, Mr. Thomas Wright, has sued the county, the police force, and others, including myself, in a civil action. But that case has not been settled, and it is still pending. But that case has nothing to do with this case. And Mr. Mallory is not involved in that case in any way."

"I'm totally involved in that case."

The judge let out a long sigh.

"Your Honor," the prosecutor continued, "if we can just focus on this one criminal case against Mr. Mallory for a moment, I may have a solution. Our office does want to pursue this criminal case. Let me make a suggestion. I don't think this case will ever proceed rationally unless Mr. Mallory is represented by an attorney. I know that Your Honor cannot force him to hire an attorney, but you do have the power to assign an attorney, not to represent him, but to advise him as his case goes forward."

"I don't need any advice from any shyster lawyer."

"Mr. Mallory," the judge raised his voice. "It has become apparent to me that you do need the advice of an attorney in order to present your defense. It's unclear to me why the prosecutor's office is pursuing this relatively minor case in the light of all the obstacles in the way, not to mention the backlog of more serious cases awaiting trial. But they have that right. It's a serious matter and your liberty is at stake. I will have the clerk's office set up a date for a jury trial, and I'll appoint an attorney to advise you going forward."

"I don't need an advisor, Judge."

# Chapter 39: Full Stop

Nell seemed determined to twist the knife even further, and her methods were nefarious. He didn't catch onto her plan until five seconds too late, until just after he announced his true address to the Cheer Committee. "I thought you said you'd moved back to your house," she announced in front of all the committee members. "But now you're saying that same efficiency apartment, the one you were staying in temporarily for your friend, is really your permanent address."

"Bunbury has had a partial relapse. I'm staying with him, just temporarily."

"Does Bunbury have any pets?" Nell asked pointedly, ignoring the quizzical looks on the faces of the other committee members. "Does he happen to have a cat in that apartment?"

"He's allergic to cats."

"My cat, Koko, is missing. He's been missing ever since the night you cat sat for him."

"I'm sorry for your loss."

Now that Nell knew where he was living, he had to be on guard all the time. But he had to be out of his apartment and at work all day, and in the evenings he had to escort Thomas on his runs. He knocked on his neighbor's door and spoke to Ava.

"I have to be gone at work all day," he explained. "Someone's trying to steal Koko. Could you watch out for that during the day. I'll leave my gun with you."

Ava's eyes grew large at the mention of the gun, then curious at the sight of his newly-colored hair, then exasperated. "I can't do that, Mr. Mallory. I work all day, too, you know."

"Oh, I didn't know you worked."

"Told you three times. And you don't need to be carrying that gun around your apartment."

"Mostly it's with me, in my car."

"In your car? When you're chasing Thomas around on his runs?"

"I'm not chasing Thomas. I'm guarding him."

"From what? The police? You gonna shoot the police?"

It had never occurred to Mallory that the police might be as much of a danger to Thomas as the hoodlums. If Officer Dempsey caught Thomas again alone on the road at night, he might be in real trouble. Mallory had suggested Thomas get a gun, a small pistol he could carry in a small shoulder holster even as he ran, but he had refused.

"I'm protecting Thomas on his runs," he said now, "and guarding Koko here at night."

"You keep your gun inside and away from Thomas and my family." She went to close the door but relented. Keeping the door just enough ajar to show her face, she added, "I thank you for what you did for Thomas's case. I truly do. But keep that gun away from here."

\* \* \* \* \* \*

He ignored the flashing lights of the police car behind him until the siren came on. Then he pulled his Escalade very slowly to a stop. Thomas, who was hardly visible in the dusky evening in his grey sweatsuit, ran on ahead. He waited as the cop slowly opened his door and approached his car. He kept his flashers on. He rolled down the window as the cop arrived.

"License and registration."

"Officer, I'm on your side. Law enforcement."

"License and registration."

It took Mallory about five minutes to find the documents, which he found on the passenger side floor. The officer scanned them briefly.

"Mr. Plastic Bag Head Man!" Mallory looked closely for the first time and saw the ruddy face of Officer Selby, the officer who had arrested him on that fateful night when he disposed of Coco. Mallory felt a surge of guilt over the abandoned ferret. But Selby, besides giving him that embarrassing name, had always been friendly and helpful to him. Mallory breathed a sigh of relief. Selby told him to stay put while he checked out the documents in his cruiser. It took a long time.

"So, you're not a real lawyer," Selby said as he approached. "I see you've got a trial coming up."

"That's right. And I intend to fully defend myself."

"That's all well and good. But, right now, I'd like you to tell me why you are driving 15 miles an hour on a 30 mile an hour road with your emergency lights flashing."

"Law enforcement, like I said. There's dangerous people running the streets these nights."

"I haven't heard any reports like that – except from you and your neighbors. What's that got to do with driving around 15 miles an hour with your emergency lights flashing?"

"If you must know, I was escorting a friend of mine, an Olympic runner, on his daily practice run. I am armed and prepared to intervene if he is attacked."

"You still have that rifle you used to carry in your trunk?"

"Yes, I feel very safe. And I have bullets for it now."

"Gus finally sell you some?"

"No, he never would. I bought a pack on the internet. Thirty percent more powerful than Winchester Super-X."

"Oh. Those Chinese bullets. Blow yourself up."

Mallory was starting to worry about that, but he was in no immediate danger of being blown up. He had never gotten around to opening up the cardboard package of bullets until the night before, and he had thus far been unable to open the heavy, sealed plastic tray inside. "It's a free country. I can buy any kind of bullets I want."

"Shoot yourself," Selby smiled. "Just don't shoot anybody else. I was going to ticket you for impeding traffic. You can't drive this slow. You can't drive with your emergency flashers on all the time. But there's not really any traffic here tonight. I'll let you go."

"Thank you, Officer Selby. You are a good man."

"I never met anyone like you, Mr. Plastic Bag Head Man.

Excuse me. Mr. Plastic Bag Head *Lawyer*."

\* \* \* \* \* \*

One of the advantages of following Thomas on his nightly runs was that he knew Koko was safe from Nell as long as the cat was with him in the car. But he made the mistake of discussing with Thomas his encounter with Officer Selby. Thomas became angry.

"You're putting a spotlight on me. I'm gonna be a target as long as you keep following me in that car. You gotta stop."

"You need an armed escort. You need me."

Thomas narrowed his eyes. "Don't make me call the police."

Mallory turned away, dumbstruck. He had always believed that no one really cared about him. He had thought Nell was an exception, but she had morphed into yet another exploiter. Now Thomas was turning down his help, sloughing off his concern. Ava had rejected him also. He now pictured his recent life as that of a stray dog, desperately searching for sustenance in the human scrap heaps of lezzies and Blacks, and still rejected all around. He thought about the bullets. Maybe he could get the package open if he tried again.

Being stuck at home with Koko, in the prime hours when Nell might come to get the cat, Mallory worried. He tried for two nights in a row to open the plastic container of bullets, but he had no tools but a dull paring knife he had taken from his mother's kitchen years before. Finally, he lost his temper. Setting the container on his tiny kitchen countertop, he raised the knife over his head and stabbed down into it over and over as hard as he could. He yelped with joy when the knife finally penetrated into one layer of the plastic. But then the blade got stuck there, and he couldn't pull it out. He started to slam the knife and plastic together against the counter, but then he suddenly remembered what both Gus and Selby had told him. Those cheap Chinese bullets were likely to blow him up. He stopped, terrified, gingerly holding onto the knife while trying to catch his breath. Then he noticed a tiny white label with even tinier print on one side of the container: *Lever to pry sharp object possible hand engagement.* He didn't know what that meant; but very, very carefully, he let go of the knife and slid the container, knife and all, back into a corner against the wall.

He still felt occasional waves of yearning for his lesbian tormentor, but those feelings were quickly turning to pure hatred. And fear. He dreamed more than once that she put him naked in a cage and displayed him for the amusement of her lesbian friend, while Koko strutted in front of the bars, just out of reach. Nell had made him so miserable in real life his dreams were hardly creative enough to catch up.

Once Thomas had vetoed his escort service, there weren't many places he could go. Koko was not allowed in the Dough and Go and did not take kindly to being cooped up in the Escalade alone. Mallory always brought along the scratching post, but the cat seemed to prefer the leather upholstery. He put Koko in the cage one night while he went to the 7-11 to food shop, but the cat peed all over the wall and wouldn't let him come near the rest of the night. The one place he could go was Rose's apartment. Rose always welcomed the cat onto her lap. Koko would purr and stir for her, too; and Mallory felt that Koko was telling him something, blessing them somehow.

Rose always put the both of them out by eleven o'clock. She told him she had a fear of the "old days" returning. She often asked him how he planned to pay off his credit card debts while driving the Escalade and buying more and more suits. He couldn't understand why she was so worried; he had discovered he could just get another credit card. Rose's old infatuation with him seemed to have disappeared, but she still liked him. She liked Koko. Koko liked her. She was a nice piece. She had a job, an apartment, the appropriate set of secondary sexual characteristics, an appreciation of his unique character. She had never met Nell, but she always referred to her as "that lesbian witch," and it was a pleasure to be with someone so perceptive. He decided he would settle for Rose. She would do.

# Chapter 40: Who Needs a Woman When You Got a Cat?

"Really big? You mean like, the size of a *tiger*?"

"Doesn't have to be that big. But big. And on a pedestal."

"A pedestal. You know we're a catering company, right?" The woman's voice was cautious, controlled. She was obviously used to dealing with customers with all kinds of psychiatric backgrounds.

"Just, maybe, two feet high and three feet long, black and white."

"You mean like, a marble or a wooden ...?"

"No," Mallory clarified. "I mean yes, the pedestal can be marble, or wooden, but the statue itself can be marble, or like, made out of cloth, or something soft, as long as it looks real and the colors are right."

"Let me get back to you."

Mallory was frustrated. He was now Chair of the Cheer Committee, and the job was harder than he expected. All the enjoyment had been in getting Nell kicked out. It had taken him only two weeks to do that. He'd promised Bob American flags and scotch, Valerie vegan food in the cafeteria, Jennifer a diet dessert at all committee events. He'd promised employees could bring pets to the Cheerboree.

He did it all just to see if he could keep Nell on edge. She accused him every day of stealing Koko, and his patronizing denial infuriated her each time. He started a rumor that she cruised the Pirate's Den for lesbian one-night stands every weeknight. He made sure Kathie heard that. He sent an anonymous letter to her home, supposedly from a neighbor, advising her that the zoning laws did not allow more than three animals per household. He still thwacked his chair against her cubicle wall, but he did it only intermittently now, the better to keep her on edge.

He wasn't sure the aggravation he caused Nell was worth the aggravation of running the committee, but he had come up with something that just might push her over the edge.

"Mr. Mallory? Sir, we have looked into this. We have located some stuffed, um, felines we could set up on some kind of pedestal. This would all cost extra, of course."

"Don't worry about the money. Are the colors right?"

"Um, no. We can't find anything black and white as you described. But our staff here came up with an idea. We have located a stuffed tiger about the right size. Of course, it's striped, not what you want. But we think we can spray paint it black and white. It won't really be *pettable* like that. The fur will be kind of rigid. More like a statue you just look at. Is that close to what you have in mind?"

"Um, okay, if that's all you can do."

"Good. Good. And about the pedestal. We called around to companies that make trophies, display cases, things like that. A plain pedestal is hard to find. We did get an estimate for a decorative wooden pedestal that size – that's a custom size – and it came to $700. But I don't think you want to spend that kind of money for a temporary pedestal. And it might need some, you know, ground preparation."

"No. That's too much. This company's pretty cheap." He really didn't care about the company's money. What Mallory didn't like was the sound of those words, *ground preparation*.

"I agree with you. That's not such a great idea. How about this? We can make a very serviceable temporary pedestal. Out of cardboard. We can decorate it with crepe paper and such. We can glue the large cat to the top, and the cardboard bottom will be flexible enough so we can make it stand up on almost any terrain. We can do that for $225."

"Deal. You won't forget the lettering?"

"No, I got it. You sure that's what you want?"

\*\*\* \*\*\*

"You didn't pay your credit card bill last month. They charged you a late fee."

"Rose, what the hell are you doing looking at my credit card bill?"

Rose flinched, caught off guard. "Sorry, Kevin. I just felt we were getting closer, and ...." She focused her dark eyes on his, grabbing his attention. "Kevin, you have to know I love you. But, how can this go anywhere if you're about to fall into a giant financial hole?"

"You're saying you'd love me more if I were rich."

"I'm not saying that. I'm saying you spend way more than you make."

"Don't you think I know that?"

"There are people who can help. Counselors ...."

"Don't give me that counselor shit." He stomped off into the kitchen. He stood in front of his counter for a while, staring at the wall cabinets, drinking the last eight ounces of his liquor supply. Well, he still wanted the little bitch. She poked her head through the doorway at an angle, her pouting face half concealed behind that sleek black curtain of hair. Oh, yes, he still wanted her.

Much later, after he'd half apologized and she'd dropped the subject, they made up in the usual way. He told her never to look at his credit card bill again. "No, I have to." She whispered it softly into his chest, but with the tone of someone who worked in an accounting office and knew what she was doing. "I know you can get out of this financial mess if you try."

Mallory got out of bed and looked for more alcohol, but he didn't find any. He was outraged that Rose had started haranguing him again. He suddenly felt trapped in his own apartment. He quickly went out the door and walked out into the murky December night. He walked more than a mile down the side of the dark road, heedless of the speeding traffic at his side. He passed the closed Dough and Go and a new apartment development. He

almost wished some hoodlums would appear so he could take
them out. He couldn't believe how he had allowed himself to get
caught up in all this shit. Looking back over the last few months,
he realized he'd re-invented himself three times, first for Nell,
then for Thomas, now for Rose. His humiliation by Nell floated
in his brain like a grim ghost that tainted and degraded his every
thought. Then there was Thomas, who'd abandoned him. Now,
Rose was trying to tear down everything good he had done for
himself with her nattering accountant-speak. He'd mortified himself for each of them, but what did it get him? Who was he anymore? Why had he strayed from the Manly Man credo? When he
got back, he would tell Rose in no uncertain terms to mind her
own business.

\* \* \* \* \* \*

"I'm filing a police report about Koko." Nell pressed her chin
out as if challenging him to hit her. This would have been difficult,
as he was sitting in his office chair and she was standing five feet
away and in the opening of his cubicle.

"I'm sorry for your loss."

"He's never been found, and the only one around the night he
disappeared was you."

"How would you know? I hear you spent the night with your
face buried in Kathie's muff."

She rushed him. He pushed back his chair to stand up, but
the chair quickly crashed into the cubicle wall. She backhanded
him across the face and then slapped him hard. He held his head
up and took the pain. She hit him again. As much as it hurt, he
was laughing inside. Physical pain was nothing compared to what
she'd already done to him.

"I hope you left a mark," he said quietly. "I know my way
around the police station. I'm going down there right now to report your assault."

"Fine. I'll go with you. I can file my complaint about you

stealing Koko at the same time."

"Where's your evidence?" he challenged her. "That cat ran outside that night just as you were shoving me out the door. I haven't seen him since. Maybe he was unhappy with the way you treated him."

"Shut up. I loved him. And it's not just me. Kiki and Florence, Galahad and Brute, they're not the same. They miss him. They're depressed, I can tell."

"Maybe you should give them more Valium. Maybe take some yourself."

Nell moved back half a step and took a deep breath. Her color returned to normal, and her mouth was set in a thin line. She was much more frightening to Mallory this way. "I've done nothing but try to help you. But you seem determined to make my life miserable. I'm consulting a new lawyer about suing you for sexual discrimination."

"What sex are you claiming to be?"

The silence from Nell's cubicle the rest of the morning was deafening. He could tell she wasn't even answering customers' calls. This put him in such a good mood he tried to help every single customer who called in, making sure his cheerful chatter with them was loud enough to be heard over their shared cubicle wall. He made one outside call.

There was a commotion on the floor during break time. People were talking about something happening in the main lobby. "Are we getting free food?" someone speculated, and people started streaming toward the lobby. Mallory waited until Nell got up to follow, then kept close behind her. At first, it was hard to see what people were staring at, but Mallory knew what it was. The caterer had followed his instructions to the letter, delivering the statue of Koko to the lobby for approval. Attached to the base, in big, sparkling, red letters, were the words *RIP KOKO*.

# Chapter 41: Ferreting Out the Truth

Mallory was furious when he opened his apartment door and saw Thomas's smile.

"I'm pissed at you! You ran away when the cops stopped me the other night! That's some thanks I get for risking my life to escort you."

"Can I come in?" Thomas seemed angry himself. He didn't sit down, but he paced back and forth the three steps it took to cross Mallory's living space. "You got to understand. I saw the cop car. That could've been Dempsey. Can't you understand I'm much more scared of the cops than of gangbangers?"

Mallory didn't respond right away. He was more concerned about his own real problems than Thomas's fanciful fears. His criminal trial was scheduled to take place the next day, and he was shaken. "It was me who got you out on bail. It was me who got you that body camera footage. I was your savior." When Thomas didn't respond, Mallory thought he'd get down to the real bottom line. "You people let me down."

Thomas stopped, stared at him, shook his head slowly. Mallory figured Thomas was finally realizing the depths of his own family's ingratitude. The young man's mouth hung open. Mallory still liked Thomas, and he was glad the truth about their one-sided relationship had finally been exposed. He waited for Thomas to apologize.

The long silence was broken by a sudden hard rap on the door. Mallory opened the door just a crack. A shot of adrenaline shook his body when he saw Nell's face. He yanked open the door and charged out at her. He had her backed halfway across the landing before he heard a familiar voice barking at him, in a frighteningly stern tone.

"Step back, sir! Step back immediately or I'll have to arrest you!" Mallory turned to see Officer Selby bearing down on him. His old fear of the police came back and turned his knees to jelly.

266

He managed to lean against a wall to keep from collapsing.

Behind them, his apartment door suddenly closed. Selby jerked around. "Is there someone else in there?"

"Yes," Mallory was glad to have Selby's sudden anger turned elsewhere. "My friend Thomas is in there. He's Black."

"I can talk to you right here." Selby, taking command of the situation, stepped forward and got between the two of them, making sure to keep them apart. "This lady has filed a complaint that you stole her cat. A black and white cat. Would you know anything about that?"

"I know that cat. She was cruel to that cat. I was there when it ran away from her, right out the door. I haven't seen it since."

"It's in his apartment." Nell had recovered from her shock.

"Prove it."

"Mind if we have a look?" Selby asked, but it seemed more like an order than a request.

"Um, I have a friend in there. He's Black, and he has a terrible fear of police." He stared at Selby, adding, "I am an American, and I know my constitutional rights."

Selby sighed. He seemed used to dealing with citizen spats. "Maybe we can avoid a constitutional crisis here. Maybe you could just let the lady go in and look around."

Nell was quick. "I'm not going in there by myself, not with this maniac and some Black man in there."

"Is that cat hair on your clothes?" Selby was clearly trying to intimidate him.

"I don't own a cat. It's ferret hair."

"Another ferret?" Selby sounded skeptical. "Thought you got rid of that ferret."

"You know this man?" Nell looked dismayed.

"I gave it to my friend Bunbury. But he got sick and couldn't take care of it himself."

"So, you do have a ferret in there. Mind if we just take a look at it? Then we can all go home."

They were interrupted by the sound of high heels clicking up the stairs. Rose was dressed in a sleek black dress. She stopped on the top step to take in the scene playing out in the dim light of the landing. Everyone else, including Officer Selby, froze. Rose addressed Mallory as if no one else were there. "I thought we were going to dinner."

"There's a problem." Mallory paused until he caught her eye. "A problem about an *allegedly* stolen cat."

"Would you know anything about that, Ma'am? Are you familiar with the premises?" Selby asked.

"And who is *this* woman?" Rose answered Selby's question with a question.

"My name is Nell."

"Oo-oh." Rose dragged out the word as if she'd just discovered the source of all evil in the universe.

"Are you familiar with the premises, Ma'am?" Selby asked Rose again, trying to get back in control of the situation.

"I told them both it's just a ferret." Mallory interrupted, meeting Rose's eyes again.

"Oh. Yeah. The animal in the apartment? I think it's a ferret. I don't mess with it too much."

Selby's sigh indicated he had lost the battle. "We have two people's word there's no cat in there, Ma'am," he addressed Nell. "I don't have a search warrant. Like he says here, this is America. If you get any proof that this man has possession of your cat, you can file another complaint."

"I don't believe this," Nell huffed and started to walk toward the steps. Then she quickly turned, edged Rose out of the way and suddenly forced open the apartment door. A startled "Whoa!" could be heard from inside.

"Is there a gun in there?" Selby shouted back at Mallory as he followed Nell in. "Miss! Miss! You can't do this!"

Mallory followed in without answering. Thomas had backed himself up to the outside wall of the kitchen and put his hands all the way up in the air.

"Stay there!" Selby ordered.

Nell was circling the room, and Selby was circling behind her, obviously reluctant to grab her. He kept asking where the gun was, but nobody answered. Nell ran past Thomas into the kitchen, appearing a half minute later with the empty cage in her hands.

"Here's the cage. Now, where's the cat?" she shouted at Thomas.

"I told her, it's a *ferret*," Mallory cried out, desperately hoping to clue in Thomas as to what was going on.

Thomas didn't say anything. Selby had found the rifle under the sofa bed and was busying himself securing it. Nell could be heard opening and closing cabinets and drawers in the kitchen. She finished there and came out and crawled around the living room/bedroom floor, looking underneath all the furniture and then pawing through a knee-high pile of empty boxes and other debris Mallory had left in a corner. Then she looked in Mallory's lone closet. Rose was trailing behind, fuming; but nobody risked stopping Nell in her frenzied condition.

Selby was holding onto the rifle like his life depended on it. "Ma'am, I'm going to ask you one more time to leave, or I'll have to arrest you for breaking and entering."

Nell stopped and stood facing him, shuddering. "Okay. But he's lying, even about the ferret. There's no ferret here."

"Oh, the ferret?" Thomas spoke for the first time as he slowly lowered his hands. "You all asking about the ferret? I was about to tell Mr. Mallory here. Mr. Bunbury done come and took the ferret back." He tried to meet everyone's eyes, but everyone else was focusing on the empty cage sitting in the middle of the floor.

"If he took the ferret, why'd he leave that here?" Selby's look was more than skeptical.

"Oh. The cage. I see he didn't take the cage. I think, um, I think Mr. Bunbury brought his own cage."

# Chapter 42: Accommodations for the Handicapped

"What the hell did you do with Koko?" Mallory yelled at Thomas the instant Officer Selby and Nell were safely out the door and down the stairs.

"I put him out the window."

"You threw Koko out the window?" Mallory could feel his eyes tearing up. He'd fought like hell to save Koko, only to have Koko thrown out like trash. He imagined Koko out there somewhere in the dark, injured, betrayed, his innocent soul merging with Coco's betrayed spirit, probably to haunt him forever. Nell and Selby had humiliated him for months, and now Thomas had thrown out the only creature who had ever loved him.

"I heard what was going on out there." Thomas tried to explain. "I figured they were coming in to get the cat."

"You asshole! I can't believe you threw him out. He was the only good thing in my life. Get out!"

"But, Mr. Mallory ...."

"Get out, now!"

Rose forced Mallory to meet her eyes. "Koko was *her* cat? You stole him from her?" Her interrogation interrupted his grieving process. "You lied to her face about it? You lied to the police? You lied to me?"

"You lied about it, too," he pointed out.

"But you're the thief. I can't believe you stole that wonderful cat from her."

"She was abusing it."

This stopped Rose for a second. She looked at him with the same little frown she probably used when talking about an accounting discrepancy she discovered at her job. When she spoke again, her voice was lower, calmer, more definite. "No, I don't believe you. That cat was in beautiful shape when it got here. And that woman was frantic to get it back. I can tell when a woman loves something. You are lying to me even now."

"I loved Koko."

"That doesn't mean it was okay to steal him. Don't you have any morals at all?"

"You don't seem to have any morals in bed."

Her mouth scrunched up like she had tasted something awful. Then her dark eyes flared as she slapped him, hard. "You're disgusting, Kevin." She turned to stomp out – but turned back again at the door. She wasn't finished with him. "You're a totally, totally worthless, evil man."

"I'm a hero at work. The Cheer Committee loves me now. I saved them."

"You saved the day *with a credit card*. Only a numbskull would do that, Kevin." She opened the door and walked to the edge of the landing, then turned back one more time. "It's a lucky thing you are such a nobody, Kevin. Otherwise, you might really do somebody some harm."

Mallory spent a jittery, restless night before waking up at sunrise. Koko was the only living being on earth that loved him, and Koko was missing. Mallory spent the morning searching through the field of high weeds behind his apartment complex, calling for Koko. His suit pants were wet to the knees. Thomas wasn't helping him. That asshole had thrown Koko out the window and hadn't even apologized. It was almost ten thirty. A middle aged woman in one of the larger apartments came out on her balcony and started calling "cuckoo, cuckoo" back at him. He wasn't surprised. Everyone had turned against him. He yelled "Fuck you" back up to her and kept doing it until she went back inside. His face hurt from the sun. His socks were soggy.

Why had all women always been so cruel to him? Now, even Rose, this common, desperate, would-be housewife, rejected him. She wouldn't be at his trial today as she had once promised. He hadn't even asked his mother to come. He didn't need yet another judge in the courtroom. He had subpoenaed Nell again, and she had to come; but now he feared she'd be harping about Koko and he wouldn't be able to prove what a slut she was. He didn't know if Thomas would come. Thomas and his family had reneged on their promise to get him out of his legal trouble. He should have expected that from those people. Nobody cared about him or would lift a finger to help. The judge probably wouldn't even make a big deal of incarcerating him. It would be a nothing case to the judge. Sending a nobody off to jail.

* * *  * * *

"Mr. Mallory, the judge told us if you aren't in his courtroom in fifteen minutes, he'll issue a bench warrant for your arrest."

"Who are you?" Mallory demanded into his dashboard.

"Joseph Ackerman, the attorney the judge appointed to advise you in your criminal case."

"I didn't ask your advice."

"It's my duty to tell you that if you don't get here in fifteen minutes you'll be arrested and placed in a cell, and it could be weeks or even months before they get around to rescheduling your trial."

"I'm already here! I'm in the damn parking lot. There's no spots."

"Oh, good. I'll tell the court right away. Come in as soon as you find a spot."

"I'm telling you, there aren't any ...." Mallory stopped talking when he heard Ackerman click off. He drove around the lot twice more, but there were no more spots. Except handicapped parking spots. Mallory had always resented these people being given the prime spots. Spots for hard working people like him were painted over and reserved for those slackers with handicapped stickers who didn't work and had all day to get where they were going. He parked in the spot closest to the courtroom entrance.

A police cruiser pulled up beside him immediately. "I don't see a handicapped sticker on your windshield, sir."

Mallory rolled his window down. "I'm not handicapped. I'm due in court. They're going to send me to jail," he complained.

"You can't park in that spot. Hey! What's that on your dashboard?"

"It's a gun. It's not loaded. People keep telling me ..."

"Telling you what, sir?"

"... I'm going to blow myself up."

\* \* \* \* \* \*

Four police cruisers surrounded Mallory's Escalade. Mallory felt a rush of adrenaline like he had never felt since the afternoon he had managed to kiss Nell. All the cruisers were flashing their lights, a crowd was starting to form, officers were herding people away from that side of the parking lot. People inside the courthouse gathered behind the glass door, but they were quickly shooed back by the police. Mallory pulled his rifle out of its case so all the cops could see it was unloaded. But all the cops were now hunched down behind their cruisers. They seemed terrified of him. He refused their orders to get out of the car. This made them scream even more frantically. Then they began using a loudspeaker. So much for being a nobody.

Nell must have found the cat outside and stolen him and taken him back with her last night. That was why he couldn't find Koko all morning. He couldn't let that go unpunished.

His lawyer Ackerman's voice suddenly surged through the Escalade's speakers so loud that Mallory jumped. "The police tell me you've got a gun, and possibly some explosives. No good can come of this, Mr. Mallory. I'm urging you to give yourself up."

Mallory was particularly annoyed by this because he thought he had turned off the speaker system. "I'm not holding the gun, you idiot. It's just sitting on my dash."

"Then get out of the car, keeping your hands up in the air so they won't think you're about to shoot it."

Mallory tried to switch off the connection, but he didn't really understand how the infotainment system worked. He compensated for this by ignoring everything the lawyer said after that.

"Mr. Plastic Bag Head Lawyer." Officer Selby's familiar voice, and the pet nickname, brought a small wave of calm into the car.

"You. Selby. You were there when Nell stole Koko last night. I can't forgive that."

"She didn't steal your cat. I drove her home in the squad car. She didn't have any cat."

"Oh."

"And Mr. Mallory, you said you never had the cat anyway."

"Oh. Yeah. Well, I didn't. But you're telling me she didn't either. So where is the cat?"

"Jeez! I don't know where the cat is! I don't think anybody knows where that friggin cat is! But right now, you're putting yourself and a lot of other people in danger with that gun."

"No, I'm not."

"Well, the tactical squad believes people are in danger. And if the tactical squad believes people are in danger, people are in danger – if only from the tactical squad. Do you get my drift?"

"They wouldn't dare shoot me."

There was a pause, during which Mallory could hear Selby mumbling something to someone else on his end of the phone. "I've talked to some people here," Selby began again.

"Where is *here*?"

"I'm in the courtroom here with your friend Thomas, your co-worker Nell, and the other people you subpoenaed. Your lawyer's here, too, and the prosecutor. Your friend Thomas gave me your number. I talked to the commander in charge outside. All you have to do now is leave that gun where it is and get out of the car, Mr. Mallory."

"Then I'll get a ticket. They said I have to move my car. But there's no other place to park, and I have a court hearing I have to get to."

"What if I get the commander to let you park where you are, just for today? Will you come out without the gun if I can get that to happen? Just give me a minute."

The phone went dead, but then lawyer Ackerman's voice suddenly boomed throughout the Escalade. "Mr. Mallory, I think you have a chance of actually winning this case. Or having it dismissed."

"How so?" Mallory liked the feeling of quizzing his own lawyer.

"There's something fishy about the way the prosecutor and the county attorney are working together. I found out they've been trying to trade off your criminal charge against your friend Thomas's civil case. That might create an ethical problem, and I might be able to use that to pressure them to dismiss the case against you."

"I'm not an expert on ethics," Mallory observed.

"I called the county attorney and claimed he was violating ethical rules. Now he's here talking with the prosecutor. I think they're afraid of proceeding with this case. I think they'll drop it. Just don't make things worse for yourself out there in the parking lot."

The cops were now standing behind their cars, some of them with their guns trained on him. They were conferring, moving their cars around. Mallory was delighted to find out he could stop all their activity and make them hide behind the cars by just feinting toward the rifle on his dashboard. After he did this a few times, though, a cop got out his own rifle and pointed it right at Mallory's head through the driver's side window.

"Mr. Mallory, this is Thomas." Thomas's whisper suddenly whistled through the surrounding speakers. Mallory jumped again.

"Hi, Thomas. There's no place to park. Can't you all just start the trial without me?"

"Listen. I didn't want to say this while that cop Selby was here. Koko is safe. My mother took him in last night."

\*\*\* \*\*\*

Officer Selby appeared in the parking lot. Another cop gave him a bullhorn, and he called Mallory's name.

Mallory stuck his head out the window. "Just come over here. Talk like a normal person."

Selby complied. He also pushed down the shotgun that another officer had trained on Mallory's head.

"Just come out of the car, Mallory. You've heard your own lawyer say it. You've got a good chance to win your case. Don't throw you chances away by threatening people."

"I'm not threatening anyone."

"Good. I'll make you a promise right now. If you get out of that car without touching that rifle, and you walk into this courtroom unarmed, we won't charge you with anything new except parking in a handicapped spot. Maximum fine for that is $85."

"But there weren't any regular parking spaces."

"It doesn't matter, legally. Pay the $85, Mr. Mallory. It's better than spending two years in jail."

"Do they take credit cards?"

"Yes."

"Okay. No. Wait. One more thing."

Selby listened, then shook his head. "There's no way we're bringing a civilian, especially a potential hostage, out into this situation."

"I need some type of satisfaction on this, or I'm not going away."

"What is it you really want out of this?"

\*\*\* \*\*\*

The voice came out clearest on the Escalade's speakers, but it was also broadcast, and even louder, from the bullhorns set up both outside on the parking lot and inside the courtroom. Everyone had been told in advance that Mallory had insisted that she read the script publicly, word for word.

*I, Nell Pickens, admit that Koko loves you better than me. He ran away because of my cruelty. Something in my twisted lesbian nature caused me to hate that prancing male cat. If Koko is ever found, I sincerely hope you will provide him with a safe home.*

# Chapter 43: Sometimes They Actually Will Help You

As soon as he came out of the car, the police threw him down on the ground, handcuffed his wrists behind him and kept a knee on his back while they awaited transport to take him to jail. Thomas then came rushing out of the courthouse, demanding to know what Mallory had done to deserve arrest. Mallory's lawyer, who had not even been appointed for the parking lot issue, could not resist the drama, and he came out and demanded to know what the new charges were. The tactical people were exercising complete control over Mallory, and the "scene of the crime," as they called the car and the handicapped parking spot it was sitting in; but Thomas and the lawyer and Officer Selby were all arguing and shouting right behind them. Selby eventually quieted the other two, then approached the tactical unit.

"I negotiated a deal with him. No new charges except for the handicapped parking."

"You gotta be kidding," the chief tactical officer on the scene scoffed.

Selby raised his voice. "Anyone here see this man point that gun at anyone? No? Anyone see him even wave it in the air? No? There's no crime here, guys." A dead silence followed while they all heard the sounds of another tactical officer clicking the lever on Mallory's rifle.

"It's not loaded," came the officer's voice from inside the car.

"You assholes should know carrying an unloaded rifle isn't a crime." Mallory contributed this to the conversation from his position face down on the parking lot.

"Stand him up!" the chief tactical officer ordered. Mallory's bow tie was hanging off loosely and there was a tear in his clothes just at the knee; otherwise, he looked fine, except for the dark stain on his suit pants where he had wet himself. Even Selby laughed at that.

Selby took control. "Look, I know this guy. He's already suing the county over another false arrest. Believe me, he can create a real mess in court. It's not worth drumming up a charge."

"Where're the bullets?" The chief turned to Mallory, his tone resigned.

"At home. On my kitchen counter."

"Where's the explosives?"

"That's the bullets. Everyone told me they might explode. Because they're from China. Officer Selby told me that himself."

The chief took a long look at Selby, sighed. Selby's argument was obviously winning the day. "Just out of curiosity. Why're you carrying that rifle, son, leaving it out there on your dashboard, if it's unloaded and of no use to you?"

"For the safety of everyone."

\* \* \* \* \* \*

As soon as the cops let him go, he followed Thomas and his lawyer into the courthouse, wet pants and all. The crowd in the courthouse was buzzing with rumors of a hostage situation outside – and with reactions to the strange confession from Nell they had heard over the speaker system. Mallory walked right up to the counsel table and called his own case. The bailiff tried to hold him back, but he was still standing, still struggling with the bailiff, when the judge returned to the bench. When prosecutor Armstrong entered through a side door he was immediately intercepted by Ackerman, Mallory's appointed attorney advisor, and the two lawyers engaged in a heated argument while the judge fumed on the bench.

"Your Honor, the prosecutor has agreed to dismiss this case," Ackerman announced even before returning to the counsel table, where Mallory and the bailiff were still tugging at each other's shirts. "Prosecutor Armstrong has agreed to dismiss this criminal complaint which was brought against Mr. Mallory for practicing law without a license."

"Is that correct, Mr. Armstrong?" the judge intoned.

"Yes, Your Honor," Armstrong agreed.

"No, it's not," Mallory spoke up. "I want a trial. I deserve a trial. I have all these witnesses here, and I have a right to put on my case."

"But there is no case if the State dismisses it." The judge's sigh could be heard over the loudspeaker system.

"And besides," Mallory went on, ignoring the judge's comment, "my friend Thomas was beaten by the police. I got a video of it. They're making him give back the video, sign a confidentiality agreement, cover up the whole thing – or else they'll put me in jail."

"Hmm. Very interesting." The judge rocked back in his chair and raised an eyebrow at the prosecutor.

"I can absolutely assure the court," the prosecutor met the judge's eyes, "there was never any such *quid pro quo* officially discussed."

"I don't know what a *quid pro quo* is," Thomas stood up uninvited and walked up next to Mallory at the counsel table. "But *my* case is over." He turned to Mallory. "Mr. Mallory here, he's not up to date on my case. The cop who beat me is fired. I still have the video. There's no confidentiality agreement. I can make it all public as much as I want."

"Oh," Mallory interjected. "Never mind, then. But I still don't see why I have to pay an $85 parking ticket when there were no regular spaces."

Thomas and attorney Ackerman, acting spontaneously but in complete synchronization, each took an arm and steered Mallory out of the courtroom.

"Thomas, why didn't you tell me before that your case was over?" Mallory complained once they were outside. Thomas just looked at him and shook his head.

"It's unethical in this state to hold criminal prosecutions over someone's head to gain an advantage in a civil proceeding,"

Ackerman explained. "That's kind of what they were doing. Close enough, anyway, for us to scare them into dropping your criminal case."

"I don't understand," Mallory admitted.

"Just pay attention to this one fact, Mr. Mallory. The case is over. That's what 'dismissal' means. You're not going to jail."

"And, Thomas, your case is over, too?" Mallory was just getting his mental bearings.

"That's what I came over to tell you last night, Mr. Mallory, but you just hollered at me and kicked me out."

"Oh. Did you get any money?"

Thomas grinned. "Enough to pay for my last two years of college if I don't get that track scholarship."

"You should stop running around at night. I keep telling you, there're dangerous people out on these roads."

"Officer Dempsey's been fired."

# 44: Advice and Consent

Mallory sat on his sofa bed, staring at the holes in the knees of his pants. The damn police had ruined his $800 suit. His face was scraped where they had pushed it against the asphalt. Altogether, though, it was a satisfactory day. Selby told him the police would eventually have to give him his gun back. He was no longer in danger of going to jail. Thomas had gotten some money out of the county. Best of all, he now had Koko all to himself, and Nell had disqualified herself from ever claiming that cat again.

He was startled out of his reverie by a quick, sharp rap on his door. Then he remembered he didn't have to worry. It was all over. He had won. He opened the door carrying Koko proudly on his arm. He saw Thomas, Ava and Edison standing shoulder to shoulder on the landing.

"What?"

"We'd like to come in," Ava responded.

He let them in. "I don't have any more Hennessy."

"We're not here to drink."

"To celebrate, right? Everything worked out fine, didn't it? Come in. sit down. You people have helped me through all of this." He moved over to make room on the sofa.

"It could have been worse." Edison didn't sound happy. The three neighbors now stood shoulder to shoulder, facing the sofa like a firing squad. But Mallory was not intimidated, because he knew these people were his friends.

"What's the problem? You got your money. Dempsey got fired. I mean, my suit pants got torn, but ...."

"The cat's the problem," Ava interrupted. "At least, it's part of the problem."

"Koko?" At the sound of his name, Koko jumped out of Mallory's arms and ran for the kitchen like he had been hit by an electric shock.

"What's the problem?" Mallory looked from Thomas to Ava

to Edison. "I had to do a lot of lying, but isn't that what it usually takes to even things out in the end?"

"We don't believe that's how good folk get on," Ava insisted.

The room went silent. Thomas broke eye contact. He looked like he was the one facing the firing squad. "I knew Koko wasn't yours," he said. It was obvious from his tone that he had already confessed to his parents.

"He belongs to me," Mallory protested. "If not legally, then at least morally. You all heard Nell admit to the world that she abused him."

"She had to say that. To save your life." Thomas's narrowed eyes showed a trace of anger, something Mallory had never seen in them before. "The tactical squad was ready to take you down."

"All I got was a parking ticket."

Edison huffed out in disgust. "You put lives in danger, Mr. Mallory. You can run your life however you want. You can go on seeing only what you want to see. But leave my son out of it. That's all I have to say."

Edison turned to go. Ava put her hand out to stop him, but then she pulled it back. The door slammed shut behind him. Ava was distressed, breathing heavily, staring at Mallory.

"Mr. Mallory, tell me something. "You buy a ferret you can't take care of. You file a lawsuit you don't know anything about. You steal a cat and tell vicious lies about its owner all over the media. You carry around a rifle you don't know how to shoot. What I want to know," – her voice was calm now, resigned, almost motherly – "what I want to know is, why do you do all this *shit*?" Her words shocked Mallory, all the more for their soft, inquisitive tone. But she looked deep into his eyes as if she expected him to answer.

Ava's words hit Mallory like a body slam. They hurt him more than any words he had heard since he was a child. And he recognized in her words the echo of what he had often heard as a child, except she spoke in a softer tone, a tone that hurt even more. He felt pinned down. He could hardly breathe. He was an incompetent eight year old again. Here he was again at the age of thirty-two, pinned to the wall still, still being examined, still being found defective.

"I don't know," he whispered into the silent room. "I don't know why I am the way I am."

Ava looked both sad and perplexed. She turned and eased herself slowly out of the room like a receding spirit, a delicate soul who could not bear the vile company. Mallory watched the door close and waited for Thomas to leave, too. But he didn't.

"I don't buy all what they said." Thomas spoke quietly. Mallory was still looking at the door. "But – one thing. That woman, Nell. She really loves that cat."

\* \* \* \* \* \*

Mallory stood uninvited on Nell's porch. The Escalade was parked out of sight up the street. Nell didn't have a peephole or a window near the door. He held Koko so he would be the first thing she saw when she cracked the door.

"You sick bastard." She grabbed the cat. "I should sue you."

He was surprised she didn't slam the door in his face. He decided he might as well go on. "Nobody believed that shit I made you say at the courthouse."

"You think so? Kathie hasn't spoken to me for days now."

"Maybe it's not you. Maybe Kathie's not really gay. Maybe that was a one-time thing for her." He said it to make Nell feel better. He really didn't have a clue about Kathie's sexual orientation. But Brad Pitt came to mind.

"So, you're now an expert on gender issues."

"I'm not an expert on anything."

"You're not. You bought your way onto leadership of the committee with your credit card."

"You can have the committee back. I only joined to get close to you."

Nell sniffed at that, screwed up her mouth. "None of it matters. We'll both be fired anyway."

"No way." Mallory was positive. "I'll make sure of that. Teitelbaum's no match for me. Dealing with the Teitelbaums of the world is the one thing I'm good at."

\* \* \* \* \* \*

Mallory's prediction turned out to be accurate. The horrendous publicity surrounding the courthouse incident caused Starganoff to order Teitelbaum to fire them both. But Mallory then reminded Teitelbaum that he had a 100% win rate in court and promised to sue him personally for the entirety of his 401(k) if he tried. Teitelbaum dithered for weeks about exactly how to fire them until he himself was fired by Starganoff – but then Starganoff left the company to take a job with the hedge fund that owned a controlling interest in UniCast. The new managers had obviously been warned that Mallory was a tough nut to crack, and they showed no interest in taking up the messy cases against Mallory or Nell.

Mallory started representing other UniCast employees who had grievances against the company. He constantly reminded both employees and managers that he had never lost a case. He could see the managers cringe each time he entered their offices. Some of the managers began to ask his advice in advance if they were contemplating personnel action against an employee. He allowed them to take action only in the worst cases.

Mallory handed the reins of the Cheer Committee back to Nell. Nell stopped sending emails discouraging attendance at committee events, and over a hundred people showed up for the Cheerboree. Mallory stayed on the committee, but only for the coffee. He never answered a customer's phone call again.